THE MATRIARCH'S DEVISE

Sharon Skinner

Brick Cave Media
brickcavebooks.com
2015

Cover Illustration by Thitipon Dicruen [xric7]

Brick Cave Media
brickcavebooks.com
2015

To Anne Lind, who knows the difference between a hot mess and a good story and isn't afraid to say so.

THE MATRIARCH'S DEVISE

Sharon Skinner

Deborah –
To the next
adventure.

Brick Cave Media
brickcavebooks.com
2015

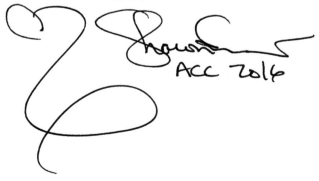

ACC 2016

CHAPTER ONE

Kira clutched the ship's railing. The storm had descended on the ship without warning. Sailors scrambled to tighten lines, adjust sails and make fast anything that had come loose in the screaming winds. Froth-crested waves broke and crashed around them, hurling salt spray high overhead, lashing against a black sky. Vaith clung to her shoulder, his leathery wings folded in close to his body and the end of his long tail wrapped around the back of her neck. He gurgled deep in his throat. Kira sensed his longing for the sky, but this blowing gale would tumble a wyvern his size out of flight before he could get a wing's length into the air. She stroked his smooth-scaled chest until he tucked his head against hers, talons clutching the padded shoulder of her leather vest.

The ship rolled as the steersman adjusted their heading, keeping the prow of the ship turned into the storm. Kira swayed, knees bending to keep her balance. The crossing had taken more than a full moon and her body had become accustomed to the rock and sway of the sea beneath her. Under normal conditions, she could cross the deck with the practiced gait of a weathered sailor, but now the wind blasted the ship from all directions and the sea roiled like a boiling cauldron. Her knuckles whitened against the wet wooden rail.

With a thrust of her arms, she pushed off toward the water barrel lashed tight to the mainmast. She ladled water into the bucket she carried, filling it only half full to keep the contents from sloshing out. After tamping the barrel's lid back into place, she hauled the bucket down into the cargo hold. Trad and Zharik were corralled on one side and though Kira and Milos mucked it out daily, the place smelled like damp straw and stable.

The ship lurched and the horses whinnied and stamped. Vaith launched himself from Kira's shoulder and landed awkwardly on a nearby beam.

"Ah, there you go," Milos said. "I told you she'd be right back." He spoke gently to calm the horses, both of which twitched and shivered, their nerves strained by the rocking of the ship. "I've worked his legs, but it isn't enough." He stopped massaging Trad's forelegs, and glanced up at Kira. "They need real exercise."

She braced herself against the heavy rolling of the ship by wrapping an arm around a nearby beam, as she held the bucket up to Trad's muzzle. "We'll have to go slowly when we reach shore. It will take days for them to regain their full strength after this long at sea." Trad's eyes were white, but he stuck his nose into the bucket and drank, even as water splashed over the sides of the pail.

"What did the captain say?" Milos stood and stretched, spreading his legs wide and gripping a length of rope that hung from the overhead to keep his balance.

Kira shrugged. "The same thing he says each time I ask."

"It takes as long as it takes," they said in unison and almost laughed despite the storm and their frustration at the long confinement they'd endured aboard the Sunfleet. The ship lurched again and Trad yanked his head from the bucket, knocking it into Kira, dousing the front of her. She gasped and reached out to calm the frightened horse. "You'd think Captain Salhker and Heresta were schooled from the same book," Kira grumbled, giving Trad's soft nose a pat. "There, now, Trad."

"This weather's turned more foul of a sudden, though." Kira frowned. "Our fine captain says we've been swept north along the coast far beyond our intended landing." She set down the bucket and swiped at her wet clothing. "They've battened down the hatches. All but this one." She nodded up at the opening that led out onto the ship's deck.

The crisscrossed covering that usually closed off the hold from above was little more than a grating to keep normal stock from escaping the hold, and had been left open as part of their negotiated accommodations for the voyage. Though, not without plenty of mutters and complaints. Most of the crew disliked the idea of a large hunting cat with free access to the decks. "I'll be glad to be back on land again and no longer at the mercy of this fickle sea." And this sour crew, she thought.

From the corner of the hold, Kelmir growled in agreement, his feline eyes glittering like amethysts in the dim light.

"Even Vaith is growing tired of fish," Kira said, with a

3

sigh, and above her the wyvern cocked his head.

Milos gave up trying to work Zharik's forelegs. The big stallion had locked his muscles to keep his balance. "We're lucky to be here at all," he reminded her. "If not for you healing the Dock Master's son—"

"And the emptying of your purse," she chided.

Milos shrugged. "It was only money," he said, standing and patting Zharik's chest. "And spent for a good cause." He reached out and pulled her close, and she leaned into him.

With a sudden lurch, the ship heaved hard to port. A shout rang out from above. Kira and Milos were tossed against the side of the hold. Vaith squawked, wings flapping. The groan of wood and the whipping of sails were drowned out by the roar of water and wind. The ship rolled back to starboard with a loud grinding of wet wood.

"What was that?" Milos clung to the wooden slats that served as a makeshift stable wall.

Kira wrapped her arm about an upright beam and put a hand up to stroke Vaith, wishing she could send him into the sky and see through his eyes. But she dared not risk him to the storm. Yet, with a smoothness that came from years of practice, her mind momentarily melded with his. She suddenly saw the hold's interior with a new precision and her hearing heightened. "Rocks," a lookout shouted. "Rocks ahead, Cap'n."

"Put yer backs into it boys. Put yer backs into it!" the captain ordered in his raspy voice.

Kira snapped back into her own body. "Rocks," she hissed. "And we're headed right for them."

Milos pushed his way to Zharik's side. The black horse pulled at his halter as the ship swayed and heaved on the sea like a writhing beast. Milos placed a hand on the stallion's nose to calm him.

"I would like to know what wisdom the Captain has for an occurrence such as this," Kira said.

Milos gave her a sideways glance. "It would have to be something special."

Kelmir prowled against the far wall, pacing to and fro, eyeing the dark sky that showed down through the ship's hatch with longing.

The ship heaved again, groaning with the sudden shift.

Milos stiffened. "If we hit those rocks . . ."

Kira nodded. She thought about their belongings. While there was nothing here she couldn't live without—aside from Milos, Vaith, Kelmir, and the horses—on impulse she reached for her store of healing herbs.

With a sudden jolt the ship pulled up short and lurched high. Kira stumbled, falling against a heavy wood stanchion. She hissed in pain. A loud crash sounded, followed by a piercing creak and grind. Zharik tried to rear, yanking at the ropes that held him fast.

Milos climbed up from where he'd fallen and grabbed hold of the horse's head. He covered the animal's eyes with his hand and wrapped an arm around his neck.

Kira's feet were suddenly wet and chilled. Water flowed into the hold.

"We have to get the horses out!" Milos shouted, untying the rope that secured the stallion and grabbing what gear he could reach.

Kira had already loosed Trad's halter from the rail. They stepped over floating debris, splashing in ankle-deep water.

The captain's voice rose above the noise. "Loose the small boats!" On the deck above them, the sound of pounding feet traveled across the planking.

Kira bent low, using one hand for balance as she led Trad up the awkward ramp toward the ship's deck.

Lashing wind whipped the horse's manes and the driving rain stung Kira's eyes. How near to land were they? She sought Vaith's mind. There would be no way to get the horses into a boat, not from the deck of the ship. In the roiling sea, they'd only be able to swim a short distance.

Vaith clung to Kira's shoulder, trilling and squawking as he gripped tight. "Vaith," she whispered. "I almost lost you once, little one. I couldn't bear it if . . ."

Vaith's eyes glowed golden, his pupils dilating with nervous fear. Then the delicate wyvern spread his wings and leaped into the storm.

CHAPTER TWO

The Sunfleet wallowed as it took on water.

Driving winds buffeted the little wyvern, and through his eyes Kira sighted the hazy outline of the Faersent coast, a distance of half a league or more. Closer than she had thought, but far enough to spell danger for all of them, especially the two horses. Vaith would find his way safely to shore, she told herself, forcing her awareness back to the ship.

Sailors had lowered the small boats over the Sunfleet's side, pushing them away from the floundering vessel. Men leaped into the water and swam to meet their companions, who hauled them into the wooden crafts.

Kelmir paced along the aft deck of the ship, muscles twitching, as Kira and Milos stood on deck, calming their frightened mounts

"We'll have to jump," Milos hollered into the wind.

"It's too high," Kira shouted back. "They'll never jump.

And if they do . . ." She let her words trail off, but she knew Milos was thinking the same thing. If the horses hit the water wrong from this height, they would be badly injured. And an injured horse wouldn't be able to swim to shore.

Milos ripped a sleeve from his shirt, and tied it over Zharik's eyes. "We have to make them jump." He gritted his teeth and swung up onto the black horse.

"Wait! The ship is listing toward port," Kira yelled to be heard above the thunder and howl of the crushing storm. "Wait until the deck is closer to the water . . ."

Milos tore off his other sleeve and handed it to Kira. "We can't wait long." The deck tilted higher and higher. Coils of rope, pins and tools rolled toward the port railing.

Kira held the fabric to Trad's eyes for a moment, then with forced calm, she rubbed his nose and placed her forehead to his. "Trad," she whispered. "Of all the times I have wished you could understand me the way Vaith and Kelmir do, now is the time I wish it the most."

"Kira," Milos said, struggling to keep Zharik calm, "we must go." His voice was urgent.

She glanced up at him, this man who had chosen to leave his home to share in this quest, and gave him a small smile. He grimaced, his blue eyes crinkling at the edges in worry. He would wait for her, but she needed him to go. Needed to know he was safe before she could leave the ship.

Without warning, she gave Zharik's rump a hard swat and the black horse leaped forward. Milos barely had a chance to pull the blinder from the horse's eyes in time to make the jump over the ship's railing.

"Kelmir, go!" she shouted, hoisting herself onto Trad's back. She dropped Milos' shirtsleeve to the deck and whispered into Trad's ear. The gray horse stood frozen for an instant as the ship gave a shudder. A cra-aaa-aack rang out like a tree bent to breaking by the wind. With a groan, the prow of the ship tilted downward.

A barrel rolled past them, barely missing Trad's hind feet. He danced sideways. Kira leaned forward and whispered again, then squeezed with her knees. He shook his head, and with a clatter of hooves, ran to the side and leaped.

They splashed into the cold sea and sank down, down, deep under the surface.

It felt as if they would sink forever, that there would never be air and sky again. Kira forced herself to stay with Trad as his struggling legs fought to stop their downward momentum and finally brought them back up again, both of them kicking hard for the surface. When her head broke the water, Kira heaved in a lungful of air, coughing and spitting when the storm-chopped waves splashed over her face.

Trad kicked, struggling to keep his head above the cresting water. Panting, Kira glanced behind her at the ship, which rolled upright for a moment before the aft end rose high into the air.

Angry waves lashed at them, pushing them toward the dying ship. Kira kicked out with her legs and urged Trad to move. They had to escape the sinking ship and the debris that pounded in the waves.

Panicked, Kira searched the water. Where were Milos and Zharik? She spun herself around in the water, waves crashing over her head. She saw only water and floating wreckage from the ship.

Trad arched his back and huffed in air, letting it out slowly. Then huffed in again. She had to get him to shore.

May Troka protect them. Kira scissored her legs, and swam toward shore, still gripping Trad's lead. After a few yards, his struggling slowed and he grew more confident in the water. The nearer to shore they moved, the less angry the sea became. It was as if the sudden storm meant to disappear as quickly as it had arrived.

She heard a shout. "Ho!" Ahead and to her left, Dahl, the ship's boy, sat in the rear of a small boat, urging her to swim to them. The sailor seated beside him cuffed his ear, but Dahl yelled something at the man and swatted his hand away. Kira changed direction and fought her way toward the boat.

"Leave her," a grizzled sailor snarled. "'Tis the wheel's own wrath she's brought down upon us."

"You'd not wish to be left to the sea," Dahl screamed back. The lashing wind and rain plastered his blonde curls against his head and he appeared even younger than Kira knew him to be. "It's not a proper thing to leave another to the salt tombs, not before their time."

"Know you that 'tisn't hers?" The sailor growled in frustration as the other men slowed their oars allowing Kira and Trad to close the distance between them and the craft.

Kira kicked her feet, struggling to swim with one hand holding onto Trad's lead. Dahl reached out to pull her aboard, but the older sailor gave him an ugly scowl.

"I'll hang onto the side and keep hold of my horse," Kira told him, grabbing onto the boat's gunwale. The boat rocked on the rough waves, but the storm continued abating and she managed to hold on. "I'd rather stay beside him. Can you help us to shore?"

Dahl nodded and pointed with his chin behind Kira.

She turned to see Kelmir paddling unhappily up beside her. "I don't suppose there's room in the boat—?"

"'Twas one thing to have a wild animal aboard the ship, though he be kept below," one of the oarsman grumbled.

10

The grizzled sailor spat into the sea. "You and that beast will get no welcome aboard this small block of pine and tar."

Kira pursed her lips together. *Swim for shore, Kel.* She sent her thoughts to him. *We'll be right behind you.*

Kelmir chuffed his disdain, then paddled his way around them and headed for land, his dark tail floating behind him like a sea snake.

"Slide abaft," Dahl told her, pointing to the rear end of the boat. "You can hang on back there and stay clear of the oars."

Loosening her hold on the edge of the boat, Kira let herself slide astern. As she neared the back, her hand slipped and her head went under. She came up sputtering, grabbing for the boat, and a slender hand reached out and caught her before she became separated from the craft. With a cough, she gasped in a lungful of air. Dahl looped a length of rope around her wrist and placed her hand back onto the edge of the boat. Then the sailors began to paddle in earnest cadence, and the small vessel turned and headed toward shore with Kira and Trad bobbing behind.

As they neared land, the swells shifted to sturdy waves that broke into whitecaps and crashed against the shore, pushing the boat nearer the beach. Rather than propelling the boat, the oarsmen now used their paddles to steer and balance it. The other men held on and leaned into the waves.

Ahead, a white sand-covered beach stretched as far as she could see. Kira was surprised to see the shore relatively clear of debris. No piles of seaweed-covered driftwood, nor other storm detritus marred the smooth curve of sand that hugged the shoreline.

Beyond the stretch of sand, greenery grew deep and lush and dark. The smell of wet forest rode out from the land, beckoning them to shore. How she'd missed the smell of earth and trees. She wondered how these men could spend so much of their lives at sea. How they could go so many days and weeks, and even moons on end, without the touch of grass, the smell of soil. She ached for the feel of steady ground beneath her feet.

As they drew closer, the sailors turned the boat and angled toward the shore. "We're putting in to leeward of that sandbar." Dahl pointed to where the water turned a lighter blue. Now that the storm had all but passed them over, the water had calmed and Kira could almost see the sandy floor beneath the waves. "If you land there, it will give the horse a better chance to gain his footing, and you'll be able to wade ashore from there."

"Thank you." She nodded and slipped the rope from around her wrist, readying herself to let go as the water grew more shallow. She swam to the place Dahl had indicated, guiding Trad until his hooves finally struck the bottom and he stopped swimming. He stood for a moment, as if dazed, then walked slowly up onto the sand bar that stretched out at a right angle from the shore. The water here rose only to his chest, but he shook with the effort of every step. Kira sloshed beside him, coaxing him to shore.

She glanced over her shoulder to where Milos and Zharik waded behind them, relief warming her. With a quick brush of her mind, she sensed both Vaith and Kelmir. They were all safe ashore, although Milos wore a grim expression. There would be words, she knew, but it appeared he would bide his time for the moment.

Five small boats had managed to escape the sinking ship. The sailors pulled their boats onto the sandy shore and several dozen men staggered onto the beach. Only then did Kira think to search for the captain. For a moment she wondered if he had stayed on board his sinking ship as the old tales said a good captain always did. But she spotted him as he disembarked from the last of the arriving boats and stomped angrily ashore.

Kira led Trad up and away from the rising tide before falling onto her knees beside him, where she began a thorough check of the gray horse's feet and legs.

Trad's chest heaved and his head hung low. He didn't even turn to look when Milos brought Zharik up a few strides behind. The black appeared unharmed, but he shivered and shied as Milos tried to check him for injuries.

"He's never been much of a swimmer," Milos said. His voice was quiet, but there was a hard edge to his tone.

With a stifled sigh, Kira stood and carried on her inspection of Trad. "You're angry."

Milos' eyebrows slammed down. His face filled with barely suppressed ire. "What were you thinking?" His tone was fierce, but he kept his voice low enough not to carry across the sand where the sailors might hear.

"I wanted you safe." Kira slid her hand along Trad's mane and patted his neck, trying to calm herself as much as assure the horse.

"And what about you? Your safety?"

Kira pursed her lips together. Why was he so upset? She had acted without thinking about anything except getting Milos off the ship and had followed right behind him. "I don't understand—"

"How can you not?" Milos ran his hand through his dark hair. "You act as if I cannot be trusted with my own welfare, nor that of Zharik."

"It's not a matter of trust—" Kira started.

"No?" Milos grabbed a handful of dried grass and used it to rapidly dry Zharik, swiping it along his coat to sluice off the saltwater and sand. The stallion twitched and reached his nose around to push against Milos' hand. "Apologies, Zharik." Milos slowed his strokes, then stopped and glared at Kira. "I am as capable of taking care of myself as you are."

"I know that."

"Do you?

Kira opened her mouth to respond. But before she could, Milos tossed the grass onto the sand and turned on her. "I have no more need to be rescued than do you. But you continue to act as if I do." He grabbed Zharik's lead, turned away, and led his horse a short distance up the beach.

Kira watched him move off. A part of her wished to go after him, but it was clear he didn't wish to continue the discussion. At least not at this time. With shaking hands, she finished checking Trad for bumps and bruises.

Standing, she reached out for Kelmir and Vaith. The big cat waited in the shadows of the thick greenery that bordered the sandy expanse of the shore. Grumpy, but otherwise fine. Above him, Vaith sat in a thick bower of leaves, ripping and tearing at a small rodent. Kira wondered at his capacity for eating. Nothing she knew of had ever put the wyvern off food, except for the time he'd gallantly, and foolishly, defended her against a poisonous basilisk and had been seared by the creature's acidic venom. But she'd been too injured from the attack at the time to care for him. That task had fallen to Milvari, Milos' niece and, at the time, Kira's apprentice in the art of healing.

For a moment, she wondered how Milvari and the people of Tem Hold fared. There were enough loyal folk to ensure the Hold would prosper as long as they worked together. But she worried about Tratine, Milvari's brother. Tratine had blamed Kira for his mother's death and hated her for it, which meant he had probably not forgiven his sister for allying herself with Kira. Often, in her dreams, she saw him with fire in his eyes, the way Toril had looked—

Kira recalled that day in the woods when she had placed herself between Milos and the basilisk. She had to admit, Milos was right. She often acted without thinking, putting herself in danger to protect others. But he would do the same given the opportunity, would he not?

"Your face has that deeply troubled expression," Milos said, moving nearer. His voice had lost some of the sharpness now, though he was still upset. "What worries you?"

"We've just come from a rather unpleasant swim," she said, turning the subject aside for the time being. "We've lost most of our supplies. And this is clearly not where the captain meant to bring us ashore. Isn't that enough?" She didn't want to worry him about a few bad dreams. Nor did she wish to revisit their previous topic. She wasn't in the mood for an argument, especially one where she was unclear as to who was in the right.

"But we're safe, and for the most part unharmed." There was still an unmistakable edge to his voice. He ducked around Zharik and moved closer to her. "You are unharmed, aren't you?"

She stared down at her hands and arms. They were raw from where the wet rope had abraded the skin and there was a bruise rising along her left forearm, only she didn't remember hitting it on anything. It must have happened when the ship had lurched and they'd been tossed about below decks. She pushed her sleeve down. "Nothing major. But I wonder how the crew has fared," she said, standing abruptly and handing Trad's lead to Milos before he could ask her any more questions. "I'd better make sure they are all right."

15

Milos shook his head. "Of course." The sharp edge in his voice had reshaped itself into a tone of condescension. "A healer's work is never done," he muttered. "Not in war nor peace."

Kira bit her tongue and left him holding the horses.

CHAPTER THREE

By the time Kira returned, the horses were grazing contentedly and Milos sat against the trunk of a tall tree. He looked up at her approach, shading his eyes against the glare of the sunlight reflecting off sea and sand. She carried a full water skin, a small hunk of bread, and some cheese wrapped in oilcloth. "With the captain's compliments, such as they are," she said, handing the food and water to Milos. "The pilot's bread is as hard as slate, and the cheese is a bit soggy, but the crew is still retrieving and sorting rations from the wreckage. So, there is hope of something more . . ." She attempted to break off a bit of the pilot's bread and turned up her lip.

"Very gracious of the good captain." Milos took a long drink of water, then wiped his mouth with the back of his hand. "We'll need to soak that to make it edible."

"You have no idea," Kira said under her breath, "on both counts. That ship was his livelihood and many among his crew are blaming us, or rather me, for our recent misfortune."

Milos glanced down the beach at the sailors toiling beneath a sun that beat down upon the stretch of sand and water as if the storm had never happened.

"Poor judgment on their part," he said. "Unfortunately, clear discernment has never been the strong suit of most people."

"Especially men." Kira ticked her eyes in his direction, wondering if his comment was meant to include her.

Milos went on as if he had not heard her. "Does Captain Salhker have any idea where we've landed?" He scraped a bit of mold off a chunk of damp cheese and popped it into his mouth.

"He says we must have been pulled off course by the north-south currents." Kira finally managed to dislodge a piece of the sea biscuit small enough to put into her mouth, followed by a sip of water, hoping the cursed thing would soften enough to chew.

"Currents?"

"That's what he said." Tension clearly lingered between them, but Kira knelt beside Milos in the warm sand and brushed his hair back from his forehead where a lump the size of a chicken's egg had appeared. "You call this unharmed?"

He threaded his fingers through hers. "It's nothing." He leaned forward as if to kiss the inside of her wrist.

She jerked her hand away with a hiss, startling him. He eyed her, first with hurt and then with curiosity, before reaching out and pushing up her sleeve. The bruise on her forearm had turned an angry dark purple, nearly black, and now stretched from wrist to elbow. His blue eyes rose to meet hers. "And what do you call this?"

She brushed a finger across her wrist and forearm, wincing. "It was only a bruise when we first came

ashore." She frowned. "I don't know why it changed
color so quickly. It isn't broken." She moved her hand
and wiggled her fingers, as she probed delicately with
the fingertips of her other hand. Pain radiated from her
wrist and shot up her arm. "Not broken," she hissed
from between clenched teeth. "But probably fractured. I
might have realized sooner, but for the excitement of our
sudden swim. And my focus on tending to the crew's
more serious injuries."

"Isn't fractured the same thing as broken?"

"In a way, except for the severity. A break is much
worse than a fracture. Displacement can cause more
pain and be problematic for proper healing." Kira
glanced around, looking for a flat piece of wood. "But
both need to be splinted and braced to limit movement."

"The healer needs a healer," Milos said, rising to his
feet. "I'm no apprentice, but I can find a splint."

Kira glanced up the beach where the ship's crew had
set up a makeshift camp. Captain Salhker had
sustained several deep lacerations and at least a broken
rib, more likely two, though he made a show of acting
healthy. When Kira had tended to him, he'd made her
promise to keep the extent of his injuries quiet. "Most of
the crew are good solid men," he'd said, "but a few . . ."

Kira had nodded in understanding while stitching up
his worst cuts and binding his rib cage, but had in turn
demanded he follow her directions for his healing, which
included substantial rest. Yet, she was hardly surprised
to see him now, coming down the beach, up and about,
ordering the work, and enlisting a scouting party of the
least injured sailors to search inland for fresh water and
provisions.

"This is a strange country, lads," he told them. "Be
wary. And watch yourselves. The laws of these folk are
different than ours and a man could find himself against

the mast for a simple gesture taken wrong. If you meet any of the natives, keep your heads down and don't look them in the eyes," he warned. "There's some of these creatures can bewitch a man into giving up his very nature. So's I've been told."

He caught Kira watching him and his eyes met hers for a moment before he turned away and sent the sailors on their mission. The foraging party nodded and whispered to themselves as they set off in the direction of the trees. All except for Dahl, the ship's boy, who cast an apologetic glance in Kira's direction before running to catch up to the men.

As Kira watched them go, the captain stepped up beside her. "No offense was meant by what I told my men," he murmured.

"None was taken," Kira said. "Why would you think otherwise?"

"While you've kept your own counsel in the matter, it's clear from your looks that you have ties to this land," Captain Salhker said.

A short distance away, the ship's surly First Mate began sorted the debris that had been washed ashore from the shipwreck. There wasn't much left of the tall-masted vessel. Lengths of wood, some chipped and cracked clay vessels, a few barrels, some filled with dried apples and other such food. The clothing and blankets that had floated ashore, hung from nearby branches or were spread out on the sand to dry.

Kira brushed fine beach sand from her hands. "How is it you know so much about this land and its people?" she asked.

"I've sailed back and forth across the Faersent Sea more times than I can count," he said. "Though I've never been caught up in so sudden a storm as this, nor one as quickly over and done." He stared out at the sea, which had lost the ugly gray storm color and sat calm and sparkling beneath a bluing sky. "I was a cabin boy on the Portent, a trader that crossed this sea at least twice every year, more when the captain could stuff his cargo hold more often. May he ride the dark side of the wheel for all time, the greedy sot." He turned his head and spat on the sand. "Though, now I've had to think on it, I never came at this land this far north. Always aimed for the southerly port. No idea how we sailed so far off course. Though, I've heard tales . . ." His voiced dropped to a murmur.

He looked thoughtful for a span, then cleared his throat. "At any rate, your eyes and hair, the way you stand tall enough to look most men in the eye. That and the glow of your skin." He held his hand next to hers, a dark mahogany beside her milky paleness. "If you're not one of them, you're at least kin."

Dropping his hand, he stared out at the white crested waves that danced against the shore and Kira gazed with him. East, toward home, toward the graves of both her parents and her mentor, Heresta. East, toward the battlefield where she had slain her abusive mate, the Warlord Toril. Forced to the act, or no, it still felt wrong to have killed with so much anger in her heart. She squeezed her eyes shut against the painful memories and the sorrows that lay across the sea.

"Kin, I'm told," she said finally, opening her eyes. She turned her back on the sea, reaching up to finger the medallion that hung about her neck, and gazed at the lush green forest that marked the edge of Eilar, the island home of her mother's kin. The place where she hoped to discover the truth of her heritage.

CHAPTER FOUR

Milos wrapped another strip of cloth around Kira's arm, keeping the length of the dried branch he had shaved smooth firm against her fractured wrist. "How does it feel?" he asked.

Kira tested it, trying to bend her wrist without success. But before she could answer him, a piercing cry rang out from the forest followed by the crashing of branches and brush. One of the sailors came stumbling out of the verdant growth and tumbled onto the sand, panting and heaving. Blood ran from a gash on his left cheek and dripped onto his torn shirt.

In a moment, Captain Salhker was at the man's side. Kira reached the wounded man close behind.

"What's happened?" the captain demanded. "Where are the others?"

The sailor tried to speak, but he was unable to catch his breath.

Kira leaned toward him, attempting to clean the blood

from his wound.

The sailor flinched. "It's them," he spat between breaths. "The ones like her."

Kira reached out again to staunch the man's bleeding, but he quickly crabbed away from her. The captain shook his head.

The other sailors left their tasks, and came running to see what the trouble was.

Captain Salhker handed the man a half-empty water skin. The sailor eyed Kira warily as he squeezed water into his mouth and gulped noisily. After a time, his breathing slowed.

"Now," the captain said. "What happened?"

The man shook his head, as if to clear it of dizziness. "I—I'm not sure," he rasped.

"Think, man," the captain urged.

"We were foraging, searching for fresh water. Just like you said, Cap'n." He threw a nervous glance over his shoulder at the deep azure of the trees. "We found what looked to be an animal track we thought to follow to a water hole or maybe a stream." He paused, as if he struggled to remember. "The Bos'n led the way. Me behind him. And then come . . ." He paused, again, and stared down at the sand.

"Young Dahl. The ship's boy." The captain's mouth turned down in a hard frown and a murmur of complaints rustled through the group of men.

Kira's heart began to pound against her chest. Dahl was a sweet-natured young boy. His breaking voice often embarrassed him to blushing, and he'd not spoken a word to Kira the first two weeks of the voyage. He'd finally been drawn into conversation with her because of his interest in Kelmir and Vaith. But unlike other boys, he'd been far more fascinated by the fierce hunting cat than the wyvern. Had his duties not kept him so busy during the journey, he would have surely spent every waking moment in the hold with Kelmir.

"Aye." The sailor continued to stare at the ground, but his body had begun to quiver.

Kira refocused on the conversation. There was no doubt the man had experienced something traumatic. She touched the captain gently on the arm, but he shook her off with a twitch of his shoulders.

"And then what?" he asked the sailor.

"Then the forest grew sudden quiet and a dark shadow rose up and reached out for us." He wiped a hand across his eyes and his body shook. "I heard a thrashing in the brush and then the screaming reached inside my head." He covered his ears with his hands and his voice grew rough with his panted breath. "It drilled into my brain, Cap'n. Pierced it like a speared fish."

"What happened next?"

"I ran," the sailor hissed. "Ran like I've never run before." His hands still covered his ears and he began to writhe and moan.

"Hold, man." The captain pulled a flask from inside his jacket and handed it to the man. "Here. This will help."

The sailor grabbed the flask with quaking hands, threw back his head and poured a draught down his throat. He swallowed, gasped and coughed. Then took another drink, before the captain pulled the flask away from him.

"Where are the other men I sent into the forest with you?"

"I don't know," the sailor shook his head. "The screaming. It made me forget . . . everything."

"Everything but saving your own hide," Captain Salhker muttered under his breath.

Kira heard the comment, but the sailor appeared not

to have. His shaking had calmed, but Kira worried the liquor the captain had given him would only mask his symptoms for a short while. She would need to find a better calmative agent for treating him. If only her healing supplies hadn't been ruined by the sea water. But wishing things different would not change them. For now, the most important task was to find the missing men, especially Dahl.

She turned to see Milos standing just behind her. He nodded when she caught his eye. "Milos and I will search for your men," Kira said.

"Too dangerous. The sun sinks quickly in this part of the world." The captain stared out at the deepening green of the forest.

"My animal companions can track in near darkness," Kira told him. "And time is critical. If any of the lost men are wounded, they may not last through the night."

The deck hand snarled, blood still dripping from the wound on his face. "Don't trust her." He pointed a weathered finger at Kira. "'Twas the Eilars that took the others."

Kira stared angrily at him and his hand began to shake. He finally dropped his arm, his eyes filled with fear. "Cap'n Salhker. Sir. You can't trust her."

"What makes you think it was the Eilars?" The captain peered into the sailor's frightened eyes.

"It's their land," the sailor's voice trembled. "It's their powers that pierced my brain. Their evil magic that made me forget I was a man. That made me run like . . . like a coward." He stood up as he spoke, turning to face Kira, his voice rising into a hoarse yell.

Hand reaching for his sword, Milos lunged toward the man, but Kira stepped between them, her arms extended to show she held no weapon. She stared at the sailor, but spoke loud enough for all to hear. "We will find your men and bring them back."

"It isn't safe in there." Captain Salhker jerked his thumb in the direction of the dense wood. "Not for anyone." He made a point of looking into each man's eyes in turn. "Anyone," he repeated, to be sure they understood. He was clearly telling them where he would stand should anything come to trouble.

Some of the sailors grumbled, but none, it appeared, were willing to take on their captain.

Kira felt Milos tense behind her, then she heard the sound of his sword shifting back into its scabbard with a shush of steel on leather and the clank of the hilt tapping home. He backed up a pace, giving her room to pass, but stood staring at the men for a moment before following her down the beach.

"What was that all about?" he asked, once they were far enough away not to be overheard.

She stared at the deep jade of the forest and shook her head. "I don't know," she said. "There's something in there. Something I can sense. Something that seems to sense me."

His eyes narrowed. "What does that mean?"

"Again, I don't know. But I intend to find out." She bent to pick up the water skin they had drunk from earlier.

Milos grabbed her around the waist, pulling her around to face him. "We'll find out together." The edge had returned to his voice and his blue eyes had gone a deeper shade.

She let herself relax for a moment and leaned against his chest. "I don't suppose it would do any good to ask you to stay here and keep an eye on things."

"Not a bit," he said.

"Very well." She slung the water skin over her shoulder and winced.

"First, you should let that heal," Milos said.

Kira shook her head. "There's no time. Keeping it steady will help it heal properly. The pain, I will just have to bear." She repositioned the strap of the water skin. "It will be fine. I will be fine."

Milos started to argue, but she set her jaw, signaling him to save his breath.

"We might as well take everything we can carry. I've no idea how far we have to go to find the people those men were talking about." Using her good hand, Kira cinched Trad's girth, but not too tight. The wet leather would stretch, otherwise. Not a good way to travel, but after what had just happened with the ship's crew, she didn't want to leave any of their gear lying here while they went after the missing men. And the longer they waited to go after the men, the harder it would be to track them and whoever, or whatever, had taken them.

Beside her, Milos draped his sodden saddlebags over Zharik's shoulder and the horse gave a small shudder at the cool wetness. "We'll want to walk the horses for as long as we can," he said, fingering the wet leather of the tack. "The dryer these saddles before we sit them, the better. Besides," he smirked. "I, for one, don't relish the thought of riding with a soggy backside."

Kira threw him a quick smile. She felt the same way about riding a wet saddle, though Troka knew she'd traveled that way plenty in the past year. She recalled the horrendous rainstorm that had beset her on the climb up the Zendel mountain pass. Then shivered at the memory of her battle with the rock troll. The dark, the cold, the rain, had all been against her. If not for her valiant companions, she would not have survived that meeting.

"You're recalling something dark," Milos said in a low voice.

"A mere shadow," she answered, picking up Trad's reins and pushing the ugly memory from her mind. How was it that Milos read her so well? He sometimes seemed to know before she did when a dark mood would strike. At those times, he was always the most gentle and understanding, even if they had been fighting. It was as if he knew exactly how much pain she had suffered at the hands of Toril, and was determined to make up for the abuse by heaping love and kindness upon her.

The only thing Milos didn't seem to be able to comprehend was her sense of guilt and loss. The confusion she still suffered. Her need to try to make amends by offering her healing skills to each and every person in need of them. If Toril had been her mate and abuser, what did that say about her, the healer who had become a warrior?

A warrior, and Toril's killer.

She found herself suddenly striding angrily toward the forest. The dark mood closed over her. Kelmir and Vaith, seeming to sense her mind, slipped under the shadow of the tree line just ahead.

CHAPTER FIVE

Kira didn't wait for Milos, but took the lead, wrapping herself in her feelings of guilt and anger. Milos held back. Was he giving her time and distance or simply expressing his frustration? After a moment, he clucked his tongue to Zharik and followed her under the shadow of the trees.

In a flurry, Vaith burst though the leafy branches before winging down to settle onto Kira's shoulder. He wrapped his long tail around her neck, tickling her ear. Distractedly, Kira reached up to brush him away, but he let out a low trill and she stayed her hand. It wasn't Vaith's fault she had become as she was. Nor was it a guilt that Milos owned. It was hers alone. The choices and actions that made her who she was, belonged to her and only her. No one else was responsible. And, truth be known, she would have it no other way. But while her guilt was hers to own, it was not an excuse to take out her anger on her companions.

She bowed her head for a moment, trying to let the foul mood dissipate, but it was useless. The black feeling would not leave her be. Yet, there was something else, too. A sense of dread that seemed to have wrapped around her as she worried at her guilt, sawing back and forth against the grain of her past actions, replaying each move, each choice she'd made since the day Heresta had found her and taken her in.

This feeling of unease nagged at her, growing in size and wearing at her like a misshapen boot that pinched and scraped. She glanced from side to side and let her mind slide out to find Kelmir in the undergrowth, where he padded quietly a short distance behind. He was wary, sniffing at the strange odors in the wood, unusual fungi and odd greenery, the likes of which he'd not scented before. But other than his cautious approach to the newness of the place, she sensed nothing unusual in his demeanor or in his thoughts. No fear, nor sense of foreboding like that which Kira felt.

She turned to Milos and saw him scowling. "Do you feel it, too?" she asked, pulling Trad to a halt.

"Feel what?" he growled.

Kira peered at him through the shadows.

He glared at her, his eyes wide and his face filling with anger.

"Milos," she whispered, stiffening. "There's something wrong here."

"Yes," he hissed. "There certainly is something wrong." He dropped Zharik's reins and strode toward her, hands balled into fists. "We never finished discussing your actions on the ship."

Kira flinched, but held her ground. She had nothing to fear from this man, she reminded herself. This was Milos, not Toril. Milos cared for her and would never harm her.

"Milos," she said quietly, "I don't mean that. This. This darkness isn't you. It's the forest. The anger you feel isn't yours."

Milos froze. His eyes cleared and he wiped his hand across his face. "Anger?" he asked. "Or is it menace?" He closed his eyes for a moment. "There's something." He shook his head. "Something gnawing at me, scraping at my nerves. I thought . . . But . . ." He shrugged and unclenched his fists, then shook out his hands. "I'm sorry," he said, heartfelt remorse coloring his tone. "It was as if something foul overcame me. A flame that seared me through with pain and . . . rage." Milos stepped back and gathered up his horse's reins. He refused to look at her.

"It took me, too," she said, intending to reassure him. "Odd." She surveyed the dense forest surrounding them. "It only seems to be bothering you and me. The animals are either unaware or else unconcerned by it. Even Vaith and Kelmir appear unaffected."

Milos pulled Zharik's head toward him and stared into the horse's dark eyes. Zharik let out a low bluster and swished his tail from side to side, but remained otherwise calm.

"I thought it was just me," Milos said. "But you're right. There's something lurking, grating at me, that doesn't appear to be bothering Zharik. And, if you feel it, too, there must be more to it . . . Do you think it has anything to do with the disappearance of the ship's crewmen?"

"I wouldn't be surprised. Though, I've no idea yet what it might be." Kira caught herself clenching and unclenching her fists, and forced her hands open. She searched the greenery for anything out of place. The entire forest was filled with unique vegetation, but nothing that appeared particularly dangerous. Yet, it all felt wrong. And the air itself seemed to thrum with malice.

They stood in silence, darting glances around them, trying to see anything that might have caused the strange sensations they'd felt.

Then it hit her.

"Do you hear it?" she asked.

"Yes," Milos said. "The forest is far too quiet."

A black shadow fell upon Kira and a heartrending scream pierced her skull. She flung up her arms to ward off the attack. A flash of light assailed her eyes and she sank to the ground, her fist still gripping Trad's reins. She tried to call out to Milos, shout a warning, but her lips refused to move. Her limbs loosened. Her fingers lost their grip, and her entire body went numb. She heard the horses whinny in sudden fear. Then a gray haze settled on her like a sodden blanket, dragging her down into nothingness.

CHAPTER SIX

Voices drifted across her disconnected dreams. Images of fire and blood swirled before her, gave way to sunlight on iridescent wings and cat's eyes that gleamed in the shadows, then spun away from her. Murmurs and whisperings rose and fell in a singsong rhythm, fading in and out, coalescing into something familiar, yet foreign. A language she sensed she knew once, but no longer understood.

She felt her body being jostled and lifted, slung across something solid. But her brain refused to tell her what, until the sturdy gait of the horse beneath her jarred her memory and she swam up through the shadows, back into the gray haze. Milos. Where was Milos? And Kelmir? Vaith?

If she could only open her eyes, she might awaken, might be able to reach one of her companions, but wherever she turned, a gray wall rose up and she could go no further. Trapped in the swirling mist, she finally stopped straining to come fully awake and focused on the only sense that seemed to be left to her, listening. The voices became clearer, cutting through the fog. But she could only understand bits and pieces of what she heard. Her sluggish brain searched for the meanings of familiar but alien words, missing others entirely.

". . . clearly of the clan . . ."

". . . more amiss . . . Matriarch's weakened mind . . ."

". . . treasonous . . ."

Kira tried again to reach for Vaith and . . . the other, but she was unable to find them in the enveloping fog that flooded her brain. Alone. She hadn't been this alone since her childhood, since the loss of her parents, since before . . . before . . .

Leafy plants brushed across her and moisture dripped onto her arms and face as she bumped steadily along, drifting in and out of the fuzzy gray that clung to her and pulled her under each time she tried to surface.

"The Physica must know . . ."

". . . of the lineage . . ."

More words and snippets of conversation floated into her ears, but she understood little of it, and what she understood made no sense.

Time became fluid, like the waves against a sandy shore, lapping at her, but leaving no imprint.

There was something she should remember, something that needed doing, but whatever it was eluded her and perhaps was not so very important after all. Finally, she felt herself heaved down off the horse and carried someplace where the heels of her captors clicked against stone floors and echoed back from rock. Where cool air mixed with the scent of strange flowers and dry rushes, then turned to damp and darkness. The dripping of moisture plip-plipped in standing pools. This too they passed through until at last she was set down on a thin mattress that smelled of herbs and something sweet and floral. And familiar. She tried to search her memories, to place the aroma, but the name of the plant eluded her. The harder she reached for it, the smaller and more elusive that knowledge became, shrinking to nothing.

Nothing.

Nowhere.

She tried to sit up, to open her eyes, but only managed to slit her eyes enough to see there was no light here save that made by the illuminated glowstones. Glowstones? How did she know that word? Before she could wonder any more about it, the darkness descended and she knew nothing.

* * *

She woke in half-light, utterly lost and alone, lying upon a pallet in a cell of some sort. A sudden fright descended on her. Where was she? How had she come here?

Pushing herself up into a sitting position, she surveyed the dim room. A large door stared at her from across the way. She tried to rise from the bed, but dizziness overwhelmed her and she sank down again. More slowly, she eased herself to a standing position, swaying as she reached out to grip the wall. Leaning against the cool stones, she slid her feet forward, one step at a time, following the wall around the corner to the huge slab door. She reached out and grabbed the handle and pulled, but the door refused to budge.

She pulled harder, bracing a hand against the wall and heaving with every bit of her strength, but it was futile. Sweat beaded upon her brow and her muscles twitched and shivered. She closed her eyes. Tears pressed against her lids. Where was she? With a jolt she fell away from the door, stumbling back against the bed. She held up pale hands in the gloom. The better question, she thought, fear squeezing her, *who* was she?

She let the raised pallet prop her up, as the panic crashed into her. Her eyes darted around the narrow room. On a low table near the pallet sat a jug filled with what appeared to be fresh water. Beside it lay a round loaf of dark bread. She leaned over and picked up the jug, bringing it to her face to sniff the contents. It smelled sharp and tangy, and somehow familiar, an herb she could not place. Like her name, she thought sourly. Or anything else about herself. There was no existence for her before now. But that could not be. She pressed the side of the water jug against her face to help cool her hot skin.

She took a tiny sip of the water. It slid across her tongue and soothed her parched mouth and throat. Her body urged her hands to tilt the jug again, to drink deeply, but something inside her told her to stop. There was no knowing what might be in the water, some voice of wisdom warned her. *Go slow*, it said. *Wait and see if the liquid holds harm.*

She stared at the jug for a moment in reflection. *If I had no past at all, how would I know to be cautious of the water? Of the food?*

With a sigh, she set the jug down upon the table and folded her hands, counting inside her head. She waited a hands span of the sun's movement before accepting that the water would do her no harm. Then she drank greedily, quenching her hot thirst.

Once more, she waited, spending the time walking the length and breadth of the cell, touching the glowing stones and attempting the door, once more. When she was certain there was no immediate way out, and nothing wrong with the water, she repeated the same process with the bread, tearing off first a tiny piece and chewing it slowly. When nothing bad happened, she hungrily ripped a fistful off the loaf and devouring it.

She had finished the water and half of the bread when she heard footsteps approaching. She stood up and moved into the furthest corner of the small room, waiting. She started to search for someone, reaching with her mind, but stopped. Why had she done that? She had no idea who she should be looking for, nor why she should be searching with her mind. No. She was alone here. Wherever she was, she was on her own.

The footsteps came closer, more than one set. And voices. No, she realized with a start, not voices. Words in an odd language that she half understood. Only they weren't spoken aloud. They were inside her head. Had this been what she had been searching for?

But, no. Nothing about the "voices" was familiar. There were two of them. And they were thinking at one another, understanding each other without speaking. She was so stunned she barely noticed as the door swung inward. Two men stood in the doorway before her, outlined in the light of the glowstones.

The younger of the two men was tall and broad shouldered, with mahogany hair. He scrutinized her and she could hear his voice inside her head. *Who are you and what brings you to the shores of Eilar?* She stared at him. His lips had not moved, yet she understood his thoughts as clearly as if he had spoken aloud. Yet something inside her, the voice that warned, made her hold her tongue.

If they thought her incapable of hearing their thought-words, perhaps she might learn something of where she was—who she was—without giving away her loss of knowledge. She glanced quickly around the room. Perhaps, they would let her go. She gave the young man a blank stare, pretending not to have heard his thoughts inside her head.

The older man, his face lined with age, leaned on an ornate walking stick and cocked his bald head to give her an appraising look. "It may be her," he said aloud. "Then again, it may not." It was only then that she realized the man wasn't actually looking at her. Not as a normal person might look. No. He was looking into her. The thought made her shiver, again.

She forced herself to continue staring blankly at the two men.

Why do you not answer? This thought pushed at her, coming from the young one, she was certain. His thoughts were hard edged and shimmered a dark blue-black when he spoke inside her head. And they shoved themselves at her, as if they would force themselves inside.

"Perhaps," chided the old man, "she does not understand the language." He gave her a friendly smile. *Or, perhaps, she truly cannot mindspeak.*

The younger man gave her an assessing look and nodded. Perhaps. "Do you understand?" he asked aloud.

She hesitated, wondering if she might learn more by pretending not to understand the language, as well. Finally, she nodded once, deciding it might be too much for them to believe she could neither mindspeak, as they called it, nor understand the language. Perhaps, in speaking with her captors she could learn something. And these two, as odd as they seemed with their unusual ability to communicate in the mind, might tell her something of value without meaning to. And why did it seem odd, she wondered. Perhaps, it was something anyone could do and she had merely forgotten about that, too. She started to open her mouth to ask, only at the last moment, that tiny voice of wisdom warned against it.

"Who are you?" the young man asked, shrugging and tossing back his red-brown curls.

She began to open her mouth to reply, but still found no answer to give. "Who am I?" she asked.

His eyes narrowed. "Do you find mockery humorous?" His lips twitched up into a sneer.

She bent forward slightly and bowed her head, her gaze directed at the floor, showing deference to the young man. "I did not mean to offend," she said in a quiet voice. "It is only that I am surprised to hear the common tongue spoken on this distant shore." Why had she said that? As she straightened, the medallion on the cord around her neck swung back against her breastbone. The metal surface, suddenly cool to the touch, made her shiver.

The old man raised an eyebrow. The movement so slight she thought she might have imagined it. "Her voice," he whispered, "it's—" but before he could say more, the younger man placed a firm hand on his arm.

"We wait upon the testing," he said. "And the Lady's wishes." A bitter note rang through his words and the old man stiffened, but held his tongue.

"I do not know why I am here," she told them, "nor who I am." Her voice sounded thin in her ears. "I cannot recall my name."

Alyana, the old man thought. Was he testing her? Was this the testing the young man had alluded to? Unlike the hard darkness of the younger man's, the older man's thoughts were sharp, but without color. Ghostly, almost. Like they had been filtered through fine meshed cloth before he sent them at her.

"Alyana," he said the name aloud this time. "Of the Eilaren Guardians' bloodline." He pulled out of the younger man's grasp and took a step closer to her, scanning her face. "You have the traits." There was recognition in his eyes, and something akin to curiosity.

"Alyana," she tried the name out on her tongue, wanting to test it against her recollections, but she had none. No connection to the name. It held not the slightest familiarity for her.

The young man cleared his throat, as if he would speak, but the old man shushed him.

"Kavyn, do not overstep. You are here as my aide only because the Second was not able to accompany me, and because you were so insistent on seeing for yourself."

"My apologies, First Meryk." The young man placed the back of his hand to his forehead.

Kavyn. There was something oddly familiar in the sound of the young man's name.

She wanted to ask them where she was, how she had come here. A million questions buzzed inside her head, but her gut advised caution, as did the echo of distant lessons on negotiating. *Before you step, seek first to recognize where you stand, or you may lose your footing.* Whose voice had that been? she wondered. Not more thoughts sent at her, but a seemingly friendly voice that came from inside herself.

How many voices will I have inside my head, she wondered, before I can recall my own?

A gong rang out, echoing down the passageways and reverberating off the walls of the room. The two men started. The young man's face warped into a scowl, but his voice was flat and unemotional when he spoke. "The Time of Tears is upon us. We must go."

The old man sighed. "Do not call it such. It belittles the memories of our ancestors," he scolded the young man. "We must leave you." He bowed his head, but kept his eyes focused on her. "For now."

The two men took their leave and she was left to wonder who the younger man was and what the old man had meant by the 'Eilaren Guardians' bloodline.'

Alyana, she thought as she sank down upon the cot. If that is who I am, why can I not remember? Why can I not recall?

She sat on the pallet and scooted back against the wall, considering. The older man seemed to see into her. It was as if he could sense more about her than she knew herself.

The two men could communicate without words. They were even able to send their thoughts at her. And she could hear them inside her head. But that was not possible, was it?

She rested her head in her hands. A hot pain had planted itself behind her eyes as soon as the two men had left the room and now bloomed into a white blaze that threatened to crush what little there was left of her mind.

CHAPTER SEVEN

"Kira," Milos called into the shadows, his mind a flurry of scattered thoughts. He stretched his arms before him, trying to feel his way through the murkiness, but there appeared to be no end to the fog that shifted and twisted around him. His left thigh ached and something sticky and wet seeped down his leg. He slid one foot forward along the ground and then the other, taking tentative steps, trying not to put too much weight on his injured leg. "Damn this mist," he muttered, brushing the clinging damp from his face. For all he knew, he was going in circles.

Something fluttered ahead, a darker shadow against the thick grayness. "Vaith?" The fluttering became a frantic flapping, as if whatever it was beat against an invisible barrier. "Vaith!" Milos called. The flapping paused for a fraction of a moment, then began again with renewed vigor.

Milos stumbled in the direction of the sound, hoping

S. A. Skinner

it meant Kira was near, fearing it meant that something had happened to her. Else why did she not answer his calls? He suddenly tripped over something and fell forward, landing in a heap atop a slender form. His leg screamed out, but he ignored it, reaching forward to touch her face.

But it was not Kira. This was someone smaller. And male. Milos felt the line of light bearding along the square jaw. The downy chin hair told him it was a boy. The ship's boy? "Dahl?" The boy lay still, skin clammy.

Milos placed his hand just below the boy's nose. Air moved in and out. Breath. The young man was alive. He gripped the boy by his shoulders and gave him a little shake. "Dahl," he said. "Can you hear me?"

The boy let out a low groan. "I didn't mean to fall asleep, sir," he slurred. "I'm sorry. Won't happen again." His words trailed off, as if he spoke in his sleep.

Milos tried again to rouse him, but the boy had lapsed into a deep slumber, like a man far into his cups.

The frantic wingbeats came again. This time from off in the distance. Milos had a strong urge to follow the sound, but he could not leave the unconscious boy to investigate, not in this fog.

He growled in frustration. His heart told him to keep searching until he found Kira, but his thinking mind told him there was no purpose in continuing to grope blindly in the murk. He could lose the boy and find nothing, no one else. He sat down beside Dahl, feeling like he carried ten stone of extra weight. His skull throbbed and his lids grew heavy.

He tried to fight the weariness that enveloped him, but soon found himself lying on the ground. He would sleep for just a short while.

CHAPTER EIGHT

The hunched woman on the high-backed throne stared at her with a look of confusion on her face. "Who is . . . this creature?" the woman demanded, her voice rasping like dead snakeskin rubbed against a dry branch.

"Do you not recognize your own daughter, Matriarch Kyrina?" the young man, Kavyn, asked. "Your heir has returned to you. Your dear Alyana. The one and only thing you have craved these long years." His voice rang flat against the hard stone walls, a bitter edge to his words. "Are you not joyful?"

Daughter? Alyana stared at the thin skeleton of a woman before her. There was something familiar about her, about the eyes. For a moment she could almost believe the woman had once been beautiful.

"My daughter is dead," the woman hissed, her blank face becoming a sudden mask of anger. "Do not speak of her." Her watery gaze roamed the room and then fell upon Kavyn.

It was clear she wasn't well. Her yellow-tinged skin sagged on her bones. Her sallow face contained no emotion. Her red-rimmed eyes seemed to stare out from a vacancy. Then her eyes fell upon Alyana.

An unsought memory rose as the woman's gaze lingered on her. Her mother—not this woman before her, but her real mother—leading her to a hollow tree. No, not hollow. Her mother had passed her hand along a seam in the tree trunk, and it had cracked open. Once she had shoved her inside, made her promise to remain there, silent and safe, she must have done something to make it appear the tree was whole again before leading the invaders away. They had passed right by the tree, following the sounds her mother made as she ran though the brush.

She shivered. Had her mother been like these strange men? Could she have spoken inside someone's mind?

The memory flashed through her mind and a name came to her lips unbidden, "Ardea."

The woman bolted up out of her chair. She stared down, shaking with anger. Her thin frame appeared so fragile, Alyana thought her bones would snap with the sudden movement. Instead, heat rolled off her in a wave that buffeted Alyana. She had to shield her eyes. It grew hot, as if she stood before a funeral pyre, but there was no fire. Only the Matriarch's singeing glare.

Then, like a wilting flower, the Matriarch sagged beneath the weight of the gold and silver chains that draped her shoulders. As she did, two women who had been standing in the shadows, one to each side of the throne, stepped forward. They took her arms, gently but firmly, and settled her back onto her stone seat.

"You are brewing some trickery," she hissed. "You are all against me! The plotting and the whispering. I can hear you." She grabbed her head between her hands and moaned. "No. No. No." A grimace of pain etched itself onto her face and she shut her eyes tight.

Alyana dropped her arm and gazed at the moaning woman. Did the woman really hear voices? Was Kavyn thinking inside the Matriarch's mind, as he had inside hers earlier? There was a whispery tickling at the edge of her thoughts. She concentrated on it and it grew to murmurs, as of many voices speaking at once, but a long way off. She reached out with her mind in an attempt to isolate the thoughts that rose and fell in the space around her, niggling at her brain. With a sudden rush, her head filled with calling, singing, shouting. She put her hands up to her ears to block the sounds, but the voices only grew louder, bombarding her with words and images.

She understood now what the woman meant. I can hear them too, she thought. She heard someone shout, "Make it stop," and realized it was her own voice. Hot tears streamed down her face. One of the waiting women rushed down the steps of the dais and put her hands upon her and the voices receded.

Suddenly, she felt a tug as if someone had reached out with greasy fingers to clutch at her thoughts. The touch filled her with an icy dread and she retreated, darting back to herself, leaving the grasping cold behind her clutching at her warmth. She glanced around the room, a shiver prickling her skin, searching for the person whose mental presence had slipped alongside hers like cold oil. There were too many pairs of eyes on her and she had no way of knowing who it had been. Or if the person was even in the throne room.

The woman standing beside her, raised a hand to her forehead in a gesture of respect, bowing toward the woman on the dais. Then, she took Alyana by the arm and led her down passages and stairways.

She let herself be led away, trying to be remain calm, but every nerve was on alert, all her senses tuned, lest the coldness come against her mind again. Her glance darted from side to side. Her head ached and every shaft of sunlight or glimmer of glowstone, stabbed her eyes.

Finally, they reached the wide wooden door of her cell and stepped inside. She sank down onto the narrow cot and the woman moved closer and placed a cool damp cloth upon her brow. "I'm sorry," the woman whispered, "that was poorly done, and the undoing . . ." She pinched the bridge of her nose between her fingers. "Nothing to be done about it now," she said, as if speaking to someone else. Then the woman laid a gentle hand on her cheek. "Rest, now. I must tend to the Matriarch, but I shall return as soon as I may."

As the woman left the room, Alyana retraced her journey from the cell to the Matriarch's throne room and back, over and over, till it blocked out all else and stuck in her brain like an oft repeated children's rhyme.

* * *

Kavyn's face might have been beautiful, but he looked as if he'd tasted something bitter, even when he smiled, which he was doing now. He held out a hand. "I apologize for our mother's behavior, Alyana," he purred. "Take heart. This meeting was but a formality, after all."

She glanced at the young man and gave him a questioning look. The name he addressed her by still chafed at her like an ill-fitting garment. Only, it wasn't the name that sent chilled fingers along her skin, but the ugly way it seemed to grate from between his teeth.

He turned his head to gaze at her out of one eye, and she sensed a scratching at her brain. She raised her hand to touch the back of her skull.

The young man's pupil appeared to contract. Surely, she could not have seen that. A trick of the light, perhaps? Though the pale glowing stones embedded in the walls of the room appeared never to waver, only to dim after she lay still for a length of time and slowly renew their glow when she stirred. She dropped her hand, wondering why she'd been holding it there at the base of her skull.

Kavyn's hand was extended toward her. She didn't know if she should touch it or if she had already done so.

He dropped his hand to his side. "As I was saying . . ."

His voice was rich, like summer honey, and Alyana became so lost in the timbre of it, she had trouble following his words.

"Mother has been outside herself for a long while now. Years, in fact. It is the Council's interview you should concern yourself with."

She closed her eyes for a moment, then blinked them open. The words meant something, she was certain of it, but for some reason, she was unable to determine what. It was as if she were attempting to translate the words into another language and back again. But that made no sense, he was speaking her native tongue, wasn't he?

He bowed to her suddenly. "I can see that you are still weary from your travails," he told her. "Why don't you rest yourself and refresh?"

Alyana nodded dumbly, and shuffled over to the pallet to sit. She hadn't remembered being tired, but it must be so. Her limbs were great weights that hung from her body and her mind sagged toward sleep. "Yes," she said. "I must rest." She lowered herself into a prone position and watched the world and the young man turn sideways and begin a slow spin that spiraled into darkness.

There was the sound of a door thudding shut and receding footsteps, then the heaviness left her body, as if it had never been there.

She sat up. What had just happened? Why had he come? There had been questions, she was certain. Questions she could not recall answering. Nor, she realized, could she remember what the questions had been.

The murmuring voices once more buzzed inside her head. She tried to ignore them, but bits of conversation crept into her understanding. Someone's laughter. Another's grief. Anger. Joy. Confusion. The emotions warred with one another, along with the voices, the words that she could almost, but not quite, make sense of. She put her hands to her temples, as if she could block out the sounds. No wonder the woman in the throne room was mad. If Alyana had to continue to listen to this noise all the time, it would drive her mad, as well.

But when he came near, when Kavyn was beside her, it had been quiet, blissfully quiet like a still lake. At the same time, it felt as if something dark lurked beneath the surface of the water. Something deadly. Suddenly, she remembered a boat, floating upon the sea. The water had not been peaceful, it had billowed and dropped, bouncing the little craft higher and higher into the air until she thought she would be tossed into the sky to fall into the salty waves and drown.

But they hadn't drowned and her father had found them. No. That wasn't right. They had come ashore someplace, someplace that Alyana could not see clearly. She rubbed her face with her hands and lay down again.

She tried to find a quiet place inside herself, a place where she could be free of the voices, but each time she tried to drift into sleep, her awareness rubbed against the edges of conversations in that odd language. The thought-words rushed by her so fast she could barely register them and had no way of knowing what was said. She wondered how these people made sense of all the conversations, how they managed to pick out single minds when they communicated.

Finally, the voices blended together in a noise like the crashing of waves upon a rocky shore. Then exhaustion overtook her and she fell into a restless sleep where hundreds of people shouted at and called to her, voices garbling like the rabble of a crowd. But a single voice, a woman's, rose above the din, *You should not have come.*

CHAPTER NINE

Milos kneeled beside the prone figure of the ship's boy and laid his hand on Dahl's forehead. Hot. Feverish. The boy groaned again, but this time his eyes flicked open. He seemed to be focused on something far off, then his gaze fell upon Milos and he gasped and tried to escape, kicking in desperation at the hard earth.

"Hush, now," Milos said, his voice as soothing as if he were trying to calm a wild horse.

"No!" the boy cried. "You're one of them."

"One of whom?" Milos asked. "What are you going on about?"

"The forest demons!" the boy shrieked. He struggled, trying to strike at Milos with his fist, but his face contorted in pain and he stiffened and fell back. His eyes rolled wildly and his breath came in ragged gasps.

Milos shook his head. "I'm no demon, boy. Let me have a look at that arm. I think it's broken." He hadn't the healing knowledge of Kira, but he could set a bone aright. He'd managed to do a decent enough job splinting her wrist. At least he could do well enough to give the boy some respite from the pain. He glanced around, searching for something to use as a splint. The fog had lifted a bit and he could make out shadows, tall shapes and lumpy spots, but still could not discern a bush from a rock.

He felt around on the ground. Hard stone, smooth but unpolished. The fluttering came again, this time from overhead, but when he gazed up it was like peering into a low cloud. The whiteness settled on him and he blinked, rubbing the moisture out of his eyes.

"Beg pardon," Dahl muttered. "I thought you were—"

"A demon. I know." Milos glanced out at the swirling fog. "Stay still and save your strength," he said. "I'll be right back." He took a painful step away, checking to be sure he could still see the boy and made a slow circle around him, shuffling his feet to keep from tripping over anything. After one full turn, he took another step out and made the circuit again. Once more he inched out from the boy and circled him. But now he could only see the shape of the ship's boy lying in the fog. Once more he moved outward.

This time his foot bumped into someone lying on the ground, someone who grunted at the touch of his foot. Another of the ship's crew? With a groan, he kneeled down to look closer and gasped. It was the boy again. But he had left the boy in the middle . . . he stared at the place he thought he'd started, but the spot was obscured in the whiteness that swirled around them.

He peered closer at the boy. Dahl's eyes were closed again and his blonde hair was matted to his forehead with sweat.

"I can't find anything to make a splint," Milos told him. "But we need to stop you from moving that arm."

He took off his tunic and gave it a thoughtful look, then reconsidered and removed what remained of his shirt. He tore the fabric into strips, then twisted the corner of his tunic into a tight roll and held it up to the boy's face. "Bite down on this," he told him. "It will help you to bear the pain."

The boy forced one eye open and then opened his mouth and bit down on the corner of the leather tunic. Milos reached over and lifted the boy's arm. Dahl cried out, his voice muffled against the leather in his mouth, as Milos laid the boy's arm across his chest and, using the strips of fabric torn from his shirt, tied it in place. He knew it probably needed to be straightened and set, but he hadn't the materials to do it right and immobilizing the arm should at least save the boy some pain.

Dahl smiled shakily and handed Milos back his vest, eyeing the teeth marks he'd made in the leather. "Sorry. It's a bit damp," he whispered.

Milos patted the boy reassuringly. "It's seen worse use." He tried to stand, but his leg burned.

He gingerly prodded his wound. It was tender, but not too deep. Still, he needed to protect the scored flesh and try to keep it clean in order to help it heal properly. Kira had taught him that much. He had nothing but water to cleanse it with, and they would need what little they had for drinking, but at least he could keep the tender muscle protected from further harm. He used the remainder of the cloth and made a bandage for his leg.

It should keep for the time being. At least, until he could find Kira.

CHAPTER TEN

"Why did they bring her here?" Kavyn collapsed onto the couch and leaned forward, elbows on his knees and his face in his hands. He was so close. And now? All he had worked for, all his sacrifice, could come to naught. "Offal and dung!" He peered up, his sharp eyes searching Teraxin's face, while seeking a way in, a chink in the man's iron-hard mental guard. Perhaps. If the old mule thought him too distracted—

"Tsk, tsk." Teraxin tilted his head, assaying him. "I thought we agreed to a truce on the matter of prying?"

A sharp pain asserted itself between Kavyn's eyes and wormed itself inward.

"Enough," he cried. Damn the old pisser for having learned all of his mental tricks. Well, not all, he reminded himself as the pain subsided.

"Perhaps, I should simply ensure that a certain young man's meddling with his mother's mind be discovered, then?"

Kavyn rubbed at his forehead, feigning more injury than warranted. "And perhaps I should explain how a young boy was first coerced into mind-meddling by his father's assassins and their conspirators," he growled.

"I agree that would be . . . inconvenient." Teraxin poured himself another goblet and raised it as if in toast. "Shall we recommit to our truce?"

Kavyn pressed the heel of his hand against the space between his eyes. "Truce." For now, he thought. "But what shall we do with her now that she's here?" He took a sip of the mulled wine, made a face and set the goblet back onto the table. Too much cinnaspice and honey. He preferred his mull less sweet. "I am so close."

"Close? Pah. The Matria is declining, yes, but your mother continues to refuse to name a male heir. Refuses to acknowledge you as Regent Esperent." Teraxin took a swig of his wine. "And the Council is in utter denial of her declination. The few who might side with us fear losing their positions more than what may happen to Eilar if we continue to slide into ruin."

"And now my dead sister is alive and well and brought to the palace by our enemies." Kavyn ran his hand through his hair, guarding his thoughts on the decline of the Matria lineage and the Eilaren. "What if she remembers?" It seemed sheer luck the veil had clouded her beyond its range. Normally, the crosser's fogged thoughts would clear as soon as the person passed beyond the veiled perimeter. Only they had gotten lucky, with a bit of help, Kavyn mused.

Teraxin raised an eyebrow. His balding head glistened in the late afternoon sunlight. "I've done my part," he grumbled. "If not for my spies, you'd not have known she was found. Nor would the Second have been so conveniently occupied when Meryk chose to visit the girl. Use your talents for something other than whining for a change." He drained the last of his wine and reached for the jug. Empty. He eyed the vessel as if it had betrayed him, then smacked it down onto the sideboard with a heavy thunk.

Kavyn glared at the old man, barely containing the urge to test him once more. "She should have drowned that night," he finally grumbled.

"Now, you're thinking." Teraxin eyed him. "It may not be too late."

Kavyn nodded, the corner of his mouthing twitching upward.

"I leave you to your musings." Teraxin stood, wobbling unsteadily, then slid out of the room as if the floor itself refused to touch him.

Kavyn paced to the window and glanced out across the city toward the sea. With sudden purpose, he stalked from the room. He needed a drink of something stronger than wine.

CHAPTER ELEVEN

Alyana opened her eyes and sat up. The cool cloth that had been placed upon her brow, slipped onto the coverlet.

"You're awake. That is well." The voice, a woman's with a rich contralto timbre, seemed to come from the shadows in the corner of the room, but Alyana no longer trusted her senses. She glanced around the room, seeking to identify her location. This was clearly not the cramped cell in which she had awoken earlier. That room, while not cold, had held no glowing hearth, and had no windows opening out upon the star-sprinkled sky as this one did.

A shadow appeared out of the darkness and grew. It approached the bed and her hands clenched in the covers, but then she found herself relaxing, as the round-faced woman appeared.

"You remember me?" The woman said, placing the back of her hand against her forehead and leaning forward.

She nodded, then cleared her suddenly parched throat and managed to whisper, "Yes."

"Good," the woman dropped her hand and straightened up. "Good," she repeated. "A beginning."

There was something in the way she said it that reminded her of another place, another time, and her heart filled with sorrow and loss.

"Shhhh. Hush now." The woman stepped closer to the bed. "Those thoughts are for another time. For now, there are things you need to know." She poured water from a jug beside the bed and placed the cup into her shaking hands.

Alyana's fingers brushed against something knotted and stiff as she took the cup. She glanced down in the moonlight to see the woman's hands. Dark shadows in the dim light, they appeared misshapen, as if melted and reformed, with not enough fingers and some of those appendages thick and twisted.

"I am Devira," the woman said, ignoring the questioning glance at her hands. "I am Physica to the royal household, and a teacher at the Mentorat." She paused as Alyana tilted back her head and drained the cup. "No need to gulp it," Devira chided in a kind voice. "The wards have not enough skilled workers to care for all the ill these days. So, the meals and water are parsed to keep the Warded well, but safe. But here there is plenty and you will have access day and night."

"The Wards?" she said. "Is that where I was? The dark room with the glowing lights?" She handed back the empty cup for the woman to refill. As she sipped at the second cup, Devira spoke to her in low tones.

"Yes. You were taken to the Wards upon your arrival, in an attempt to keep your identity secret. But, despite the Matriarch's denial, you are known." Devira sounded both relieved and worried about what had happened. "So, now that there is no point in hiding you, you should not be among those who are so ill they may be a danger to themselves or others."

"I will teach you to control your mental shields, but you must first let me in. This will require trust, I know, and I have no way of earning that trust beyond sharing what I can." She paused for a long moment. Then she slowly let out her breath in a long sigh. "Unfortunately, I have not the time to tell you all you need to know. Not now. Nor, can I entrust much of the knowledge I hold until I can be certain your shields will hold against assault."

Alyana handed her the empty cup. But when the woman reached for the pitcher to refill it, she waved her off. "I do not pretend to understand any of what you are telling me," she told her. "And I do not know whom to trust." She rubbed at her aching temples. "But if you can help me to quell these voices in my head, I will at least be willing to hear you out."

"Then we begin with who you are." Devira glanced about the room, as if the shadows might hide spying ears and eyes. "And why you were brought to me."

CHAPTER TWELVE

Kavyn's thoughts spiraled around the problem of his sister, the Matriarch's Heir. What purpose had she sought to serve by coming here, now? Who had found her, sent for her? Who stood to gain the most from this twist? Kavyn had to find a way to be rid of his rival sibling without revealing his plans.

Fortunately, she appeared to have no real mindskills. At least, none that he had been able to discern. But that was no guarantee. He was powerful, yes, likely the most powerful mindbender born in more than a few generations. Hard to know for certain what might have emerged had one of the more promising children lived. Luckily his gift, however, had not been harnessed and broken before he could turn it to his own uses. His tutor had seen to that.

Teraxin had bowed and scraped before the Matriarch and her Consort, Kavyn's father, denying the burgeoning power they thought they'd seen in the boy, convincing

60

them of his ordinariness, his lack of "special" abilities. Sworn to secrecy, Kavyn had played what he had thought was a game of lords and spies with his tutor. Trying his best not to slip up and show off his gift. Hard though it was when they cooed and fussed over his bratty sister simply because she'd been born a girl.

He'd thought her gone. Drowned in the river, or at the very least cast off onto a distant shore. But here she was. Arriving just as his plans were coming to fruition. Complicating things.

So be it. There were ways to deal with her. He just had to be subtle. Unfortunately, that meant waiting. Again. And he was getting sorely tired of waiting.

He stepped into the bedchamber without knocking and smiled charmingly at the attendant's gasp of alarm.

"How fares the Matriarch?" Kavyn asked the waiting maid, plucking a ripe berry from the basket beside the bed. His mother lay sunken against the pillows, soft coverlets tucked around her. She looked as pale as the sheets, her eyes sunken and her cheekbones a stark outline. He had once thought hers the most beautiful face he had ever seen, but the years and her selfish focus on his sister had changed that. Now she was simply the ugly husk of what had once been a powerful woman.

"The same, your . . ." she paused, searching for the correct word.

Once, there had been no question of his place in the royal lineage. He had been the Matriarch's son, Consort Verun's spring. Then, with no female heir to the throne, he had stood to receive the Council's blessing to be the first Patriarch of Eilaren in more than a hundred years.

"Grace," she finished at last.

Clearly, word of his sister's return had already clouded the issue in people's minds. Even those of the lower classes.

Kavyn turned up his lip in a sneer, but then his features smoothed out once more and he smiled and nodded to her. He plucked another sunset berry from the basket and held it up to admire its shape, the blush of color that rose from pink at the end to bright red near the stem. A sunset of color. Odd that they were only picked at the end of the day, when the sun left the sky. The farmers swore that this was the best time to ensure the sweetest berries, but Kavyn preferred them with a hint of bitterness left within. His own life had been bittersweet, and he liked the idea that this special fruit should share his position.

He popped the berry into his mouth and chewed until all that remained was the brown fibrous bit of stem. This he spat unmannerly onto the floor before rising from the chair. "Have her dressed and brought to the Guardian's room for the midmorning lists." He gave the girl a wicked smile. "And be sure to drape the royal charge about her. We all know how important appearances are to her, and we wouldn't want her to seem to have lost control of the Seat." He knew the charge, made of heavy metals and memory stones made it difficult for his mother to sit up straight, but that somehow she would force herself to bear the weight of her position with as much grace as she could muster. Fine, he thought, let her continue to bear that weight until she decided to step aside and name him regent and heir, if not fully abdicating her position to him, the stubborn old sow.

He paused beside the door, staring back at his once beautiful mother. Then, without blinking, sent a powerful blast of mind-thoughts at her. The maid flinched, then her face went blank as he sent the barest trickle of power across the room to erase all trace of what she had just witnessed.

With a satisfied smirk, he sauntered from the room, leaving the door ajar, as he would that of a common doxy's chamber.

CHAPTER THIRTEEN

Kira slouched low. She jutted her chin toward the grate that stretched across the opening. "It's loose," she said. "I tried it. When my mind was still clouded." She shook her head. "I don't know why. I just felt . . . trapped."

Milos grabbed the rusted crosspieces and tugged. The grate gave a metallic shriek, but barely inched outward. He searched the ground for something to use as leverage. There were rocks, but bashing at the grate would rouse the entire palace and bring the guards down on them. He didn't want to face that gray dream again, become lost in the fog. He gazed at Kira's face, the line of her chin, her green eyes glittering in the moonlight. He couldn't let anything come between them again.

He reached down and took hold of the grate once more. This time he strained until his muscles turned to fire. Kira sat watching him in confusion. Then she began to laugh.

Her laughter reached icy fingers up his spine. No. Not again. It couldn't be happening again.

The moonlight shifted into fog and Kira drifted away from him and dissipated into a gray cloud as he awoke.

He growled in frustration. What was this place? What was happening to him? Where was Kira?

"Was it the same?" Dahl asked, his young voice breaking from low to high.

Milos grunted, unable for the moment to find words. He turned and stared off into the depths of the gray shadow that surrounded them. Formless shadows, rock or tree or enemy, he knew not. "We need to find the way out," he said, not for the first time. "Perhaps, if we begin again."

The boy shook his head. "We've water here," he said. "We don't know what's out there. You said so before."

Milos dragged himself up onto his feet. He swayed weakly, his torn leg hot and tender.

Dahl reached up to steady him. "I knew you weren't taking your share of the food you gathered." His voice was quiet, but the accusation was mild. "There's none left, either."

"Then we need to find our way out, or starve." Milos gripped him by the shoulder. "There must be some way of marking our passage."

Dahl pulled a scalloped seashell from his pocket. "Perhaps we can score the trees with this."

"Now you're thinking, boy," Milos said. "Lead on."

Dahl walked slowly. Milos could see the boy's arm pained him, and his own hunger had made him weak. He stumbled, then righted himself. Dahl tried to offer him support, but he was in no shape to bear the extra weight, so Milos soldiered on. He tried to see beyond the gauzy fog that continued to blanket them. They would be no match for any danger that might lurk in the gray shadows that enveloped them, but neither could they linger where they were. There was nothing for it, but to move on and hope they might find their way out of this confounding murk.

CHAPTER FOURTEEN

The Matriarch sat upon her throne, staring blearily out of the eastern window. Or was it the southern? Clouds scudded by, dappling the blue sky like sheep on a hillside. Only hillsides were never blue, were they? She sagged for a moment, then caught herself and jerked upright. As long as she could keep command of her body, she might yet regain the use of her mind, she reminded herself. Or was it something else she was supposed to remember?

The white clouds suddenly began to swirl into a gray mist that covered the sky. Or was it the hillside? She rubbed her hand across her eyes and looked again. The sun shone. She heard the children calling to their father. Kavyn whining again that he should be allowed to go down into the garden, rather than stay with his tutor. Alyana giggling as her father swept her up into an embrace. Then the screaming and the shouts. The stamping of feet. The smell of death that swept over her as she fell upon her knees in the dark grass, wet with blood. His ebbing life staining her skirts as his eyes pleaded with her. His last breath whispering out of him. Alyana's name, in a gurgle of blood.

Her own voice, distant in her ears. "I don't believe it." Her eyes burning, the last of her tears long gone. "He would never betray me in such a way. Nor would he harm his . . . our daughter." She pushed a strand of hair off of her forehead, her hand numb, her face feeling like underworked clay.

The buzz and murmur of voices changed into a low chant.

Traitor. Murderer. Usurper.

The incessant voices. They never let her rest. Her mental shield felt fragmented. Her insides cracked, like broken eggshells. The separate rooms she'd created in her mind had sprung holes, thoughts and memories leaking into one another, like water through a sieve. Useless. She didn't have the strength to bother repairing the rips and tears anymore. So, she grew to trust the voices. Relaxed into the familiarity. The quiet, loyal hum of words that sang to her over and over.

Betrayed. Lost. Alone.

CHAPTER FIFTEEN

Milos sat, listening for . . . anything. Aside from the never-ending fog, there was something else terribly strange about this place. In the time—sunspans, days, weeks?—they had been lost in this fog, he had not heard the sound of bird or animal. Nothing trod the underbrush. No wild calls rose on the air. No wind cut the fog or fluttered the leaves of plant or tree.

Beside him, Dahl slept fitfully. They had found no more water, no more food, no way out of the misty forest. When they finally decided it would be wiser to return to where they started and begin again, the marks they had made on the trees as they passed, had vanished into the fog. They were unable to retrace their steps and so had been forced forward. They moved slowly, stopping more and more often to rest, aiming themselves on a straight path.

The ship's boy sat up with a sudden shout. "No!"

"Peace, boy," Milos said, his voice weak and raspy. He

tried to stand to go to where the young man sat whimpering and shivering in fear, but his limbs were like limp rushes and his stomach ached with the need for food.

"I . . . I thought . . ." The boy wiped a hand across his eyes. "I'm sorry," he murmured, embarrassment coloring his voice. "I've not cried out in my sleep like a babe since before I can recall. Now, I do so every sleep."

"No matter," Milos reassured him. "It's this place. It's working on your nerves . . ." Milos' voice trailed off. Something itched at his brain, something important, if only he could grasp hold of the thought. But the fog had gotten into his brain. It covered his thoughts, his memories, in a layer of gray that fuzzed the edges of everything. Everything except Kira. Her visage glowed in his mind's eye, as if a special aura surrounded her and lit her face with soft golden light. She was the only light and color left to him in this dreary place, and he clung to her glow, as if it were the last candle left to a man trapped in a deep cave.

"I need to rest." He let his shoulders sag as he leaned against the trunk of a tall dark tree. "I need to sleep for just a short while." His eyes drifted shut.

"I'll keep watch," the boy told him. "I cannot sleep, anyway."

Milos drifted on the damp fog, the boy's voice fading before he finished speaking the words.

She was there. Her smiling face, framed by that golden light, leaned over him as she held a damp cloth to his forehead. "Kira," he rasped. He tried to reach up, tried to brush her cheek with his fingertips, but she rose, backing away from him.

"Why do you cling to me like a drowning man clings to a bit of flotsam?" she hissed. Her smile turned to a sneer. "Why don't you die?"

Stunned, Milos choked back a sob and forced himself to sit up. He placed a hand on the trunk of the tree and dragged himself up to stand, his leg burning under his weight.

A shadow moved in the gray fog. Something large and lithe padded toward him. Milos stretched out his arm and something large and covered in fur brushed against it. He cocked an ear toward the sound of a low growl rumbling in the throat of an animal . . .

Realization dawned.

"Kelmir!" Milos nearly threw his arms around the hunting cat's neck in joy and relief, but he drew up short and glanced around. "Kira?" he called her name into the drifting mist. Kelmir hissed. Milos lowered his voice. "Where is she?" he asked. The strain in his voice rang in his own ears. He must remain calm. He didn't want to spook the animals. Animals? Where was Vaith?

As if reading his mind, the little wyvern soared down and alit beside his hunting companion. Kelmir sat and stared at Milos. Vaith eyed them both, turning his reptilian head first one way and then the other.

"Where is she?" he asked again, keeping his voice low and calm. "Where is Kira?"

The grey mist swept over him once more and the cat and wyvern dissipated into the curling fog. "No!" he cried out. "No."

A whisper swirled around him, a thin, desperate voice that rose and fell like dark waves lapping against a deadly shore. ". . . returned . . . loved . . . betrayed . . ."

71

CHAPTER SIXTEEN

Alyana woke to buttery-yellow sunshine that sifted through the arched window where gauzy curtains ruffled in the morning breeze. She rolled onto her side and scanned the room. Certain she was alone, she sat up and swung her legs over the edge of the bed, stopping suddenly as an overwhelming dizziness rushed in. She shut her eyes and remained still until the wooziness cleared. When she opened them again, her head wanted to loll on her neck like a broken doll's.

A few steps away, a fresh basin of water and clean towels sat beside the dressing table, but the distance between it and the bed seemed like leagues. She clung to the silken coverlet to keep herself from teetering forward onto the floor.

What was it the Physica had said about these dizzy spells? They were likely related to her loss of memories.

There was the feel of a question in her mind, the face of a man with arresting blue eyes flashed before her, then the dizziness rolled up and swallowed her again. This time, the accompanying queasiness that filled her stomach made her want to retch. She gulped in air, letting it out in a rush as the door swung open.

A young woman with bright skin and a mane of coppery curls—what was her name again? She searched her mind, thrashing about inside her skull as if in a dark ocean before coming up with it; Keliss—entered and stopped in the doorway, a look of concern on her face. She set her tray on a table and walked to Alyana's side, her wide-legged pants swishing beneath her long tunic. "Are you well?" she asked, reaching out a hand to help her.

"I'm fine," Alyana told her, taking in a deep breath before pushing herself slowly to her feet, one hand clutching the sturdy bedpost. "It's just the dizziness, again. It's already passing." She started to shake her head but stopped herself, afraid she would be sick again. Her brain seemed filled with harz sap.

What had made her think that? She closed her eyes, once more.

"It's as if you are of two minds," Keliss mused, her voice a soft monotone. Light footsteps crossed the room as the young woman moved away from her. "You'll want your breakfast." There was a rattle of dishes and the sweet scent of oat porridge steamed with goat's milk wafted across the room.

Alyana felt hungry despite her recent sickness. She slowly opened her eyes and crossed the room to where Keliss readied the morning meal.

"Are you like Devira?"

A smile flashed and the young woman let out a small sigh. "I've not yet been in love," she said. "But I favor young men . . ."

Alyana seated herself at the table, giving Keliss a

quizzical look. "Are men healers, as well?"

"Oh." The girl blushed. "You mean a Physica?"

"Yes. Physica." Kira seated herself at the table. The porridge smelled of honey and spices, with a hint of tartness that must be the little yellow-orange fruits that floated in the dish. She toyed with one of the berries with her spoon.

Keliss looked thoughtful. "I have some empathy skills. I can sense emotions, but not read thoughts. However, I do not have dual gifts, as Devira does. Sadly, that has become an exceptional rarity among innates. So, I will likely be able to help only with mental healing." Her hands suddenly clutched at her bodice. She gaped down at them in surprise, then dropped them to her sides, anger and confusion twisting her face.

"Are you well?" Alyana did not need empathy skills to know something was wrong.

"I . . . I'm not sure. I feel as if . . . as if I have done something shameful, but I cannot recall what."

There was something about the girl's words, about the fear wreathed around them that caused Alyana's spine to stiffen. A shiver crawled across her skin.

Keliss seemed to register her discomfort. "Nay. You need not worry for me." She tucked a strand of copper-colored curls behind her ear. "You're the patient, remember? Not I."

Alyana nodded, staring at the cooling porridge, its honeyed scent no longer appealing to her. Rather, the attraction of it frightened her for some reason. She stabbed her spoon into it, watching in satisfaction as a golden berry exploded.

Keliss' eyes narrowed, her mouth twisting into a frown. She turned away, suddenly, as if the food repulsed her. "I'm sure it is nothing. I will speak to the Physica about it when next I see her."

CHAPTER SEVENTEEN

Milos sat up and wiped the sleep from his eyes. The fog remained, thicker than it had been. He reached out to the huddled shape beside him, tentatively touching the boy's arm. Dahl's shoulder felt cold and stiff. Milos leaned over the boy, brushing his fingers across his throat to find the place on his neck where Kira had shown him to feel for a heartbeat. His fingers found the place, but the boy's skin was cold and clammy and there was no warmth or movement beneath it.

Holding in his breath, Milos put his cheek near the boy's face. Not a whisper of air. Nothing.

Milos sat back on his heels in despair. No. Not Dahl. He was so young. Near the same age as his niece, Milvari. Grief ravaged his chest and mind. A raw pain that he'd thought he would never feel again. Not after his brother's death. But here it was, awakened and alive, and tearing him apart from the inside.

Milos raged at himself. Why had he not done something? There must have been some other action he might have taken. But now, it was too late. Hot tears burned at his eyes and he tried with all his might to push them back. He was a grown man. Tears were not appropriate. Then, in a rush, he realized that tears were always an appropriate response to the death of a friend, especially one so young and bright. He'd not known the ship's boy long, but Dahl had been cheerful and kind, when others in his place might have been surly and mean. He'd snuck tiny bits of gizzards to Kira for Vaith and had carried water for the horses each day, when all his other duties had been finished.

"I'm sorry," he told the boy, feeling his helplessness like a wound. The same helplessness he'd felt when his brother lay dying. Milos wiped his eyes with his fingers. Standing, he stared into the horrible fog, a great anger rising inside him. Regret seethed through him. He should not have left his home and everyone he loved.

Everyone except Kira.

And now she was lost, could be dying, inside this cursed wall of mist.

His emotions tangled in his throat. He pictured Kira's face, saw her as she had looked the day they rode out from Tem Hold together. He punched at the gray mists. The wisps swirled away from him, unharmed, and his anger rose. With a sudden fierceness, he tore at the fog, screaming and cursing like a madman. "Kira!" he shouted. "Kira! Where are you?"

Confusion blurred his thoughts. Had he seen a ray of light, or was his now crazed brain playing with him? He took a step toward the place he thought the light had been. Then another. The fog seemed to waver before him. He took another step, and another, then he was stumbling in the direction of the golden ray that flickered in and out of view, leading him forward . . .

Milos opened his eyes. They were crusty with sleep

and his body ached. Bright light nearly blinded him, but he needed to see it, needed to know. So, he forced himself to look, blinking aside watery tears. He tried to turn and discovered he was lying on the ground beside a fallen tree. He sat up and stared around. He was still in the forest, but the fog had gone. Not a wisp or tendril remained. His vision was clear and he could see the dappled sunlight that poured through the overhead branches and danced on the ground below.

Something swooped down, landing on the fallen tree, knocking crumbs of bark loose. Milos froze. With careful movements, he rose to his knees, peering across the top of the weathered trunk at a familiar glitter of color. Vaith looked him in the eye, flapped his emerald wings and squawked like an excited chicken. It reminded Milos of the way Tem Hold's cook, Brilissa, had scolded him for stealing her best berries before she could get them baked into a pie. Despite everything else that had happened, Milos couldn't contain his smile.

"Vaith," he said, "is it truly you? I cannot say how relieved I am to see you." The little wyvern twisted his head to the side, then closed his wings and waited, as if expecting Milos to do something. Milos scanned around again in sudden excitement. "Kira?" he called.

He rose to his feet in a rush, ignoring the dizziness that washed over him. "Kira!" The forest grew hushed, but there was no response. He called again. His voice growing louder and more desperate. "Kira! I'm here. Where are you?"

He turned back to Vaith. "Where is she?" he demanded. "Where is Kira?"

Vaith gave Milos a one-eyed stare.

"Is she all right?" Milos pleaded. "Can you take me to her?"

Vaith continued to stare at him, as if trying to

understand.

A rustle in the underbrush made them both turn. Milos felt hope rise inside him as Kelmir stepped out from between the trees. "Kira?" Milos limped past the big cat, searching for her. But his heart stalled when he saw she was not there. Only the shape of a thin body lying on the ground.

Dahl.

Milos' heart clenched inside his chest. He would have to bury the boy, but he felt so weak, his arms and legs rubbery.

And he needed to find Kira.

He scanned the forest, his vision blurring in the dappled light that filtered through the trees. "Where is she?" he asked again, desperation causing his voice to crack. She could be anywhere, lost in the gray fog he'd been trapped inside. How long had it been? It had felt like days, but so much of it had been unreal, like a swirling nightmare wrapped within a fevered dream. It could have been only a few spans.

Kelmir sat in the sunlight and growled, deep in his throat. The sound was familiar, but it took Milos time to place it. When Kelmir yowled again, it was there. Fear and discontent. The sound Kelmir released now was exactly the same as when Kira lay injured by the poisonous basilisk.

Milos' heart sank. His crazed brain had dredged up yet another hopeful vision to torment him with. A low moan caused him to spin around. He gasped at the sight of the ship's boy sitting up, hugging his broken arm to his chest.

"Dahl?"

The boy grimaced, then blinked his eyes hard. "Another dream?" His voice was raspy and there was a tired edge of frustration in it. "I want the other one. The one where my arm is whole," he lamented. "Even if I do have to swab the deck endlessly."

Milos narrowed his eyes at the boy. Then he realized that his own pain was bright and hard edged, unlike in the illusion, where everything had been dulled. Was that the difference between what had been a dark dream in which he'd been trapped and the real world. That here the pain was sharp and clear. His eyes roamed around, taking in the trees, the sky.

This was real.

Dahl was alive.

Kelmir and Vaith were truly here.

But Kira remained lost.

CHAPTER EIGHTEEN

Leaning out of the window, Alyana searched the sky. She had no idea what it was she was looking for, but she felt as if she bore a great loss. Each time she glimpsed a speck of color, a bird or small-winged creature flitting across the cloudless expanse of blue, her heart tumbled up toward her throat. And each and every time the creature soared past her window and winged out of sight, her forlorn heart dropped, not bothering to stop in her chest where it belonged, but slamming into the pit of her stomach with a near physical pain.

The door opened and closed behind her and she turned with a sigh, expecting to see Keliss or Devira. Instead, she was caught off guard by the tall woman who stood outlined against the oaken door. Her delicate features were a contrast to Devira's round face. Her red-brown hair framed a thin face, the soft curls contrasting the severe line of her mouth and the hard set of her jaw.

"Your Graceling," the woman placed her hand against her heart and bowed her head just enough to be polite and to acknowledge her station.

It was clear the willowy woman questioned that status as much, or likely more, than Alyana did herself, but Devira had clearly schooled her in protocol these past few days for a reason, and until she understood who and what she was in this place, and to these people, she would play the role assigned her. She nodded in return, her head tilted just enough to show deference to the stranger without relinquishing her position. Her vision grew suddenly blurry and a numb tingle skittered along her scalp. The odd sensation shook her, but it passed quickly and she managed to keep her balance.

"Have we met?" She allowed herself the question. There were too many things in her memory that remained lost. She had no idea how many of those things were names and faces, but she refused to pretend there were no missing pieces. Such an act would never hold up under scrutiny, so she allowed herself to ask at least the most necessary questions. She rubbed at her temples, still troubled by Devira's assertions that she was connected to royalty.

The woman's eyes scanned her, as if searching for something she was certain would be visible if only she looked hard enough.

Alyana pulled her dressing gown closer, clutching the collar tight around her throat, hating that she'd allowed the woman to unnerve her, but feeling the need to shield herself. Though from what she had no idea.

Finally, the woman looked away, her gaze going to the window. "You were seeking something." It wasn't a question, but a statement of fact.

She hesitated for a moment, then nodded. "Yes," she murmured. "But I have no more idea for what than do you."

There was a long silence, a quiet space in which they both seemed to float for a moment. Then, with a more formal bow of her head, the woman cleared her throat. "I am Aertine." She said. "Sister-kin to . . ." she paused for a moment, glancing around the room and then once more toward the heavy door. "Ardea."

Alyana felt that strange numbness again, and a shiver ran up her body. She glanced down at her feet, expecting them to be bare on the cold stone floor. But a pair of soft slippers enveloped them and she stood on a thick carpet. She should not feel chilled. Perhaps the fever that had caused her to forget was returning.

Aertine watched her closely. "You recall the name?" she asked.

"No," she said. "Yes . . ." she hesitated. "I'm not certain . . ." A fist of nausea gripped her insides.

The woman waited, a sudden hunger in her eyes.

"I'm sorry," she told her. "I think I'm growing feverish, again." She stepped backward, her hand reaching behind her, feeling for the bed. Her fingers brushed the coverlet and she longed to crawl beneath the soft layers, to return to the warmth she had left only a short while before this stranger had entered her chamber. Only something held her in place.

"But there was recognition in your eyes," Aertine said, reaching out to her. "I saw it. Surely, you remember . . . something." Her voice was pleading, as if she were drowning and begging to be thrown a rope.

"I know not what you saw," she said. "But I have no recollection . . ." She paused. Did she? Visions passed before her eyes. Faces. Fields. Then smoke.

And fire.

Her hands shook and her knees weakened.

Aertine's face grew angry. "I don't believe you," she

hissed. "Why are you lying?" She glanced behind her at the door, then took a step closer. "Tell me what you know of my sister." A desperate edge colored the woman's words. "Tell me at the least whether or not Ardea lives."

"Ardea?" she whispered the name and a swirl of a memory trembled at the edge of her mind. A woman's voice. She raised her hand and brushed her fingertips across her cheek where she felt a warm breath. She stood inside the heart of a tree, unable to breathe. Thunder rumbled and the ground shook.

The world spun. She sank down onto the bed, feeling as if her skull would shatter. The fist of nausea tightened.

Aertine stared at her.

The mask of misery the woman wore, tore at her and Alyana's eyes filled with tears. She tried to shake her head, but dizziness overwhelmed her. She fell back against the bed, her body jerking in great spasms.

* * *

"Someone, come quick!" Aertine called, panic in her voice.

Devira rushed into the room. "What have you done?" she shouted, rushing across the room to the bed. She gripped Alyana's arms to stop them thrashing. "Hand me the spoon," she demanded. Aertine obeyed. Devira took the utensil from her and wedged the wooden handle into the girl's mouth, between her teeth. "I knew I should not have allowed you in."

Aertine looked heavenward.

"Don't roll your eyes at me. I should never have left you alone with her," Devira chided in a hushed voice. She placed her hand upon the Matriarchess' forehead and sent healing energy through her fingers into the girl's mind. As before, there was too much resistance there. Like slogging through thick mud. Perhaps, it was the sickness. Or the years the poor girl had spent without proper training of her gifts that had done this to her. "Hush, hush now." Devira cooed as she tried to ease the fit. It took too much of her, too much pressure, as if there were a wall inside the girl that kept Devira from reaching her mind. Finally, she managed to push past the barrier. Not far, but enough. Alyana's limbs stopped jerking.

As soon as the Matriarchess stilled, Devira stood and pointed toward the door. "You need to leave. Now. Before anyone hears what happened. I told you not to push her." She let out a heavy sigh.

Aertine's jaw tightened. "I don't know what happened," she said, glancing at the girl, who had lapsed into a fitful sleep. "I only asked about her. Whether or not she lives or . . ." Her shoulders slouched. "We have abided in this dark shadow for too long."

"Not we," Devira hissed. "You. You have lived in this darkness. Trapped within your own stubborn refusal to let go." She hovered above her patient's still form and gently slid the spoon out from between her teeth. "Some of us have continued to live our lives. To work toward healing." She gave Aertine a measuring look. "And some have more to lose than others," her words were filled with meaning.

"Always the first to push away," Aertine said, her voice swelling with anger and disgust. She thrust back her shoulders and straightened her spine. "We have a right to know the truth of what happened. Some of us," she said pointedly, "need to know." She turned on her heel and stalked from the room, swinging the door wide and slamming it shut behind her.

Devira watched her go. Then she sat on the bed beside Alyana, who had not stirred. "You are right, dear sister, we do have a right to know. But at what cost?" she murmured, stroking the girl's brow. "At what cost?"

After a time, she stood and straightened Alyana out on the bed to make her more comfortable. Although, she knew in her heart there was little comfort for the young woman. And far less for Aertine and the rest of their family. Not only had they lost a sister, but . . . She let it go, picked up the soft coverlet and draped it over the girl. Alyana spoke in her sleep, a single whispery word. "Ardea."

Tears sprang into Devira's eyes and she wiped at them with the back of her hand. "Ardea," she echoed. "What have you done? And why?"

CHAPTER NINETEEN

Milos stared into Kelmir's lavender eyes. The big cat sat on his haunches with nary a twitch of ear or whisker, as if waiting for Milos to speak to him. Vaith sidled along a nearby branch, tail twitching and whipping, his nervous movements in direct opposition to the statue-like pose of the big hunting cat. One thing the two animals shared, the air of loss that hovered over them.

"Where is Kira?" Milos asked them for the hundredth time. He almost laughed aloud at his own foolishness. There had never been a connection between him and these two animals. At least, none beyond the bond that all of them had with Kira. The worst of it was, he couldn't fathom why they remained here with him, rather than beside their mistress, as they always had before. Unless . . . No. He dare not even think it. But what other explanation might there be for her absence, and their presence?

He shook off the dread that clutched at him and sank piercing talons into his heart and soul. An invective slipped past his lips and he fell to his knees, begging Troka that it be not so. That after so long in darkness, finally having found such a light, it could not be snuffed out so soon. That this quest of Kira's would not end with her ending. Not after all she had already been through. She, too, deserved a chance at life. At happiness.

Milos let out a low guttural cry that sounded more like a wounded animal than a man, and slumped forward in abject sorrow. For a moment, he wished that Kira had never awakened his own lust for life, had not opened his heart to the world again. But he quickly felt remorse for thinking such a thing. Better to have had one day, nay, one hour, one moment, with Kira than to never have met and loved her. He closed his eyes tight, willing himself not to think of her as gone.

Vaith winged down from the tree, landing beside Milos in the grass. The little wyvern warbled low in his throat. Milos opened his eyes and stared at the creature. "Would that you and I could connect as you and Kira," he whispered. "Perhaps, then I might know why you are here with me and she is not."

Vaith tilted his head, peering out of one eye and then the other. Then he hopped forward, nudging Milos' hand with his snout and pushing it beneath Milos' warm fingers. Milos began to pull away. Then, sensing what Vaith intended, he stroked the wyvern's neck. "You're as lost and confused as I am," Milos said, his voice cracking, as realization struck him. "You're as confused as I am," he repeated. "You'd know, wouldn't you? Know if Kira were . . . gone?" He sat back on his heels. "But you can't tell that, can you? That's not what you sense, is it?" Hope lit upon him, like warm sunlight.

Milos ran his fingers down the little dragon's neck.

87

Petting him the way one might pet a cat, albeit an odd hairless one. Milos chuckled then glanced at Kelmir. Perhaps not a hunting cat.

Sensing the change in the man's mood, Vaith flapped his wings and stepped back, stretching his neck to get a better look at Milos. Kelmir's tail twitched ever so slightly. "No," Milos said. "It's true, I can't communicate with you. Not the way Kira does. But I can listen." With my heart, he thought. The heart she reopened. The heart that holds her in it and will never let her go.

He offered his arm to Vaith. The little wyvern eyed the wrist extended toward him. Then, he took a tentative step forward. And another. He climbed onto Milos' arm. Carefully, Milos stood and held up the diminutive dragon before him. "I know you probably have no idea what I am saying," he told Vaith. "But we need to work together, if we are to find her." He thought for a moment, then pulled out the heavy chain Kira had gifted him when they were in the Gnome King's hall. The links were imperfect, but each one had been made with care by her hands and he treasured the gift all the more for its imperfections. Surely, it would no longer carry Kira's scent, but perhaps Vaith would recognize the object for what it was, a gift she had wrought with the help of the Gnomes' master silversmith.

Vaith examined the chain for so long, Milos began to wonder what the creature could be thinking. As light as Vaith was, Milos' arm grew fatigued, but he kept himself steady until, with a high-pitched trill, the wyvern took to the air and began flying in circles overhead, as if searching for prey.

No, Milos corrected himself. Searching for Kira.

Making one more loop, the wyvern soared higher and disappeared from sight.

* * *

Milos scanned the sky, waiting.

Vaith had last looped past more than a sunspan ago, but hadn't yet returned. Kelmir remained where he'd lain. The big cat's eyes were lidded, but Milos sensed he was being watched. He paced to and fro, worrying at the knot of the problem, his aching leg screamed at him, but his nerves would not allow him to be still. If Kira lay unconscious somewhere, or addled by that nefarious fog that had plagued him and the boy, it would explain why Vaith and Kelmir were unable to find her. Or connect with her. Or whatever it was they all did.

Milos had never quite been able to grasp exactly how Kira communicated with the two animals. He only knew that it was some sort of mental connection. He had tried to fathom it, but had finally chosen to take on faith what she was capable of. It was clear the way the animals responded to her—and to none another—that she could truly communicate with them, even if it didn't entail any language Milos could comprehend.

He checked once more on Dahl. The boy was sleeping too much. He needed food and water. As did Milos. The small amount of dew that had been captured in the wide leaves he'd layered together had been worth only a few sips. The boy appeared flushed, but his skin was not hot. Milos sighed in relief. At least the boy's broken arm had not caused the fever that could complicate such injuries and turn them fatal. He shivered, recalling the fog-driven nightmare in which Dahl had died and swore such a thing would not come to pass.

Kelmir sat up and yawned. Milos stood as a flash of color and flapping of wings alerted him to the return of the wyvern. Vaith dropped to the ground, the remains of a tiny rodent clutched in his claw. He stepped away from the mangled mass of fur and flesh and turned a bright eye on Milos.

Milos stared at the bloody mess in disappointment, tempted for a moment to try and skin the tiny animal. But no, there was not enough flesh to make it worth the effort. He needed to check the snare he had set, but likely with all his pacing this close to where he had set the trap such a short time ago, it would be fruitless.

He regarded Vaith. "No, thank you?" he said it as if it were a question, unsure of what Vaith wanted. The reptile stepped from foot to foot, then leaped on the remains of the puny animal, tearing off meaty bits and swallowing them whole.

Startled, Milos turned to Kelmir, who sat watching Vaith stuff himself. "I don't suppose he's planning to share with you. Though, if you could find something larger, we all might partake," he said, then laughed at himself. He must be going sideways, attempting to speak with the pair.

Kelmir stretched, sticking his tail end high in the air and ripping at the ground in front of him with his extended claws. Then he turned and bounded into the forest. Milos sat on a fallen tree trunk and shook his head. Of course, they would be hungry. His own stomach growled at him like an angry dog. He should find some sustenance for himself and Dahl. He'd spent enough time in the forest outside of Tem Hold, hunting and trapping, before his brother's tragic accident. He was no stranger to the woods. At least not the woods surrounding his home. But this place was different in so many ways. He worried the plants here might betray him.

"Only one way to find out," he told himself, standing up with a groan and brushing stray bits of bark from his trousers, before limping off between the trees. It wasn't long before he spied a cluster of beehive mushrooms. He picked one of the oddly shaped fungi and sniffed it. It was larger than those that grew in the forests of Sedath, but smelled exactly as he remembered, and it had the same rounded shape, the same honeyed coloration. He popped it into his mouth and chewed. Woody with an underlying hint of sweetness, which would, if like those back home, become more prevalent with cooking. He picked them all and carried them back to the clearing where Dahl slept.

His stomach grumbled for more than the single fungus he had eaten, but Milos forced himself to wait until a full sunspan had passed. He could probably find other edible plants to pair them with, build a fire, cook them until they lost their bitter edge, but he was too hungry for that. He separated the mushrooms into two scanty piles and having had no feelings of sickness, he ate his share, barely bothering to chew. He swallowed the last mushroom, then placed Dahl's share on a flat green leaf beside the sleeping boy before limping off to search the brush and leaf mold for more nourishment.

He returned a short while later with a few skinny white tubers to find Dahl sitting up, resting against a tree, stroking Kelmir's ears. The hunting cat raised his head when Milos approached, watching him expectantly.

Milos stopped himself short of tripping over three fresh-killed rabbits lying in the shade of the little clearing. He fixed an eye on Dahl.

The boy tried to shrug, stopping with a grimace of pain when he moved his arm. He pointed at Kelmir with his chin. "He brought them."

A sharp chirrup caused them all to look up to where Vaith sat upon a branch eyeing them.

"I suppose you helped," Milos said.

Vaith stood and flourished his wings, then settled

once more onto his perch.

Milos thanked Troka again and again as he dressed the rabbits. His mouth watered and his stomach rumbled as he spitted the carcasses and offered the remains to Vaith and Kelmir. The fire he'd managed to build had grown to a dancing flame and he was impatient for the bed of coals he knew would be needed to properly roast the tender meat. He rinsed his hands with the last of the water from his water skin. The rivulet he'd found not far from off was a thin trickle, but it was cool and sweet. After they ate, he would return and refill the bag.

As he rinsed the last of the blood from his fingers, he thought once more about Kira. What had become of her? Of the other sailors who had been lost in the forest? He glanced up at Dahl. The boy's color looked better, but he needed more care than Milos could provide. And Milos needed to move quickly, to find Kira before . . . he dared not think about what might happen to her.

The evening shadows spread along the ground. Milos knocked the fire down and hung the meat close to the glittering coals and placed the washed tubers on a hot rock beside it. "On the morrow," he said, "we must find our way back to the beach. Return you to your captain and crew."

Dahl shook his head. "What of her?" he asked.

"I will find her." Milos said, voice gruff with emotion. He cleared his throat. "I will find her, but I will move faster . . ."

"Without me?" Dahl asked. "And what of you? I've seen how you favor that leg."

Milos shot a look at the boy, then gripped his leg where he'd wrapped the gash in the strips torn from what had remained of his shirt. The muscle was still tender though the bleeding had abated. "I will manage," he told the boy, hoping his worry and fear did not betray the confidence of his words.

"But I can help you," Dahl said, his voice breaking on the last word.

Milos didn't bother to respond. He'd said all he would on the subject. It chafed at him to lose the time it would take to return the boy to the beach, and he had considered taking him with him on the search, but he could not properly care for him out here and he had no idea how long it might take to find Kira. No. Dahl would be better off with his crew.

If they could find their way to the sea. Milos gnawed on that worry again as the boy continued to protest.

"And if the fog comes again, I could be a help," Dahl said.

Milos paused. What of the fog? He knew it was unnatural. What if he managed to return Dahl to shore only to be taken by the fog again afterward? "It is a risk," he said. "One that cannot be helped."

* * *

They followed the sun's path through the dense woods. Vaith and Kelmir kept pace with them, intermittently disappearing and reappearing as they traveled. More than once Milos caught himself searching for a sign of either animal and feeling they had been abandoned, only to discover Vaith sitting on a branch just ahead or catch a flicker of Kelmir padding beside them in the shadows. The forest, now free of mist, was a bright mixture of mottled shade and sunlight.

"Doesn't feel so brooding, now, does it?" Milos asked as they sat beside the remains of the fire that night. He tossed the clean-gnawed bones of the brush fowl Kelmir had brought them into the embers. Overhead, Vaith slept with his head tucked beneath one wing and Milos turned to scan the growth for a sign of the big cat, but the shadows were too deep to see much beyond the glow of the dying coals.

The following day brought the smell of salt air to their nostrils. The many leagues they had seemingly traveled in the mists turned out to be no further than a tired man and wounded boy could traverse in little more than a day and a half. Perhaps, the dreams had distorted time. Or they had been going in circles.

"I can help you," Dahl repeated, for the hundredth time since they'd set off in the direction of the sea. "I still have one good arm." He flexed his muscle to demonstrate, wincing when the movement pulled at his injury.

"You should save your energy for healing," Milos told him.

They trod quietly as they neared the edge of the forest, where the long stretch of sand led down to the ocean.

"Be watchful," Milos cautioned, moving carefully. There was no telling what might have transpired on the beach while they had been lost in the mists.

Dahl followed his lead, tiptoeing forward, hardly making a sound.

Peering through the trees at the rough camp the crew had erected, Milos spotted Trad and Zharik, picketed beside a narrow patch of tufted grass a short distance from the tree line. Relief at seeing the horses safe and sound rolled through him. Hope surged and he searched the beach for Kira. Perhaps, she too, had escaped the befuddling fog-ridden forest.

Men worked and lounged beside rough lean-tos, but there was no sign of Kira. His relief turned to fear. Kira could be injured. Or worse. And Milos needed to find her. Now. Hungry and thirsty as he was, he had no time to deal with the sailors and their fears. He needed to be moving.

Milos glanced at the horses again and felt the urge to rush forward and take hold of Zharik's bridle, but the stallion would be more hindrance than help where Milos was headed, and would no doubt be safer here on the beach.

He motioned for Dahl to go, but the boy stood firm and shook his head. "I want to go with you," he whispered. Milos shushed the boy as Zharik raised his head, nostrils flaring for a moment before he resumed his grazing.

"Dahl," Milos murmured, "I need you here."

Dahl began to protest, but Milos cut him off. "To watch over Trad and Zharik." He nodded in the direction of the horses. "I need someone to care for them and assure no harm comes to them until I . . . until we return."

Milos waited until the reluctant boy crossed the sandy beach to where Captain Salhker stood staring out at the watery expanse of the Faersent sea. He watched as the man spun around and went down on his knee, catching himself just short of hugging the injured boy. Then, without observing the rest of the reunion, he slipped away, Kelmir and Vaith keeping close.

CHAPTER TWENTY

The afternoon sun cast long shadows across the Keep garden. The Hour of Memories, what Kavyn referred to as the Time of Tears, always left Alyana unsettled. Nearly every person in the citadel spent this time tending to their ancestral memory gardens, or at some other meditative activity. It always somehow left her feeling as if she were alone in a city of ghosts. She shivered, realizing that in many ways, the memory gardens actually contained the ghosts of people's ancestors. She glanced around, feeling as if the spirits of hundreds of generations drifted in the gardens where she walked.

Hushed voices floated upon the evening breeze. She paused, her body tensed. Nothing. She nearly laughed at herself. Ghosts. What a silly notion. The spirits of her ancestors would be riding the wheel, not tarrying upon the earth. But the voices came again.

They were not of the deceased, however. These were

voices she was certain she should recognize.

She shouldn't intrude, shouldn't eavesdrop, but something in the tones of those urgent whispers made her creep off the path and ease her way closer. She slipped behind a crooked elm and silently tucked herself in close between the garden wall and the tree's comforting trunk, straining her ears to hear above her own pulse and the flow of sap that hummed beneath her fingers.

She started, barely keeping herself from gasping. She could not possibly have felt the tree's lifeblood. She tentatively reached her fingers toward the bark again, but froze as the voices grew louder.

"Though she was not raised among us, she is still one of us," a man said. "One of the lineage."

"She should have been drowned at birth," another hissed.

The first man barked out a short laugh, but there was no real mirth in it. "Is this a matter of sibling rivalry? I have allowed you many indulgences over the years, but jealousy does not become."

"Jealousy?" The younger man's voice was filled with heat. "It was not jealousy that caused the death of the Matriarch's Consort."

"Politics, my boy." The older man's voice held a quiet warning. "Merely politics. Not that I expect you to understand, despite my many attempts to tutor you in that regard."

"I understand well enough," the younger man fired back. "You have no care for her lineage, for the blood that pumps within her veins. You made that clear on this very ground. You only think now that she'll prove useful."

"There may be hope for you, yet." The older man's voice was mocking.

"Horse piss," the young man hissed. "And you're wrong about her usefulness. News has spread fast. Too many are already weeping in joy at the Matriarch's Heir returned. She's more dangerous than she could ever be useful."

"She was a mere babe when the witch stole her from us before we could finish what was started. Although, that may also prove to our benefit in the end." The other man's voice faded, as if he were walking away. "Besides, there will be no memory of it left . . ." his voice trailed off behind the gurgle of the little stream and she could only wonder at the meaning of his words.

She leaned against the garden wall. What did it mean? The older man, she was certain she had heard his voice before. Who was he? She rattled the voice around in her brain, searching to put a face to it.

Clearly, they were speaking of her. The young man seemed to have no use for her. Strange, in a culture that honored the leadership of women, that a young man could be so filled with spite and anger against her. What had she ever done to him? Could he have been a spurned suitor? No. The man had accused him of jealousy, not the anger of rejection. His voice sounded so familiar to her, but she could not for life nor blood remember why. She wished she could see through the thick flower laden hedge, but she dared not push aside the leafy plant. Dared not make a sound. To be caught listening in on another's words without permission was criminal . . . No. It was another's thoughts she shouldn't listen to, not their words.

Words can be a knife. Capable of skinning the truth when need be, but liable to cut through the heart . . .

She had the urge to shake her head, to loosen the thoughts and memories stuck inside her, to make sense of the bits and pieces of things that seemed unrelated, yet somehow connected. It felt as if, like a string of beads, she could pull all the fragments together, and the story of her life would unfold, moment by moment. But there were too many pieces missing. Too many pearls that had rolled away from her to lie hidden in the shadows of her mind. The voices of the two men disappeared as she stood beside the tree, fading to nothing as they turned the corner of the garden wall.

Frustrated, she put her hands to her head and willed herself to recall her past. Anything of who she was, or where she had come from. A single day, a moment. But nothing. She pushed off from the wall and wandered along the path beside the splashing rivulet. Watching the sunlight glint off the water, she wondered how she might possibly be useful, much less dangerous. A woman with no memories, no past.

There was something important in what she had overheard. What was it that had been left unfinished?

CHAPTER TWENTY-ONE

Kavyn paced the length of his chamber, his soft boots making no sound on the plush rugs covering the stone floor. His dull headache had become a throbbing pain and a glittering halo obscured his vision. Yet, his overtaxed mind felt clearer and sharper than it had in days. Exhilaration was a pleasant side effect of his use of the touchstone. And he'd suffered mild headaches afterward in the past. But this pounding was different. So pronounced. Could it be tied to his attempts to invade his sister's mind? Instead of the usual mental guard—a barricade he had learned to readily surmount in most minds—her thoughts were clouded. Trying to look inside her, was like attempting to see through too many layers of gauzy curtains into a smoky room. Almost as if a corner of the veil itself existed inside her mind.

Exactly. He let out a low chuckle with the realization. It was just like the fog that could be laid upon the weak minds of those without the ability of thought-speak or mind-guarding. So easy to leave such a mind lost until they stumbled back beyond the veil, or the body gave out. The Eilaren elders believed their way was so much simpler than the bloody wars fought by other peoples. Simpler. More humane. Pah! Not that it was of particular concern to him. Invaders, of any kind, deserved to be dealt with like a destroying species of pest that attacked a castle's garden, or a country's crops. Quickly and decisively. Before they did any real damage.

He stopped pacing and threw himself onto an ornate couch covered in soft cushions. Interesting. If her mind had never been trained and once taken by the veil, a bit of it had somehow lodged inside her head . . . He wondered if such questions might be worth asking, but decided against it. His use of the device must be portioned out and there were more important issues to deal with.

The spiced wine still steamed in the cup where the steward had left it only minutes ago, entering and leaving as quietly as a mouse. His fear of Kavyn's discontented anger and foul mood still hung in the air. Kavyn inhaled it like a perfume. Funny, how much obedience and loyalty could be earned by a few well-placed false, yet vivid, memories.

He put his feet up on the padded stool and took a sip of the wine, the heat of it warming his mouth and throat, but not his heart. He'd seen what happened to rulers who led with their hearts. His mother was a prime example of such inane self-indulgence. Look at her now. A drooling mess. He threw back a large portion of wine, hoping it would dull the pounding in his head. A Physic could easily relieve his pain, but allowing anyone else through his mind-guard was far too risky. There were rooms within his mind that were not yet walled off enough from one another.

And secrets that must never be shared.

Another gift of his tutor, Teraxin. The man seemed to be a bottomless well of information that was not common knowledge. Finally, Kavyn had discovered his own source of knowledge and could be done with the man. Probably the reason Teraxin had kept that resource so secret all these years, guarding it as if his life depended on it. He had apparently known, someday, it would.

Kavyn rubbed his hands together briskly, then cupped them over his closed eyes and rested against the cushions. The glistening halo remained, flashing against the backs of his eyelids, but the wine was beginning to do its work. The throbbing pressure melted into a dull ache. Though the vivid clarity of his mind had not abated.

This was a fresh facet to his gift and he relished the thought that he might be gaining something new, another aspect of his unique abilities. He was, after all, just nearing his twenty-third season. True, he had once believed that like most youths he had reached his full majority at eighteen, but there were many histories that included late maturing skills, especially for those most blessed by the ancestors, and Kavyn's gift had proven to be beyond anything known even in most of the Eilaren histories. And now, with the amplification of his powers . . . His fingers twitched to hold the stone, but he'd suffered a malaise for weeks the last time he had returned to it too soon.

If Teraxin had not recognized the premature onset of Kavyn's gift as more than an early manifestation, who knows how his training and education might have suffered. He did owe that much to the man. Then again, his tutor had been repaid in lavish ways over the years. And he clearly enjoyed such recompense and all the luxuries it allowed him. Their most recent altercation had been a sure sign that Kavyn owed the man nothing beyond a solemn silver cloaking at his burial.

But first, there was the problem of his tutor's machinations. The time had come for Kavyn to become the sole owner and architect of his destiny. Teraxin had served his purpose and needed to be retired, as an old horse might be pastured. No, he corrected himself, more like an aged plow handle that had become useful only as kindling for the fire.

Kavyn let his hands drop from his eyes and scanned the room, assuring himself his vision had cleared. He needed all his faculties in full working order for his next foray.

CHAPTER TWENTY-TWO

Aertine fussed with the silver band, smoothing out a rough spot in the fitting before slipping the polished gem into it. It still sat unevenly, wobbling beneath her fingertip. She dropped the stone into the padded box and tossed the shiny band down onto the table.

Her apprentice glanced up at her. "Was the stone not cut properly?" he asked.

Aertine started to scold him, but held her tongue at his nervous habit of biting his lower lip when he'd erred. Although she was dual skilled, she had never taken on a metallist apprentice. Only a stone innate. Only Varnon, whose family had remained steadfast despite what had happened with Ardea and the Matriarch's family.

"The stone is fine," she grumbled. "I am the one not properly cut today." This fine work was beyond her while her mind remained so disturbed. Devira's voice echoed against the walls of the workroom, "Breathe. Breathe and center yourself." But Aertine knew her own nature.

She gazed out the open window. "Put up the tools and go home, Varnon," she told the boy. "Go home and work on your sister's pairing gift."

He glanced up at her in surprise.

"Your mother told me. She's very proud of you. As well she should be. It will be a thing of joy and make a beautiful centerpiece for the new couple's hearth."

The young man smiled at her praise. "Thank you, Mistra Aertine." He bent to pack up his tools, but paused a moment, biting his lower lip again. He held out his hand to her, palm up. "Would you . . ." His hand shook and he stared down at his feet.

Aertine waited, giving him time to speak his mind.

"Would you lay the capping upon it?"

"You wish a metal capping?"

"Yes," he murmured, nodding, his hand still held out in the manner of one requesting a favor.

"Then I shall be honored to cap the hearthstone centerpiece for your sister's pairing."

"Thank you, Mistra," Varnon put his hands to his heart. "Thank you."

"Now, go on with you."

"Ancestors grant you mindfulness," he said, gathering up the last of the tools and placing them on the side bench before heading out the door.

Aertine sighed as she watched him go. Mindfulness was beyond her reach at times like this. Her sister, Devira, had always been the calm one, her tendencies running toward quietude and making people whole.

But Aertine had an edge to her, a fire that smoldered. Always. Even when they had been children, Aertine had been the one to burn hot. Devira had been the grounding force. But Ardea, the nurturer, she had been the one who had held them together. The one to smooth hurt feelings and bruised egos. Why then had she stolen the Matriarch's heir? Why had she doomed the family to years of defending themselves against the accusations that rained down upon them?

Betrayal. Complicity. Treachery.

There must have been a reason. And Aertine wanted to know what it was. No. She needed to know. Needed to put this restless curiosity to bed. And she needed to know where their sister was now. Why had the girl, the Matriarch's Heir, returned without her? And without her memories?

She wiped her hands on a buffing cloth, leaving a smear of tarnish, a streak against the light-colored fabric. A dark smear like the one on her heart. Like the smirch upon their family name. No, she reminded herself. Not the entire family. Devira had been able to work her way once more into the good graces of the Keepers. Her calm composure and mental grounding abilities had finally won her a place in the Matriarch's current household. That, and the way she suffered in silence, the wounding given her by the Matriarch when she had lashed out in her mind-wounded sorrow and grief. It was Devira who, without regard for her own safety and without complaint for the harm done her, had calmed the Lady then and ever after at the worst of her sideways edging.

Aertine stepped through the arched doorway and out onto the patio. She strode past the murmuring fountain, followed the twisting pathway to the sympathy field, and wended her way between the memorial stones. She knew she should be glad Devira had made the way clear for their family to once more become welcome in the surround. But it only made her feel as if her sister had abandoned Ardea to the fate of traitor, relegating her memory not that of a trusted nurturer, who had been as close as non-blood could be to the royal family, but that

106

of a despised betrayer.

This could not stand. Not without clarity. Not without understanding. Aertine could not allow her sister's memory to molder in such a fashion. She must know. And she would not rest until she did.

But Devira was right. She should not have pushed at the girl. She had thought the illness a ruse, the girl's lapses a lie. Had thought Devira was being duped. She cursed herself for being a stubborn fool. Chastised herself for her impatience. Hated herself for being unable to let go of the past and Ardea.

She stopped beside the remains of the obelisk that had marked her family's memory ground. The stone, once tall and smooth, had been broken and toppled by the Matriarch's anger after the discovery of her Consort's body and the disappearance of her daughter. Such had been the woman's grief and rage that the stone had been cracked, shattered and scorched by her mental energy. Her mind had followed suit. Until Devira had foolishly stepped in and had guided the Matriarch to her center, calming her long enough to be reminded of who she was.

But not before the damage had been done.

Aertine could still smell the burning flesh of Devira's hands. Her sister hadn't screamed, nor made any sound at all, when her flesh had been seared by the white hot anger of the Matriarch's mind, her Guardian's power lashing out as if in defense of the realm, but targeted against a single family and, ultimately, a lone representative. Had it not been for Devira's sacrifice, what untold damage would the Matriarch have wrought? And what would have become of their family lineage?

Aertine knelt beside the shattered pieces of the memory stone. "Lend me strength and patience," she whispered to the spirits of her parents. The urge to reach out and touch the bits of broken granite was overwhelming, but even as she brushed her fingertips against a pile of rough stone chips, she knew what she would find.

The memories of the past, moments that should have been preserved for all eternity, were as shattered as the shards of stone. Not a single recollection remained intact. Just bits and pieces of what had been left behind: Her grandfather's laughter, cut off in mid chuckle. A great-grandmother's glance. A whisper of their mother. A half-thought. A breath.

Nothing remained of their sister, Ardea. Nothing. The Matriarch had burned it all away, every image, every thought, every word.

Aertine yanked her hand away and wiped it on her canvas work apron. She reached inside herself, searching for her lost sister. But Ardea's smiling face appeared blurry and indistinct. Guilt and anger seized her. She pushed herself to recall the shape and color of Ardea's eyes, dug inside her memories to sharpen the image of her sister's forehead, her lips. She sat back on her heels and sighed in relief as the memory grew sharper, clearer. It was not her nature to let go. She would not rest until she knew the truth. Like the scorpion that stings instinctively, Aertine would continue to search for answers, whether she wished to or not. But today had shown her that she needed to tread more softly, find a more subtle path to the truth.

She placed her hand upon the remains of the memory stone, letting the jumbled shards of memories buzz against her fingertips. "I will learn the truth," she swore. "I will see that our family name is restored, or I will pass away my gifts trying."

* * *

108

"I cannot allow you in," Devira hissed, when Aertine rapped upon the chamber door. "Not after the last time."

"I must speak to her, once more." Aertine lowered her lids and placed her crossed hands over her heart. "I will not push. My heart rendered word." She glanced up at her sister, older than her by mere minutes. How was it, she wondered, twins could be so different, so opposite? "Devira, you know what this means to me. To us."

Devira narrowed her eyes. "Her health is my priority. I cannot forsake my oath for any reason, no matter how personal." She let her voice drop. "No matter how dear."

Aertine heard the despair in her voice, but she saw too the stubborn set of her sister's jaw. To argue further would be fruitless. "I'm sorry, Devira. I know I have been a burden to you, that my need for answers has caused you endless pain."

Devira shook her head. "No," she said, a quiet catch in her voice. "You're wrong, Aertine. The pain I carry is not of you, but for you." She glanced behind her, into the shadowy room, lit by a single illuminating orb in the far corner. Aertine followed her gaze to where the draped bed hugged the corner of the room. There was a stirring of rustled coverlets and a frightened whimper, then all was quiet once more.

Devira's eyes flicked sidewise along the corridor then she returned her gaze to Aertine. She shrugged her shoulders and lowered her voice. "I cannot bar you from walking along the garden paths at midmorning, nor again at eventide during the Hour of Reflection." She gave Aertine a knowing look, one eyebrow raised, then resumed speaking in a normal tone, "Please, do not come here again unless you are called for."

Aertine backed away and Devira closed the door with a quiet snick and set the latch in place. She leaned against the heavy wood and sighed. Had she done right to tell Aertine where the girl would be? Would it help? Or had she only further complicated things, supporting her sister in her relentless quest for answers that she might never find? Or if she did, might find to be more painful than not knowing.

CHAPTER TWENTY-THREE

Alyana paused beside a flowering bush. The petals of the flowers glowed golden in the sunlight. She reached up and pulled a willowy branch closer to her face and inhaled the heady scent. Strange yet somehow familiar, the perfume of it warmed her.

"Jesmapine." A woman's voice said behind her. "A late blooming tree."

She jumped and twirled around, heart pounding wildly.

"I'm sorry," the woman said. "I didn't mean to startle you."

She shook her head, forcing herself to calm, to breathe normally. She recognized the woman from their previous encounter. The one who had been so desperate for information. Answers Alyana was unable to provide. "No. It's me," she told the woman with a sigh. "I seem to be afraid of every little noise." She shrugged. "I wish I knew why, and . . . I wish I could tell you what you want to know." She searched around inside her brain, seeking any clue, even the most insignificant memory, but there were only blanks. Emptiness.

She considered the woman for a long while. "You're Aertine." At least that much seemed right.

"Yes." The woman looked hopeful, then reached up and touched one of the golden flowers. "Ardea loved the scent of jesmapine," she said, "and the way the petals fell and swirled in the river eddies in late summer." She appeared for a moment as if she were traveling in time, returning to another day, another place.

Alyana waited quietly until the woman's eyes refocused.

"I'm sorry I pushed you," the woman told her. "I truly thought you might remember something of her. Of Ardea." Aertine gazed into her eyes, a sad expression etched upon her features, as if carved there by years of sorrow. "You remind me of her."

Alyana's fingers slipped to her throat, touching the medallion that hung about her neck.

Aertine sucked in her breath and stared.

Alyana started, her hand froze and she peered down at the medallion. "What is it?" she whispered.

"Nothing," Aertine said. "It's just that . . . I thought I recognized your amulet." She stepped closer. "It's lovely. May I see it?"

Hesitantly, Alyana let her hand fall from her throat.

Aertine reached out, brushing her fingertips across the metal.

A jolt ran through Alyana and she jumped back, hands clutching at the medallion. "What did you do?" she asked, her voice a hoarse whisper.

"I'm sorry," Aertine smiled warmly, her face flushed with what looked like embarrassment. "I have a sympathetic connection to precious metals. It's my key talent and enables me to cast the settings and set the jewels of my . . . craft. Though, I am dual skilled and am also stone affined, as well." Aertine shrugged. "Your medallion looks much like one I've seen before. Where did you come by it?"

"I think it may have been my mother's," she said, reaching up to finger the metal disc. "But . . . " Her head began to ache again, the familiar throbbing starting up. She let the thought drop along with her hand.

Aertine appeared concerned. "Are you unwell?" She reached out, but Alyana took a step back, stumbling and catching hold of one of the yellow laden branches. Soft golden petals rained down and tinkling laughter echoed around her. Dizziness gripped her, but not the dizziness of illness and fainting. This was the giddiness of a young child being twirled around and around beneath falling leaves, with the chill of autumn flushing her cheeks and the warmth of a mother's hands holding tight to hers. Then the world rocked, her head exploded and everything went black.

CHAPTER TWENTY-FOUR

Devira paced the room. There must be some way to get inside this young woman's mind, to access the thoughts and memories still being blocked. She rolled her shoulders to ease the tension from them. She wanted nothing more than to share her deepest thoughts with Aertine, but the secrets she held on behalf of the Council, the Matriarch, and even those few she had discerned of her young patient, could be shared with no one. Not even her twin.

She understood Aertine's frustration. While they no longer shared the depths of one another's thoughts, their emotions were another matter. This was the crux of the ties that bound them, the ties that had once brought them closer than other siblings. Now, these same ties were in large part the cause of the ever-widening breach between them. If Devira could have shared her thoughts, the secrets she held so close because they belonged to others and not to her, her sister might not be so angry at her. And the world.

But her oath precluded that. And now, she had risked that oath by allowing Aertine to disrupt Alyana's mental healing. Not once, but twice.

She sat on the edge of the bench beside the tall window overlooking the river. Below, blue-green water tumbled and flowed between grassy banks dotted with tall shade trees. Hawthorn and Flamebranch reached skyward, leafy branches swaying in the persistent breeze. The soughing of the wind recalled happier times spent with her siblings picnicking and playing beneath those trees.

They had all been happy once. She and her sisters. Though older by nearly two turns, Ardea had been as close as any sister could be to the twins without being a triplet.

All three had chosen differing paths. Dual-skilled, Devira had become a Physica, healing minds as well as bodies with her talents of soothing and her skills for guiding the mind through the healing paths. Aertine had never been happier than when she'd mentored and taught the younger children, helping them to find and master their skills and to find their own paths. Her dual mindskills in stone and metal work had surfaced early and provided a path for making that few others could master as she did. But her talent for teaching younglings to use their abilities for the arts of creation, though not a true mindskill, had been no less a gift.

Ardea had had no such calling. She wanted no more than to serve her best friend, Kyrina. So, she had given her life in service to the Matriarch. Until . . .

Devira closed her eyes. Why had her sister done what she had? What could have driven her to such an action? The loss of her babe had been a great blow, yes, but she had seemed content to nurture the Matriarch's Heir, to wet-nurse and raise the girl as her own. Had even appeared to thrive in doing so.

If Ardea had known the cost she would pay, the cost to all of them, would she still have chosen to walk in those fateful footsteps? Devira let out a heavy sigh. She knew the answer to that without having to consider it.

Her patient stirred and she rose to tend to her. Alyana sat up and blinked, squinting against the late summer sunlight that streamed in through the open window.

"How are you feeling?" Devira asked, placing her cool hand against Alyana's cheek. She sensed the girl's confusion, then jerked her hand away with a gasp. Tumbling images rushed into her mind. They came too fast, too frantically for her to see clearly, but one final image rested in her brain before slowly fading out. Ardea, laughing, as a red-haired toddler, Alyana as a child, flopped down in a huge pile of leaves, disappeared momentarily from sight, then burst forth in a shower of red, gold and brown.

Alyana stared at her, eyes wide. "What?" she asked, her voice breaking. "What was that?"

Devira stood frozen beside the bed, her hand still raised in the air. She forced herself to reply in a calm voice. "What did you see?" she asked.

"I don't know. Faces. Places. Things. People. People I should know, but . . ." She swallowed. "They look so familiar, but I can't . . ." Her lower lip trembled.

Devira reached out and took the girl's shaking hand. "It's all right," she told her. "No need to push."

But inside, the Physica was trembling, as well. This was the breakthrough she had been hoping for. Though she had no idea why it had come now. No matter. The girl would begin to remember. And with her memories would come the answers she and Aertine had both awaited so long.

CHAPTER TWENTY-FIVE

She drifted in darkness, shivered and clutched the coverlet to her. Coming wide awake with a start, she pushed herself into a sitting position, trying to unwrap herself from the tangled fabric. Faint coals flickered on the hearth, and the room had taken on a wintry chill.

She finally managed to extricate herself from the blankets, and slid out of bed. Through the shutters, starlight shimmered in an indigo sky. The keep seemed to shudder in the chill silence of the wee hours of morn. The deep cold before the dawn slipped icy fingers into the room and caressed her cheeks. She slung a thick woolen coverlet across her shoulders, pulling it around her like a cocoon, and tiptoed across the floor to the fireplace.

She kept her fist tightly wrapped in the blanket to keep it from falling from her shoulders, while she prodded the coals with an iron poker. Sparks rose and scattered like a cloud of fireflies, glittering as they flew upward, before glinting out. A stack of kindling lay piled beside the hearth and she tossed the bits of dried wood onto the glowing coals. The morning caretaker would likely be put out having to fetch new wood, but she cared not. She wanted heat and light and she would use the furniture if need be to chase away the licking cold and the darkness that closed in around her, threatening to swallow her once again into forgetfulness.

She knelt before the blaze and wondered when she had grown afraid of the dark. She had a feeling of certainty that she had been alone in the dark many times, but had never feared it the way she did now. Not even after her fight with the rock troll. The blurred vision of that stormy night had passed, almost as quickly as the storm had. But this was different. This dark fear clutched at her, groping for her, seeking her out, attempting to writhe its way inside her. It grew inside her brain like a voracious weed sending blackened tendrils to steal her thoughts and memories. The need to guard against this invasive blackness exhausted her.

She paused. Her arm outstretched, clutching a stick of kindling as if it were a knife. No. That couldn't be right. When had she fought with a rock troll? She slammed the wood into the fire and sparks flew. Another dream mixing itself with memory inside her head.

What little memory there was.

She stared into the licking flames, nodding before the fiery warmth. Then, she was beside a rushing river. It was cold, wet, dark. Something rose up before her. It let out a roar, deep and sonorous, filled with feral danger. She was fighting, her companions leaping into the fray. A horse screamed. She battled with all her might, but the hulking shadow continued to attack. She struck with her knife. Again and again. But the creature grabbed her arms and pinned her down.

"Hush," the monster said. "Hush now. It's only a night terror." The creature's claws shrank and grew small, fading into fingers, scarred but human. Her companions faded into the shadows. The fire crackled, bathing the side of her face in glowing warmth. Devira knelt beside her, holding her wrists gently but firmly with her gnarled hands.

"You're awake now," she told her. "Awake and safe."

Alyana relaxed and the firm grip on her wrists lessened.

She stared into the fire, then shook her head. "It seemed so real," she whispered, her dry throat raw, as if she'd been screaming.

Devira put a hand to her brow and leaned forward to peer into her eyes. "Do you wish to talk about it?" She asked it calmly, but there was tension in her voice, as if she were afraid of what the answer might be.

She gave her head a tiny shake and felt Devira stiffen, but it was impossible to tell if in disappointment or relief. She tried to stand, but her legs quivered and she sat down hard upon the thick rug. "I'm sorry to be such a bother," she told the Physica. "I've not been plagued with bad dreaming before. At least . . ." She paused, somehow doubting her own words. Suddenly, the fire burned too close. Before she knew what she was doing, she had pushed herself up and away from the flames, stumbling back from the hearth.

The Physica was at her side in a flash, guiding her to the bed.

"What is wrong with me?" she asked in a weak voice.

Devira shushed her and patted her forehead with a cool cloth. "Do you recall what happened yestereve?" she asked.

She tried to recall the day before, but visions and

119

memories snarled in a web of tangles, like balls of string a litter of kittens had been at.

"You had a visitor," Devira said. Her words were matter-of-fact, but there was a tone in her voice that said this was more important than she wanted to let on. "A woman with red-brown hair and rosy skin. You spoke with her by the river."

She struggled to find the thread of memory attached to this visitor. She should remember someone who would stand out against the pale skin so prevalent in this place, but each time she came close to catching at the end of the thread, it slipped through her fingers and she found herself staring at another knot so tangled and unfamiliar it left her reeling. She lurched to the cleansing basin beside the bed and splashed cool water onto her face.

She felt seared. Something burned her skin. A basilisk hissed in the darkness and reared up at her . . .

She straightened and turned. Shadows flickered across the walls, reflecting a strange vision of another room layered over the dim bedchamber. She glanced toward the shuttered window. Darkness still cloaked the sky and land outside. The blanket had fallen from her shoulders, but she was no longer cold. She was sweating and out of breath, as if she'd been running at high speed. The room cantered and she felt as if she were spinning in circles, spiraling backward.

Where was she?

The world lurched, then swung about and clicked like a bit of paving slate that had finally settled into its correct place in the road. With sudden clarity she found herself at rest on firmer ground.

I know my name, she thought with a surge of conviction. I know my name, and it is not Alyana.

S. A. Skinner

CHAPTER TWENTY-SIX

Milos rolled onto his back and stared up at the stars. They sparkled just as those at home, but their shapes were different here. He recalled the nights aboard the Sunfleet when he and Kira had stood at the railing looking up into the vast sky and the endless stars that reflected their light onto the frothy waves. The bright greens and blues that glowed against the ship's hull as they plowed through the water had mesmerized them.

"Stardust," the captain had told them. "The water in the Faersent sea is filled with the dust of falling stars. That's what makes the water glitter at night when the ship churns it up."

They had laughed, thinking it a bit of whimsy, but the old sailor had insisted. "There is real magic in this world and it resides in more places than in a healer's hands," he'd said, before turning and heading into his cabin for the night.

Milos sifted that through in his mind, wondering if

the glowing orbs in the city below were filled with stardust, as well.

This land of magic was beyond him and he understood why people feared it. Feared its people. But Kira was of this bloodline. And she was the farthest thing from evil he had ever known. Though he could not deny what had happened in the forest, the hours, or days, he had wandered in his mind. The evil dreams that had fed on his worries, had embraced him and held him close, refusing to set him free.

But he had broken loose.

He still wondered what had finally allowed him to escape the dream mist's clutches. Shivered at the thought of what would have become of him had he remained within those foggy illusions. Shuddered at the thought of a power that could capture and confine a man in a realm that seemed to be set apart from the real world and keep him there until he starved or died of thirst.

Thankfully, he and Dahl did not succumb to the dreams once again during their return journey to the shore at the edge of the forest.

Prepared to be caught by the demon mist at any moment, Milos had been surprised to find himself able to retrace the path he and Dahl had followed. With Vaith and Kelmir bringing in game every evening, food was no longer a problem. And once he had found the stream again, he'd followed it through the forest, until an eerie glow drew him up over the foothills. He'd ducked as he approached the top of the last ridge and lay on his stomach, staring down at the shimmering city below.

Kelmir shifted in the grass beside him, tail twitching impatiently. "Yes," Milos said, "we must find your mistress." He sat up and brushed off a bit of dried grass. "Since we've no idea where to look, this is as good a place as any to start." He stood, but Kelmir lay still, ears pricked in the direction of the glowing city. "Yes," Milos agreed. "It's larger than any keep or settlement I've ever seen. But if she's there, then that is where we are bound." He eyed the cat. "But we cannot just walk in the front door and announce we are seeking a red-headed woman. Not with the way they treat uninvited guests to their shores, their power to inflict dark dreams. No. We must find another way in. And we must do it unnoticed." Milos stared at the lights below and considered. "That means, I cannot take you with me," he said, finally.

Kelmir growled deep in his throat, as if in agreement. At least Milos hoped that was what was in the big cat's mind. Without Kira's connection to his feline companion, he really had no way of knowing. He wished once more that she were by his side. Together they could devise a cunning scheme. Their successful rescue of his nephew from the bounty hunter Lagos Surrat and his hired thugs had proven that. It wasn't that he was devoid of the ability to plan on his own, just that together they were more capable than either alone.

In the pale dawn, Milos slipped around the edge of the city, marking the roads in and out, points where the river ran under walls and along throughways, and the thickness of the walls. He stayed inside the tree line where he could, ducked below the scraggly scrub oaks where he could not. Despite his wishes, he sensed Kelmir pacing him, keeping to the shadows. At least the big cat kept out of sight.

Expecting armed guards, or at the very least watchmen, Milos was surprised to find no one watching the gates. In fact, there were no gates. The stone walls, while high in places, in others appeared no higher than a tall man's reach. What magic, he wondered, could secure a place so well as to allow the people to come and go freely through wide open lanes in and out of the city? Their guards must be formidable. He thought of the misty curtain that had fallen over him in the forest.

Would he stumble into another dream if he entered the city? He forced down his worry and considered his next move. He had to find Kira. His heart insisted she was alive, and that meant there was a reason she had been cut off from her companions. She might be ill or unconscious. What if she was being held captive? She had managed to keep Kelmir and Vaith secret from her abuser, Toril, despite the warlord's power. Had worked in fact to ensure it, choosing to send them away to keep them safe. Were she to find herself in danger, it would be like her to choose to remain disconnected, rather than risk her beloved companions.

He made a half circuit of the city before being forced to retreat in frustration. Though fewer than he expected, as the blush of dawn receded and was replaced by a cloudless sky of pale blue, too many people moved about the wide lanes for him to slip into the city unseen. The river that spilled out of the lush forest edging this part of the city was too wide and too open to ford. He retraced his steps to the dense patch of grass where they had started. Vaith still perched upon a high branch, head tucked beneath a wing, his tail looped around the limb.

"It appears our friend has slept on as we worked," Milos said to Kelmir. Vaith started awake with a flap of his iridescent wings and chirruped in annoyance. "My apologies," Milos said.

The big cat yawned, showing his huge canines, his dark tongue stretching out. Then he clamped his mouth shut, and sat waiting.

Milos weighed his options. He needed to enter the city unseen. And he must be able to retreat quickly should the misty dreams threaten to cloud his mind again.

He looked out across the valley at the glowing city. Lighted orbs suspended between tall pillars dimmed as the sun rose. They burned without the wavering of firelight or candle. Once more, he wondered what strange magic might be at work here. What other powers might these people possess? He put the thought aside.

Kira was still alive. He was certain of it. And, though he had no way of knowing where she might be, his footsteps had led him here. She too might somehow have found her way to this place. If that was the case, what sort of welcome might she have encountered?

He heard a noise behind him, tensed, then relaxed as Kelmir crept up beside him. The big cat stood still, flicking an ear, then settled down onto his haunches and turned his lavender eyes on Milos, tail twitching in the grass.

Milos resisted the urge to reach out and stroke the big cat. They had become allies in their search for Kira, but there was still an uncertainty about the big feline. An edginess that made Milos remain cautious. Vaith, however, had no such compunctions. He flitted down onto the ground beside them and trilled excitedly.

"I've nothing for you," Milos chided the wyvern. "Unless you'd like to finish off the withered remnants in my bag, you'll have to scratch up your own rations."

Vaith tilted his head, and cocked one round eye at Milos before opening his wings and leaping up into an overhead tree branch to preen. If he didn't know better, Milos could almost believe the tiny dragon understood his every word.

He ate the last of the rubbery tubers he'd dug the day before. Then he settled in to wait out the day. At dusk, he would explore the other side of the city.

CHAPTER TWENTY-SEVEN

Kira wandered along the edge of the water, the fading sunlight reflecting gold and pink off the surface of the stream. She had a name now. A name and the faces of her parents, but little else to fill the dark void where her memories should be, aside from the nightmares full of fire and blood. She shuddered, though the evening air was warm.

A sudden flash of color glittered in the last rays of the sun as something small and quick darted toward her. She ducked and let out a tiny yelp as the miniature winged reptile swooped out of the trees and flew directly at her. The tiny wyvern chirruped as it swerved past. It landed on a low branch and trilled and chittered in annoyance.

Kira watched the creature, fascinated. Its fine wings and graceful tail, the curve of its neck, the iridescent coloring. Something about its eyes drew her. She walked toward the tree in which it perched and gazed up in wonder. "You're a beauty," she said.

The dragonet's eyes glowed gold, the oval pupils dilating as it watched her. She unwrapped the chunk of stale bread she had carried with her to feed the waterfowl and held it out to the creature. The wyvern tilted its head to peer at her, but stayed on the branch.

Her heart thrummed inside her chest and she wanted more than anything for the little reptile to come closer. That's silly, she thought. A wild beast would as like take my finger as a crust of bread. "You must prefer fresh game, or at least meat," Kira said and dropped her hand in embarrassment. "Or perhaps you're simply too wild a thing to coax with food." She watched the creature for another moment, then forced herself to turn away toward the central keep. But before she had taken two steps, the wyvern soared down from its perch and landed on her shoulder, wrapping its thin tail around her neck.

Kira froze, panic and excitement faced off inside her, both pushing her to act, but instead she stood as still as the trees. She breathed in and out, very slowly, wanting the moment to last. Afraid of what the creature might do, but for some reason longing for it to stay, longing to run her fingers between its eyes and down its long neck.

A fine-scaled head appeared in her vision and golden eyes peered into hers, as if trying to see inside her mind. She held her breath, afraid of startling the animal into biting or attacking. Then, with a loud chirrup that sounded uncannily like disapproval, the wyvern opened its wings, leaped into the air, circled once overhead and, with a flash of light off glittering scales, disappeared beyond the treetops.

Kira let out the breath she had been holding. What a glorious little creature! She tilted her face to the sky, thankful for this moment; the first of true happiness she could recall.

"You have a gift with animals." The voice that purred behind her sounded silken, but there was a hard curious edge to it. With a slight quick gesture of her hand, she let go of her prayer, sending it singing into the world. Why she felt the need to hide her actions from this man, she knew not. Only that something about Teraxin made her skin feel oily and unclean. Was this another emanation of the skills Devira had spoken of? Or did Kira just not like the way the man behaved, as if there were always more to what he said than his words betrayed. Or the way he parsed every word Kira spoke as if seeking to decipher a hidden meaning, as if she held all the secrets of the unknowable.

She glanced over her shoulder to acknowledge the man, then walked to the edge of the water to coax the wading birds with the bread she had brought with her. "I like to feed the birds," she said, tossing a handful of crusts upon the water.

The tall birds lifted their thin legs high as they waded toward the crumbs and arched their graceful necks to grab up the morsels in their bright bills. Kira watched them tilt their heads back, beaks pointed at the sky to swallow her offerings, much the same way she had been thanking the Goddess before being interrupted.

A word of wisdom crept into her brain, something about trust being the weapon of liars. Could it be some sort of farmer's lore? Or was it some hedge-wives saying? Perhaps, something she might have picked up from Devira? No, something about it felt older, not something that had been given to her of late.

She realized that Teraxin had been talking to her as her thoughts wandered. Had he just asked her for her thoughts on the troubles in the Council? Were there troubles in the Council? Was she supposed to know about them?

She shrugged and feigned boredom. "I know not what wisdom the Council might seek of me," she said, hoping this was the correct answer. "But should they ask me, I would say that, trouble finds its way to the doorsteps of both those who prepare for it and those who do not." Where had that come from? She tried not to look startled by her own words while ignoring Teraxin's surprised reaction.

"You are correct, of course," he finally managed to sputter, confusion contorting his brow.

What had made her say such a thing? It had almost been as if someone else had spoken through her. Kira tossed another handful of bread upon the water and watched a swarm of tiny, bright feathered birds dive to scoop them up before the graceful water birds could get to them. The tall waders, nonplussed by the smaller birds, squawked and cawed until Kira threw them the last of her offerings.

"Do you not sit among the meditation stones at this hour as most others here do?" She asked it quietly, not wishing him to think she was anything more than curious.

"There are times for quiet reflection," he said pointedly. "And there are times for more overt activities." Teraxin watched her closely, eyeing the birds, as if he expected them to do some odd trick or something. But when the birds merely continued to squabble over the few remaining crumbs that floated on the water, he finally took his leave, muttering to himself as he walked off. "Meditation and prayer will not save this land, nor our people."

CHAPTER TWENTY-EIGHT

There was something more to this girl than what she let on, Teraxin thought as he made his way to the Council chambers. And he knew he should probably say something to Kavyn, tell him of his suspicions, but he wasn't entirely certain what it was he suspected, nor how it might be proven. Besides, if there was something hidden here, Teraxin preferred the opportunity to move it to his own advantage, an outcome that could be better for him. Perhaps he could strike a new deal. It was clear his young student now believed he had outgrown his tutor. Perhaps, a new student would be more open to guidance, especially since she had no troublesome parents to get in the way.

Odd, he thought, how one's world can shift. One day there is an heir being groomed for the throne, standing in the way of a man's greatness and needing to be gotten rid of, and in the next moment it turns out that same heir may be the one to pave a man's way to greatness.

He merely needed to discover exactly how much she knew and how deep her skills might run. And, depending on her malleability, perhaps find a way to get rid of Kavyn. Sadly, it would be a more difficult feat than attempting to drown a baby. And that had not been so easily attempted. Nor achieved. No. His path had been set long ago. Though, it might set his enemies off balance were he to feign a change of heart on the matter of the Eilaren rulership.

Teraxin took his seat in the Council chamber, trying not to stare at his former pupil. The board was set and the pieces teetered on the edge, a point of uneasy balance. Neither could make a move without upsetting the play. But neither could they allow the board to stand. A move must be made. The rise and fall of voices pulled him back into the room where the councilors continued to argue and discuss without coming any closer to making a decision.

As the council members kept their mental guards at high level during their gatherings, the argument was vocal, the raising of voices an annoyance that preyed upon Teraxin's nerves. The traditionalists versus the progressive thinkers. Those who preferred to maintain the matriarchy and those who would follow another path. A path untrod for nearly a thousand years. A path he had striven to pave for more than two decades. One that should have been embarked upon years ago and would have, had it not been for a stubborn nurturer and a matriarch of such mental strength, she had managed to maintain a delicate hold on her sanity despite the manipulations of her gifted son. Her brief moments of clarity were the threads by which the Council clung to their indecision.

He snorted, then composed himself, covering his face and feigning a sneeze. "My pardon," he mumbled to the white-haired councilor sitting beside him. Meryk gave him a feeble nod. The old man, who served as First of the councilors, hunched in his chair, leaning heavily on the padded armrests, his age weighing heavily on his thin bones. He appeared unsteady, as if he might teeter and fall out of his seat, if not for the layer of cushions that surrounded him. But his sharp eyes shone bright and alert. His composed face showed no weakness, and Teraxin, though tempted to test the old goat's mental guard, knew better. Meryk might be a fool, but he was not to be trifled with.

The councilors droned on, their voices as ineffective as the buzzing of annoying insects. Kavyn toyed with a quill, balancing it first upon one hand and then the other, projecting disinterest in the current rehashing of old arguments. Only the tiny tic on the right side of his mouth revealed his level of stress. Hopefully, only Teraxin recognized that tic, that single miniscule, telling facial movement he had never been able to train the boy to school.

Teraxin raised his cup to hide the sneer that threatened to cross his face as he contemplated the failings of his protégé. Had he been born with half the skills of Kavyn, he would have wrested control of the Guardian's Seat long before now. The realm would be under his control and they would not only be prospering, they would be ruling the lesser lands. As it was, their country continued to decline. Its people had long ago rejected the art of war, depending instead upon their Guardian's abilities to shield them from external harm. They used their gifts only for arts and crafts and growing flax to spin into cloth, even the defensive arts waned when they should be taking the offense, growing outward, conquering the barbarians, not trading with them.

The First raised one hand, spread his fingers wide and then closed them together, in a call for silence. Meryk still held the authority of the First Seat. The bickering ceased and respectful quiet settled over the gathering. He shifted, attempting to sit up straighter, as all eyes turned to him.

At one time, as Councilor of the First Seat, Meryk would have addressed them all in thought-speak, having been one of the few among them who retained such strong power and control. But, with his increasing age, his mental prowess had faded, so he spoke aloud, his voice breathy and trembling. "Would you have us relegate one of the last defensive minds among us to the Wards?" he asked.

Protests broke out among the gathering, but Meryk held up a palsied hand, palm out, and the councilors grew silent once more. "A broken mind, admittedly. Yet, the strength of past generations still resides in our Matriarch. A strength we have not seen repeated in this generation." He examined the faces of those seated around the table. "No one now among us can match her. And a broken shield is worth more than none."

Teraxin bit back the derisive laughter welling inside him. Unlike Kavyn, however, he schooled his features into a flat mask, giving away nothing of his thoughts as he regarded the factions that fought for control of the realm. If only they knew, but he dared not reveal himself. Should they now discover Kavyn's powers, which had been hidden from them for so long, and the uses to which he had put them, there would be questions. Tribunal. Perhaps even a formal interrogation panel. They might never question the boy directly, nor would they likely be able to ply beyond his mental guard, but Kavyn's close, almost exclusive, relationship with his mentor was no secret. Teraxin could not stand against their combined powers. He knew all too well his own limitations. They would crash in upon his barriers like a stormy sea against an unprotected shore. And he would break, like the frail dwellings of poor fisher folk dashed against the rocks.

He raised two fingers in the respectful gesture for permission to speak. He may not like these games, but he was more adept at them than his impulsive pupil.

Meryk placed his hand on the table, palm facing upward, fingers pointing toward Teraxin, granting him the opportunity to voice his mind.

With a nod to the old man, Teraxin cleared his throat, then took a sip from his goblet, forcing the others to wait in silence for him to speak. When he finally did, he began with a mild sigh. "True," he said, "a broken shield may still deflect an enemy's weaker blows, but," he surveyed the assembly, one by one making eye contact with each of them, "a shattered shield is worth nothing at all."

Cries erupted from around the room. The arguments flaring up once more.

"How dare you," one of the female councilors cried out above the din. "She is wounded, not dead."

Teraxin gritted his teeth. No wonder their race was failing. How could a people ruled by such an emotional gender last? It was a wonder they had not fallen into utter ruin already. These women who had lost children, even before birth, acted as if such a loss was a great tragedy. As if it were some badge of honor. They even used it as an excuse to shirk their duties, to hide in their beds and mourn for days, weeks, or—like the current Matriarch—too many turns.

Once more, Teraxin held up two fingers and the room quieted. "I did not say our Matriarch was shattered, but I fear we risk that happenstance should we allow her to continue as we have. It is for the Matriarch's own safety that we must strip the Guardian's Seat from her, sever her connection with the Warding stones, and place the chains of office upon the shoulders of another."

"We know your thoughts on this." Council Second Zoshia folded her hands together upon the table. "And there are some on this council who see the wisdom of such a change—"

"And the Council has ruled against the actions you have proposed." Meryk cut her off with a frown that wrinkled his old face into that of a toad.

For a moment, it appeared Zoshia might say more, but she held her peace, smoothing her face into an unbiased mask.

"I have only the security of our people in mind," Teraxin countered. "When I advocated for such a change, I believed we had no other option. However, that happenstance appears to have changed."

* * *

"What are you suggesting?" Kavyn half rose from his seat, the feather he had been toying with falling to the floor. His was not the farthest chair from the First, yet it was one of rituality and he held no actual rank here in this room amongst these councilors. At least none beyond what he had thus far been able to wrest from some of them by hacking through their dream shields and planting tiny seeds as they slept. Some of these had taken root and were growing. A shift had begun to weave its way through the Council, but some councilors remained merely doubtful. They needed more time.

But now. This betrayal. His tutor continued to be filled with surprising moves. By offering the Council another option, another heir, a female heir, Teraxin, the old fox, had made a move that upset all of the pieces on the gambit board, setting the game up for concession or defeat. The Council had no idea yet, but Kavyn could see it as clearly as if the imaginary board were real and sitting on the table before him, jade and silver pieces shimmering in the orb-light. How many moves ahead Teraxin had planned was as big a mystery to Kavyn as was how his sibling had managed to not only survive all these years, but how and why she had returned to them, at this time, as he hovered, finally, on the brink of assuming the Guardian's Seat. If any of the conspirators were still alive, aside from Teraxin, Kavyn might have suspected them. But he and his tutor had ensured their own safety. Together, they had secured silence and secrecy through the most guaranteed means.

Meryk waved at him with his gnarled hands and Kavyn realized he was still standing. He sat, slowly, his hazel eyes burning into Teraxin's ocean colored ones. "A thousand apologies," he said, his voice barely cracking with the emotion that seethed through him.

Kavyn could not expose his knowledge of Teraxin's involvement in the Consort's murder those many years ago. Not without exposing his own secrets. But he needed to find a way to stop this. He had worked and waited too long for his turn upon the Throne of Eilar to let it be stolen from him now. He raised a hand and held up two fingers and waited until Meryk laid the back of his hand upon the table and opened his fingers to point in his direction.

"Venerable First Seat Meryk, and honored Second, Zoshia. Respected Councilors," he nodded to each of them in turn. "I know I have no voting power here, but I feel I must warn you, our Matriarchess, my sister," he said the word deliberately, "is untrained and unwell. I fear we have but two broken shields," he glared at

Teraxin. "Two halves that do not make a whole."

The Councilors sat in silence, none wishing to be the first to speak after such an openly detrimental statement regarding not only their current monarch, but that of her heir, their lost hope, only recently returned to them.

Kavyn glared around at them, a sour look growing on his face. Imbeciles. They were weak. "You talk and talk and talk," he told them. "Yet, you decide nothing. Your words will not bring us back from the brink. They will not stop the inevitable tide that washes over us and drowns our very existence. Our children are born weak, and pass before their maturity." He stood and leaned forward, his hands on the table, shoulders tight with anger. "Already there are rumors that the Outland horde that swept across the Aestron continent is poised and preparing to strike again, seeking a more bountiful harvest guarded by a weaker enemy." Even as he spoke, he raised additional shields around the source of his information. It would not do for any of the councilors to detect his part in the creation of those rumors, nor what part he played in the weakening of the Eilar bloodlines.

A part of him wanted them to know. Wanted Teraxin to understand how outmaneuvered he truly was, how many moves behind he was . . . but it was too soon. That time would come. How proud his mentor would be of him to learn how patient he could be. For now, he must redirect the councilors, yet keep them from making a move that would delay things too long. A move that would keep him from the Guardian's Seat beyond the first wheeling moon of Autumn, which was less than a fortnight distant.

A few nodded, but several of the councilors shook their heads in weariness, clearly tired of this argument.

How was it the truth could not stir them to action?

How could they not see that their lives, their very existence depended on this decision? "Traditions are no excuse for damning us all to be crushed beneath the weight of our forbearers mistakes," Kavyn shouted, no longer able to contain his ire.

* * *

Idiot! Teraxin cringed. Heaping blasphemy upon insult. Kavyn would ruin everything. This was not the way to set the final gambit into motion. Teraxin tried to catch his pupil's eye. He clenched the edge of the table, his nails digging into the polished wood. How many hands had touched this wood, polishing it with the oil of skin and sweat? How many times had such a council been convened? Yet, over the thousands of years since their system of governance had been established, there had been only a single male monarch. And he had nearly brought them all to ruin in a single span of years. Had his pupil been deaf during every history lesson he had ever taught? He calmed himself and gestured around the table. "Councilors," he said in his most ingratiating manner, "we are all tired and the evening shadows grow long. Perhaps, we should adjourn until the morrow."

The First Seat glanced around the room, and his eyes met Kavyn's, as if he would tear down the mental guards that held all his secrets in place. Then the moment passed, and Teraxin let out the breath he had been holding.

"I agree," Meryk said, his voice shaky with exhaustion. "We shall reconvene at mid-morn on the morrow."

Kavyn's face twisted. It was clear he had lost this battle. He turned on his heel and, ignoring protocol, left the room without waiting for the First and Second Seats to rise, leaving a stunned silence behind him.

The councilors looked to the Seats, but Meryk waved them off. "Leave us," he told them. "I would have a word with the Second before I retire." He remained seated, watching the others disperse in small knots, their voices low whispers that susurrated against the walls and slipped behind the tapestries like slithering snakes.

Teraxin dawdled, ensuring that aside from Meryk and Zoshia, he was the last to remain. "I offer apologies for my student," he said when the three of them were finally alone.

With a quiet sigh, the First Seat sank into the chair cushions, settling his hands to rest upon his lap. "His youthful passion might be put to better uses," the old man said.

Zoshia snorted, but quickly covered it with a small cough.

The First Seat closed his eyes. He was quiet for so long, Teraxin began to think the councilor had fallen asleep on them. Again. He glanced at Zoshia and raised an eyebrow.

She shook her head in warning.

Meryk's eyes remained closed, but he opened his mouth and spoke. "There was once a kingdom that sat at the pinnacle of a tall mountain," he said, his voice dreamlike, as if he had gone into a mind-trance, but Teraxin knew full well the old man had no such gift, so he sat and waited for the story Meryk had decided to tell him. It was a story he had never heard before, and Teraxin knew the old man was intent on making a point.

Meryk's voice droned on and Teraxin shifted in his chair and leaned his elbows on the table, attempting to appear interested, but instead of listening to the old man's story, his mind raced. He needed to put a stop to this talking, needed to force the councilors to make a move, but it must be the right move and he must first regain Kavyn's trust. Clearly, his student felt betrayed by what had just transpired, but that could not be helped. He needed the rest of the Council to conclude for themselves the monumental mistake it would be to place Alyana on the Guardian's Seat for this plan to work. The unforeseen luck of her presence would move them forward and secure their plans in a way that Teraxin could not have hoped. Two broken females in a single line would prove beyond doubt that the time for change was upon them.

There had been no time to discuss or prepare for this particular circumstance, which was just as well. Kavyn's anger and surprise were the perfect tone to establish before setting up the pieces to fall in line. Shift of tradition did not happen without the pain of crisis. This Teraxin had learned through all his studies, political and historical. Had his student, so much a prodigy in the art of mental skills, only been a better student of books and learning. He, too, would understand the need for disaster to strike in order for the councilors to embrace the change they needed.

The room went silent. The old man had paused his blathering for some reason and Teraxin realized he had missed nearly everything Meryk had said. "Is there a moral to the story?" he asked politely.

Zoshia gave him an odd look.

Meryk opened his eyes and stared at Teraxin for a length of time. "If the young do not honor the wisdom of age," he said, his breath wheezing out of him as he arose from his chair, "then they will be doomed to gain their own through trial and fire."

Zoshia stood as well, and went to the old man's side, holding out an arm for him to lean upon. Meryk grasped her arm with one hand and picked up his walking stick with the other. Together, they left the chamber, leaving Teraxin alone in the spacious room attempting to respin the threads of his plot into some semblance of a plan.

CHAPTER TWENTY-NINE

A wave of images flashed inside Kira's head. A jumble of color, movement and sound. Then a cascade of memories.

A man with red-gold hair and beside him a woman with hazel eyes, leaning over her, smiling, their minds coalescing inside hers, filling her with a sense of love and warmth.

A young boy staring at her in curiosity.

Her own chubby hand, gripping a glittering coin.

The images played out, as if she were watching them in real time. Her father strolling along the river with her small hand clasped warmly in his. Him kneeling to show her a fragrant pink flower.

Her father alone on the shore. The sudden rush of men. Father's angry voice raised in question before the thudding sound of a club hitting him, knocking him down.

The rush of the wind and a panting of breath, as she

was hurriedly carried away from the keep, her mother's arms—no, the arms of her nursemaid—wrapped tightly about her. The lapping of the water against the sides of the small sailing boat, as they drifted downriver and out to sea. The hand of the woman straining at the tiller, a look of fear in her eyes, though her words were soft and reassuring.

The look in the eyes of the farmer—the man she had known as her father—when he took them in, offering food and shelter from the raging storm outside.

Kira gasped and pulled free of the amulet at her throat. Sorrow smashed into her like a mailed fist.

All she thought she knew about herself was a lie. Her mother, the woman she had loved and who had appeared to love her back, was . . . a lie. Her father. Her dear, sweet father, who had truly loved them both. Had he been merely a safe haven? Or had her mother—no, not her mother, but the nursemaid, Ardea—had she even loved him?

Kira turned her face to the wall and let her body go limp. Her shoulders shook as she took in a shuddering breath, and told herself how little good it would do to cry, even as the tears slid across her face and dripped onto the bedding.

Finally, she let go and wept. For the loss of her life. For the loss of her real father, murdered by assassins. For the loss of her mother, the Matriarch, who had been permanently damaged, her mind cracked open like a rift, by the theft of her only daughter by a woman she had trusted.

When the door swung open and the attendant brought in her food, Kira was cried out. She watched as the evening's meal was set upon the table. "I hope this eve finds you well," the young woman said, placing her hand at her heart. When she received no response to her formal greeting, she backed out of the room, closing the door quietly behind her.

Kira rose and paced the floor, leaving the food to cool on the tray. Her thoughts moved with her, backward and forward. She sifted each memory she had, poking and prodding at the most trifling of moments. Why had Ardea stolen her from her true parents? Her actions had mentally crippled Kira's mother, and broken her family the way a storm breaks a ship upon the rocks of the shore. Had she also helped to kill her father?

There had been no clues that Ardea had not been her mother. No cause to have ever doubted the love that Ardea had shown her. The little kindnesses, the warm embraces, the gentle drag of a comb through her hair and sudden stopping at the slightest snarl, and the patience taken to untangle the fine hairs. Even the way Ardea had treated her father. No, Kira amended, the farmer, Sef, whom she had thought was her father.

Never had she any doubt that she'd belonged.

The one true sign of her not belonging had been her looks, and some secret Ardea had made her promise to keep. Something about a gift. But what gift? She owned nothing of value, aside from the amulet that hung about her neck.

Kira pulled on the leather cord and held the gleaming disk near one of the lights recessed into the wall. In the crystalline glow, a pattern emerged, a coil of snakes all tangled together, guiding her thoughts back, back along the trail of memories . . .

Kira sat on the smooth stone and stared into the water. Beside her, Ardea murmured soft words that she could not understand. She tried harder to listen, but the words sounded funny, like another language. Kira fidgeted. "Concentrate," Ardea told her. "Focus on the water below the surface." Her voice was hushed, as if she were telling Kira a tremendous secret.

Kira slowed her breathing and tried again. She stared at the water until she could feel the tension, then she pushed against that tension and felt herself go deeper, until her thoughts settled just beneath the surface. The water was cool and thick, but it didn't feel wet. Instead, it pressed against her like the brush of flower petals, tickling her skin. She suddenly giggled and lost the connection.

Ardea said nothing. Kira knew she had done something wrong, but what she was uncertain.

The memory blurred, as if it too had sunk beneath the water.

A warm breeze ruffled Kira's hair. She and Sef stood on the little hill that overlooked the farmstead. The sun glittered golden off the stalks of barley in the field below them. Sef took her hand and touched her palm, tracing the lines there. "You were born for something more than this," he told her, his normally smiling face serious and intent.

Kira gazed up at him, all the warmth of his love seemed to reach out and fill her heart. "What do you mean, Papa?" She looked down at her tiny hand, dwarfed by his.

He shook his head. "I don't know," he said. "Just that I think someday you will leave us and go far beyond the nearer steads." He laughed, letting go of her.

The summer wind felt cool on her skin after the warmth of his hand holding hers and Kira shivered. "I'm never going to leave you," she said, her voice firm. "I'll always stay here with you, Papa. With you and Mima." She'd used her baby name for Ardea.

Kira shuddered and gasped, flinging away the medallion as if it had stung her. It landed on the floor with a clink. What had just happened? She put a hand to her forehead, trying to push against the sensation of dizziness that wrapped around her skull. She needed to remain present. Her face felt wet and she reached up a sleeve to wipe at the salty tears that still leaked from her eyes.

The memories had been so vivid, as if she were reliving them. A sob erupted from her, pushing from her chest all the way up past her lips before she could stop it. Her eyes exploded with new tears. They weren't her real parents, she knew that now, but they had been good people and they had loved her. Both of them. Why then, had Ardea done what she had? Why had she kidnapped Kira and taken her across the sea, far from her real family?

Perhaps there was a way to find out. Kira dried her face and eyed the golden coin. It lay on the floor where she had heaved it, the leather cord trailing from it like a thin snake. She kneeled, grasping the ends of the cord, and raised the medallion up to eye level. It dangled in the air, glinting in the light as if mocking her.

She reached out and gripped the medallion, squeezing until the edges of it bit into her skin. Her fingers cramped in pain as the flood of memories struck her. She fell back, reeling, against the pallet. Pain exploded behind her eyes and the vision became real.

Her mother, the Matriarch, bending down, dangling a glinting object that caught the sunlight and gleamed as her tiny hand batted at it, the cooing voice of her mother sounding in her ears.

"That's my beauty, my precious kit." Her mother smiled, her red lips curling and her eyes bright. "One day, this will belong to you, along with everything else. An entire realm and all its people. The whole kingdom."

"Momma," a child's voice whined. "I want a kingdom, too."

"Such a handsome boy, but a silly one," her mother sang sweetly. "Only a woman has enough heart to rule a kingdom properly." The golden object was lifted out of Kira's reach and then a skinny little boy peered down at her from their mother's hip. "You shall be a great advisor when you are older," the Matriarch told the boy. "It will be your place to provide wise counsel to your sister when she is Matriarch, but it is with heart that people must be led."

Kira's brother stared down at her and she shivered under the cold malice of his glare and the angry jealousy behind his pale eyes.

Kira's eyes opened wide and she released her stranglehold on the medallion. Her body shook and her hand ached. Did this simple-looking item truly hold even her earliest childhood memories inside it? Or was this some kind of mind-trick? Her eyes searched the room, her ears pricked up to hear the tiniest sound. Then, she let her awareness float outside herself as Devira had taught her, opening up to the mind-talk conversations that pervaded the keep. If someone was sending her memories, surely she should still be able to hear or sense the sender, even when she wasn't clasping the medallion.

She pulled back and sagged against the wall. It was so frustrating to feel locked away like this, to have little ability beyond her own sensing. What she wouldn't give for a pair of eyes and a set of wings. . . A deep emptiness overwhelmed her and her throat constricted. She covered her mouth to muffle the sob that sought its way free from her lips. What were these odd longings that haunted her without explanation?

She pressed her fingertips against her pounding temples. Each time she accessed the medallion, the pain came on more swiftly, and even the whisper of her own rushing blood grew to a towering roar. She gritted her teeth against the wave of pain that crashed down upon her.

Each wakening grew harder, but she forced herself to continue, to relive and recall what had transpired, to learn what had caused Ardea to flee with her. When the memory came, it tore at her, crushing her heart into a thousand tiny fragments. She was a child again. A child called Alyana. Evening, by the river, her father tall and proud walking beside her, telling her stories of the fish that darted in and out from under the fat lilies. She had laughed when he told her the lilies were thrones for the frog princes who sat upon them each night calling for their servants and demanding their supper of juicy flies to be served on silver trays with worm sauce.

Her laughter was choked off suddenly when she slipped in a patch of wet moss and fell into the water. Ardea had grabbed her up in an instant and hugged her tight, scolding her father for letting her get so close to the water. Then they were all laughing again, strolling along the garden path, when they heard the sound of raised voices.

Ardea had frozen in midstep and put her fingers to Alyana's lips, setting her down behind a Harcanthia bush and signaling her to be still. The nursemaid tiptoed down the path and hid behind a blooming fire tree, watching something down by the river. There was shouting and Ardea was suddenly beside her, whimpering. "They've killed him, by the Guardian's Light, they've murdered him." There were tears in Ardea's eyes and fear on her pale face as she scooped Alyana up in her arms and began to run.

All the while Ardea was whispering, muttering to herself. At the time, she hadn't understood, but now the words were clear, as the young woman veered off the path. "They'll stop at nothing," Ardea hissed, her voice filled with anger and fear. "I will keep you safe, my precious heart. But where can we go? Where can I hide you?" They were running now, the heavy jostling causing Alyana to cry until Ardea shushed her. "Nay, nay, my dearling, don't cry. Hush now." Her voice broke and she fought her own tears. "I'll not let them harm you."

The darkening sky grew black as the last rays of the sun flashed across the castle keep. Darkness covered the gardens. There was a sound of rushing water beside them and then the quiet splashing of water as Ardea waded into the narrow rivulet that wound through the gardens and down to the broad river. All the while, she cooed to Alyana, humming to her under her breath, her lips against Alyana's ear as she hugged her small body close to her.

The sound of hurrying feet and hushed voices came toward them and Ardea ducked low, dipping them both into the cool water. Alyana reached out and splashed the water, but Ardea gripped her tiny hand and brought it to her soft lips. Her eyes were open wide, a terrible fear filling them. Slowly, careful not to make a sound, she moved between the tall rushes, hiding them from the view of anyone who might be on the path.

The voices grew louder, then the footsteps stopped.

"It is done," a gruff voice said. "Now pay me the balance."

"It is only half-done," a smoother voice intoned.

"I told you," the first man said again, "I'll not kill a child."

"And I told you," the second man growled. "I don't like unfinished business."

There was a shout and the sound of something wet. A gasp and the thud of something heavy falling onto the paving stones, then a splash as something large rolled into the water.

Back along the waterway a cry rang out, then heavy boots running.

"Guards! To me! To me!" It was the smooth-voiced man, his call raised in alarm.

Ardea retreated further into the tall green plants that grew along the bank and quietly waded into the darkness. They moved away from the running feet and the shouting voices and the clattering of arms. Away into the deepening waters of the widening stream. Under cover of night, Ardea took them to a quiet street, hugging Alyana to her to keep her warm. She rapped thrice on a polished wooden door and waited, hushing her charge, who had begun to shiver and fuss.

The door opened and light bloomed from inside. Ardea ducked her head as a man ushered them in. He was tall, with a ginger-colored beard gone white at the edges, and he stared at them without seeing. He moved aside as they slipped inside and then pushed the door closed behind them.

Kira roused from the waking dream. The room had grown uncomfortably hot and she wiped sweat from her face. She needed air, needed to see the sky. She stood and grasped the door pull. The door swung inward, opening out onto the brightly lit hall. She leaned against the doorjamb, looking up and down the passageway. Empty.

She took a tentative step, then another. No alarms rang out, no shouts exclaimed. Using the wall to brace herself, she staggered down the hallway to the first turning and saw a broad staircase leading down. Her legs shook with exertion and her head had begun that dull throb that preceded the horrible pain that always came after the memories. What was she doing? She couldn't escape in this condition. But, escape from what? For a moment she stood bewildered and confused. Then the memories jumped out at her. In a sudden rush, she realized they weren't hers. The memories she'd seen this time had been Ardea's.

Tears sprang to her eyes and she slumped against the wall, giving into the overwhelming sorrow that filled her like a rising tide. She let go, riding that tide, weeping in earnest. For her father. For Ardea. Even for her poor mad mother.

She felt lost and alone. There was something else she needed to remember, someone she was forgetting. There was something she was supposed to do, but every time she got close to the memory, it all melted into a gray fog inside her head. She tried to push against the fog, to brush it aside and peer through, but it was no use, and she was so tired. She returned to her bed, rolled her face to the wall and willed herself to fall back to sleep.

She awoke to darkness. Fingers fumbling beneath the bedding, she searched for the cold metal object, almost afraid to touch it, yet needing to know it was still safe in her possession. She wondered again how it had lain dormant against her breast for so long. Why only now had it begun to make her remember?

Her fingertips finally found the medallion and the touch of chilled metal sent a cold shiver through her.

CHAPTER THIRTY

Kavyn pushed his plate from him. The meal should have been adequate, should have sated him, but the hunger he felt was a gnawing need for power, and now, vengeance. Perhaps, he could serve up a potent helping of each.

Although he had been quite young and had played no direct part in his father's murder, he had willingly concealed his knowledge of events for more than a decade. Such concealment was more than guilt by association and a treacherous act. He knew this. Knew that this was as his mentor had intended, but it bit into him with venomous fangs, poisoning his thoughts and gnawing on him. He needed to find a way to circumvent whatever plot Teraxin was now putting into play. The old goat thought himself the ultimate strategist, but he was weak. His soft spots would be his doom, but Kavyn needed to act fast.

He glanced across the room to the waiting girl. Her

coppery curls hung down in swirls that caressed her neck and shoulders. Her high cheekbones, and dark eyes, scintillating in the lamplight. He sent his thoughts at her, a tentative nudging at her guard as she bent to tend the fire. Minimal resistance met his probes, so he pushed deeper, slipping inside her thoughts, listening in as she thought about the chores remaining to be done before she could leave and go to her home on the eastern edge of the citadel. "Keliss," he whispered, having caught her name from a memory. Ah, yes, he remembered this one. A sweet he had tasted before. Excitement rose in him.

She started, and turned toward him, surprised he recalled her name, her cheeks flushed with emotion. "Is there something you need, Your Grace?"

He looked her up and down, his eyes feeling their way across the curve of her breast, sliding along her hips. She blushed harder and her face grew taut, making it clear she did not share his desire. His next push inside her mind was sudden and less than subtle, causing a sharp intake of breath, but it mattered not. As before, the girl would remember nothing of the encounter, and besides, he liked the way her bosom rose when he forced his way fully into her mind and overwhelmed her thoughts. The way she fought for control. The way she struggled against him. The fight was invigorating and it made the physical domination so much more exciting.

Her hands came up and began unlacing her bodice. She fought against it, her eyes those of a trapped animal, but she no longer controlled her own actions. Kavyn played her like a puppet as she stripped out of her overdress, watching with unbridled excitement as her consciousness shifted, until finally, she dove deep inside herself and the light went out of her eyes.

CHAPTER THIRTY-ONE

Kira stood on the edge of the river, staring out at the swirls and eddies. The rushing water filled her head with a shushing sound that was oddly comforting. This place dredged up a staggering assortment of emotions, anger, joy, love, fear. Her stomach twisted. Her legs ached to carry her far from this spot, but something stronger forced her to stay.

"Oh, Heresta," she whispered into the sluicing sound of the flowing river, "where is your wisdom now?"

"Heresta?"

Kira jumped at the sound of the voice inside her head. She spun around in a fluid motion and stood her ground, poised on the balls of her feet, prepared to flee. There was something about Kavyn that seemed intimately familiar, yet she felt no kinship to this young man, despite the knowledge that they were siblings.

He placed a hand upon his chest and inclined his head. "My pardon," he said, aloud. "I was not sure if you would hear me. I know you are untrained at mindspeak, but it appears you are not deaf to what is sent directly to you, after all." His face was flat and composed, but his eyes shone with keen interest.

Kira tried to remain calm, but she felt the pull of fear along her spine and up the back of her neck. If she had been a cat, the fur on her back would have been standing on end. She stopped for a moment, the odd thought giving her pause. A memory rubbed itself against her mind, warm but faded. With a start, she realized Kavyn was watching her and she let her face go blank. Had it been some sort of test? She would have to be more careful. There were too many odd things going on. Too many machinations playing out around her. And she still had no idea why. Only the constant nagging feeling that she could not trust anyone. Least of all this young man.

"I'm sorry. I thought I heard a yelp or bark behind me. I thought a wild animal might have gotten into the garden."

A scowl crossed his face, almost too quickly for Kira to see. But she had seen it. She was certain.

"A wild animal? Indeed." He made a show of searching the grounds, eyes squinting as if they might be weak and unable to discern what lay around them. "I should be more careful in the future, if I were you, straying out in the wild." His words oozed out like oil.

Kira knew scorn when she heard it, but she pretended not to notice. "My pardon," she said. "I should not have wandered so far from my rooms. I'm not as well as I had supposed." She rubbed at her temples and let her eyelids droop down to half cover her eyes.

"Certainly," he said, and nodded as if agreeing with her.

Kira wanted nothing more than to flee, to distance

herself from his prying mind, but she forced herself to move at a sedate pace. She skirted along the main path, heading deeper into the welcoming garden.

"There is more to you than meets the mind's eye," he murmured as she walked away, but he did not move to follow her.

She forced herself not to hurry, but she wanted to escape from him. There was something feral in the way he examined her, something dark behind his eyes, something that made her scalp itch. No. Not her scalp. The inside of her skull, as if tiny claws scritched at her brain. She had a terrible urge to try and scratch at that itch and a shudder ran through her.

She finally paused beside a low wall covered by a creeping ivy. Mesmerized by the way the plant caught the light, she reached out to caress its silver leaves.

"Alyana! Don't touch that," Devira slapped Kira's hand away from the glowing tendrils.

Kira stumbled back, clutching her fingers, as if she had been burned. "What is it?"

"Blockweed." Devira gave the plant a nasty look. "I'm sorry," she told Kira, reaching for her hand. "I didn't mean to hurt you."

"I'm fine," Kira said, wondering why it was that everyone seemed intent on accosting her this day. "You only startled me." She held up her fingers and wriggled them to prove she was unhurt.

"I am truly sorry." Devira pushed a stray lock of hair off her forehead. "It's just that we already have so much work to do. I don't want you to have a setback."

"Setback?" The glistening plant seemed to call to her, but she forced herself to stay put.

Devira nodded at the plant. "It's used for the young, the old, and the feeble. To block their minds, when they are unable to do so, or have lost the ability to shield their personal thoughts and feelings." Devira rubbed her hands together. "There is enough of a barrier in your head, without creating yet another wall. And we have come so far along in your training," she paused, assessing Kira.

"You're staring again."

"Your mind is truly an odd puzzle," Devira told her. "For one with no training, you learn quickly, and . . ."

"And?"

"It's of no consequence," Devira brushed aside the comment. "Come, we have much more work to do." The Physica's voice sounded strained.

Deciding not to question her further, Kira allowed Devira to lead her out of the garden. But as they went, the plants called to her, singing radiant songs of health and vigor and sleep and wakefulness, each with its own voice, its own special music. She covered her ears with her hands, but the lilting calls remained, only fading as she followed the Physica into the keep. Within the silence of the stone walls, Kira thought she heard a whispered cooing, as if someone were shushing a crying babe.

CHAPTER THIRTY-TWO

Milos slipped within the edge of the tree line and turned back to observe the sleeping city below. The odd, steadily glowing lights gave the setting a surreal, almost dreamlike quality. He shifted his thoughts away from the idea, focusing instead on the thin light that tinted the edges of the trees. The sun's light had not yet crested the horizon.

Vaith stirred on his perch, spread one wing outward, then refolded it. The little reptile seemed to always be either eating or sleeping. No. Milos corrected himself. The wyvern apparently spent his days out hunting for things to eat, returning only in the evenings to sleep in the branches overhead.

Milos had made this night's foray alone and returned to find Kelmir curled beneath the tree in which Vaith now stirred. It comforted Milos to have the animals nearby. Although, he continued to wish he had a way of connecting with them as Kira did.

The sun rose above the edge of the earth enough to cast a pale light upon everything, turning the dark silhouettes into silver-gray versions of themselves. Milos had just settled down to give his aching leg a rest when a high-pitched shriek pierced the dawn, startling him into a crouch.

Vaith leaped from his branch and winged high into the pale sky. Kelmir jumped up and arched his back, a low growl emanating from his throat. The shriek came again. A scream, followed by a sound that sent shivers down Milos' spine. The snarl of an angry boar.

Milos sprang to his feet and ran. He exploded through the brush, ignoring the crashing sounds he made, trampling brittle branches and dried leaves, his only thought to stop the creature from extinguishing an innocent life.

The screams, a child's he was now certain, grew louder and more frightened, broken only by frightened sobbing. Milos hurled himself forward, heedless of the branches that struck his face and arms. Beside him, Kelmir ran, too. Leaping fallen trees and disregarding the thick undergrowth, they came to an open vale, surrounded by tall white-trunked trees. Backed against a tree trunk, a young boy, no more than five or six turns old, held a heavy stick, pointing it like a weapon at the snarling beast that pawed the ground only a few strides away. The boar was old and gnarled, and it stood taller on all four legs than the child before it.

"Hold!" Milos shouted, hoping to attract the animal's attention. But the boar merely bristled and pawed the earth again, preparing to charge the helpless child, who had now stopped screaming and stared at Milos, eyes pleading for help.

"Be still," Milos told the boy, drawing his sword. It was not the proper weapon for this fight, but it would have to do.

"Kelmir," Milos began, but before he could finish the hunting cat let loose a fierce yowl and circled around behind the boar. The animal turned its heavy head to stare at the big cat. There was no fear in its red eyes. Only anger. Kelmir hissed and continued circling left and the boar turned to keep the cat in its view.

Milos gauged the size of the beast and realized it would be an unfair fight, weighted in the boar's favor. "Ho!" he shouted, drawing the animal's focus to him. "That's right," he said, his voice low and threatening. "Come and fight with someone more in keeping with your stature." He circled to the right, still talking, and the boar was forced to turn again to face this new threat.

Caught between two enemies, the animal huffed and roared. It shook its tusks at Milos and Kelmir, swinging its huge head to and fro, trying to keep them both in sight. Suddenly, it lowered its head, eyes fixed on Milos. With a snort of ire, it charged. Milos crouched, leaping aside and rolling away as the animal trampled the ground toward him, raising its hoary tusks to gouge him. He used his momentum to roll back to standing as the boar passed and stabbed at it with his long blade. But his wounded leg set him off balance and he missed the animal's heart.

The boar screamed in pain as the sword raked a deep gash across its side. Blood ran from the wound, but the enraged animal turned and charged again. Before it could reach Milos, Kelmir leaped onto its back and clamped his jaws onto the nape of its neck. The boar squealed and bucked, trying to free itself from the cat's jaws. It swung its mighty head around and caught Kelmir with a broken tusk. Flipping the big cat off its back, it turned to attack.

But Milos was already beside it. He thrust his sword deep into the animal's chest. The boar swung around, ripping the sword from Milos' grasp. It thrashed wildly, attempting to remove the instrument of pain from its body, but Kelmir charged in once more, and it stumbled and fell, driving the blade in deeper.

It let out a final scream of pain, twitched and stilled, blood pouring from its chest.

Milos rubbed at his elbow. The boar had pulled the weapon from him so hard, his sword arm was wrenched in pain. Much more of this and he would be worthless in a fight.

The little boy still stood with his back against the tree, eyes wide, shivering now as much from cold as fright.

Milos took in the boy's disheveled hair and dirt-smeared nightclothes. "Are you all right?" He kneeled in front of the child.

The boy nodded slowly, wide eyes glued to Milos, fat tears running down his red cheeks.

"What is your name?"

"S-S-Solin," he stuttered and wiped at his eyes with his small hand.

"Solin, I am . . ." Milos hesitated before giving the boy his true name, then shook his head to clear his doubts and suspicions. The boy needed succor, a friendly face, after the trauma of the boar's attack. "I am Milos." He glanced around. "Where are your parents?"

"I . . . I don't know." The boy swallowed hard, clearly forcing back more tears. "I was asleep. Something chased me. I thought it was a bad dream, but when I ran and fell . . ." He held up a skinned and bloody arm for Milos to see. "It hurt so much."

Milos examined the boy's abrasion. "I know it stings, but it will heal," he told him. "For now, we must get you home."

"Of course, it will." Solin nodded and squeezed his wounded arm to his chest in tight concentration.

Milos glanced at the dead boar. "Stay here," he told the boy. "I'll be right back."

Solin whimpered, but stayed put as Milos went to check on Kelmir. The big cat stared intently at the dead boar, but appeared unharmed. "Kelmir," Milos whispered, hoping the animal would understand. "Enjoy your well earned feast. I'll return as soon as may be." He retrieved his sword from the animal's carcass and wiped the bloody blade on a patch of lichen. Wincing, he sheathed his weapon, then limped across the clearing and held out his hand to the boy.

"But you are hurt, as well," Solin said, his face solemn.

"Like you, I will heal."

"Yes, but I cannot reach. You are too tall."

Milos kneeled once more beside the boy and reached out to him. "Do you wish to be carried, then?"

The boy stood up as tall as his few years allowed, and looked Milos in the eye. "Only babies need to be carried."

"Of course." Milos moved to stand.

"Wait." Solin reached out toward Milos and gently placed one hand on his leg and the other on his elbow.

Sudden warmth tingled beneath Milos' skin and he nearly jumped back, but Solin had shut his eyes and sunk into a deep concentration. So, Milos remained as still as possible and steadied his own breathing, finding it easy and natural to fall into and match the rhythm set by the boy.

Moments passed. Then Solin took a deep shuddery breath and dropped his hands to his sides. Milos sighed and flexed his arm. Astonished, he prodded the wound on his leg. Still sore and clearly bruised, but amazingly improved. "How did you do that?" he asked.

Solin shrugged and held out his arm. "I'm not as good nor as quick as the trained Physicas and Physics, but my mother says I'm an innate." His own wound appeared only red now, as if he'd not even torn the skin in his fall.

Milos nodded slowly, though he had no idea what the boy was saying. "I think we had better get you home."

* * *

Milos glanced up and down the wide lane, eyeing the lampposts that spilled huge pools of light down onto the street. The glowing lights he'd seen from the distance, were actually large spherical crystals that grew dimmer as night faded from the land and the rising sun streaked the sky with pinks and golds.

Solin shivered beside him, pulling him along the lane in a hurry to reach his home and his warm bed. "It's this way," he nearly shouted, pointing left at an intersection where a narrower street crossed the main throughway.

"Ssshhhh," Milos hushed him. "We wouldn't want to wake the entire city, would we?"

Solin stared up at him and nodded solemnly. He pointed again and said in a loud whisper. "My house is just down there. The white one with the gray fisher bird on the door."

Milos squinted, but all the houses appeared the same to him; tall, stone buildings with narrow windows facing the street.

Solin padded along the street, his bare feet slapping the ground.

They stopped before a house that, aside from being

white, appeared to Milos no different from the others along the lane, which were painted in different shades and hues of color. Solin signaled for Milos to lean closer. "This one," he pointed up at the door, which did indeed bear a crest that contained the image of a bird.

Milos glanced up and down the quiet road, then kneeled before the boy and placed his hands on the child's narrow shoulders. "You'll need to go this last stretch alone," he said. "I must return to the woods."

"But my parents will want to thank you," Solin said.

Milos glanced around. "Your thanks and knowing you are home safe are all I need." He waited until Solin reached the door. Then, he turned and slipped into the gray shadows of the early morning.

CHAPTER THIRTY-THREE

"There you are," Devira's voice brought Kira up short. "The councilors are asking for you."

"Councilors?" Kira asked, forcing her hand away form the medallion at her throat.

"As I have told you, our Matriarch is guided by a council. They wish to see you." Devira took her hand gently, placing her fingers against Kira's wrist. "You're upset." She said. "Has something happened?" She peered knowingly at Kira.

How was the Physica always able to tell when she was unwell or unhappy. Kira glanced at the woman's hand where it wrapped about hers and something inside her fell into place. Gently, she extricated herself from the Physica's grip and placed her own fingertips against the place on her wrist where her heartbeat echoed in tiny throbs like a bird's.

A shifting of the light distracted her. She glanced around. The plants and trees appeared different. Some of them seemed to shimmer and others were shadowed. "These plants . . ." she pointed to a batch of long-tendrilled leafy stems. "What are they?"

Devira's forehead wrinkled. "They're Placaria. A plant used in calmatives," she said. "But we haven't time for an herbals lesson. The Council wishes to speak with you." She ushered Kira toward the high keep.

As she waited outside the council chamber, Kira wondered what the councilors might possibly want with her. The Matriarch's denial of her appeared to have made a number of people unhappy. To make matters worse, she had not regained the rest of her memories even with Devira's healing support, and the magic of the amulet. What purpose might she serve?

Something nagged at her. The face of a man with dark hair and blue eyes kept floating in and out of her mind. The cries of battle mixed with laughter and the flames from her nightmares were all, somehow, tied to this man. Yet, she did not fear him.

Something shimmered past outside the window, a flash of rainbow-colored light glanced off something that soared past and her heart leaped. She rushed to the window just as the door to the council chamber opened and a voice called out to her. "They will see you now."

She glanced at the door, then turned once more to the window, her heart in her throat, but it was gone. The flash of light, whatever it had been, had disappeared. With sudden embarrassment, she wondered what had called her to fly to the window like a child expecting to see her father returned from a long journey, or a young girl watching for a returning lover. Heat crept up her face as she smoothed her features and slunk back toward the chamber door.

A moment later, the door swung wide and she was ushered inside.

When she stepped into the room, she paused to catch her breath. Instead of the dark room full of frowning old faces she had expected, the council chamber was ablaze with sunlight reflected between polished disks placed at angles to catch the sun through wide open windows and reflect it onto a shimmering globe of polished stone that hung from the center of the ceiling. Most of the women and men seated around the table were elderly, but a few were younger and one woman appeared to be still in her prime, the glow of her cheeks as bright as any young maiden's. Her eyes, when they brushed over the Physica, Devira, seemed to fill with light.

Then her gaze settled on Kira, and she stood, waving her over. "Welcome Alyana, daughter of Kyrina and Verun, Matriarchess of Eilar." A murmur rose among the councilors and Kira thought she heard someone grumble something about a lack of proof. She felt color rise to her cheeks, remembering the Matriarch's denial of her.

The woman who had spoken glanced sharply at the men and women seated around the table and the whispering quieted. She reached out to Kira in an odd formal gesture, hand flat and palm facing toward the floor.

Kira hesitated a moment before recalling Devira's lessons in etiquette and greetings. She raised her hand, palm up and placed it beneath the woman's.

"I am Zoshia, the Guardian Council Second," the woman said nodding in approval. Her face remained serious, and Kira sensed a frown behind the woman's gray eyes as she lowered her hand.

Kira followed suit, feeling out of place. The large room seemed to echo with the voices of ages, yet she also heard laughter and felt a delicious sense of belonging. She raised her eyes to the glowing mirrors that reflected the sunlight. A flash of light and color struck her eyes and her heart leapt up and for an instant, she was flying. Then, as suddenly as it had occurred, the moment passed and she felt herself slam back into her body. Her knees crumpled as her weight became a huge anchor that threatened to drag her down below an ocean of darkness.

She struggled to remain aware of her surroundings, fought the rising blackness. Dimly, she felt a warm presence at her side, heard Devira's voice soothing her as she led her back to her room and tucked her under the soft coverlet. Only then, did she let herself drift away.

CHAPTER THIRTY-FOUR

Devira rested her palms against Alyana's temples. The young woman's eyes flicked open, then closed again. She tried to open her mouth to speak, but her body seemed paralyzed.

"Hush now," Devira told her, sending currents of thought to quiet the girl's swirling mind.

With a final push along the mending pathways, Alyana stopped struggling and floated into the dark. With a sigh, Devira pulled the coverlet up to her chin, then turned to Zoshia. "I told you she wasn't ready," she chided.

"We never even got to the testing," the Council Second said, frustration in her tone. "We had only just begun introductions. Yet another impediment in a world of delays."

Devira clucked her tongue. "Something sent her into the mind-rift again," she said. "Knowing what the cause was would help me to help her. Have you no idea what it was that might have sent her drifting?"

"There was a shift of energy, but I have no idea of the source," Zoshia responded. "Aside from that, I sensed nothing beyond her own leap into the pathways. But this does not help your case. Nor hers." She dropped heavily into a chair. "The Council remains at odds. We cannot continue in this manner. If she cannot plead her own case, we must look elsewhere for a solution."

"We don't even know that it is her case." Devira finished tucking the coverlet around her patient's shoulders.

"Why else did she return to Eilar?"

"I do not know. Nor can we guess at what might be in her mind when her thoughts and memories are beyond even her own grasp."

"We need to move forward," Zoshia grumbled.

"I realize that. The longer we delay, the stronger Kavyn's claim becomes. I cannot abide the thought of that dark mind in the Guardian's Seat." She filled two cups with sweetened wine and crossed the room to hand one to Zoshia.

Zoshia took the cup, but shushed her lifemate. "Watch your tongue. You speak of the young man who well might become the first Male Guardian in more than a thousand years."

"Bah! You know as well as I that such a move would send us beyond the brink and into the chasm. Just as it nearly did the last time." Devira sat in the chair across from Zoshia.

It was an old argument and an even older bias, but Zoshia only rolled her eyes at Devira's remark.

"As to the dark thoughts behind his glittering smile, you must see it, too." Devira shuddered at the thought of what someone like Kavyn might do once ensconced upon the realm's seat of power.

"I know you believe it to be true, but you have not seen inside the young man's mind any more than I have. We need the Matriarch to name an heir while still lucid enough to do so."

"I well know how desperate the situation has become, but we do no good to force the issue. These riftings take a toll each time she falls into them. Do you want to lose her completely?" Devira set her cup onto the table, no longer in the mood for drink.

"Of course not," Zoshia snapped. "But we need a Guardian upon the seat."

"Our isle, our way of life, our very existence is at stake," Devira's voice rose in pitch. "Kavyn upon the throne will be our final undoing."

"Don't be so melodramatic," Zoshia told her. "Our people have survived generations upon generations. We have even been known to survive a Patriarch."

It was yet another old argument and Devira wasn't sure why she had even brought it up again. They were apart so much of late, she didn't wish to start another fight. But her first duty, as always, was to her patient. "The Matriarchess is our only hope, and she has been placed in my care. I will not fail my charge. I am oathsworn."

"Don't remind me," Zoshia spat. "And don't lecture me. Sometimes I regret granting you leave to speak to me as an equal."

"You have always regretted that," Devira told her. "Since we were girls. But you also know that I am the voice of reason to your emotions." She placed her hand on Zoshia's shoulder.

"True," Zoshia whispered, "But were we not paired, I wouldn't put up with you." Her gentle, chiding tone belied the words she spoke. She placed her hand on Devira's scarred fingers and smiled weakly at her, tilting her face up expectantly. Devira glanced at the bed and her patient. The girl lay quiet, eyes still closed, her breathing steady. Devira spun around, took a quick step forward, and brushed her lips against Zoshia's, then pushed away. "Not very professional behavior," she sighed and busied herself straightening the room.

"But we see one another so seldom," Zoshia said. "Our duties can't always come first."

Devira paused to look at her lifemate. "Yours always have," she said. Then, seeing the hurt on Zoshia's face, she quickly added, "I do not hold it against you. I know the weight you carry. I have sensed it in the darkness as we lie abed. I feel your roiling mind, the restlessness of your thoughts." She crossed the room and leaned down to wrap her arms around Zoshia and hugged her tight. "It's all I can do not to reach out and move you to rest— all I can do to keep my promise never to interfere with your thoughts or your mind."

Zoshia pulled Devira into her arms and buried her face in her neck. "I know," she murmured. "You've always been the best thing in my world, and the one person I can trust to keep her word. Always."

They remained like that for a long moment before breaking apart. "Speaking of duties," Zoshia said, her voice filled with reluctance. "I must return and report to the First that the testing must be further delayed." She rose with a tired sigh. "He will not be pleased."

CHAPTER THIRTY-FIVE

Milos strained at his bindings. He was not able to figure out the workings of the damned things. There were no knots or ends that he could discern and the ropy ties cut into his wrists when he struggled, refusing to stretch or yield. He'd thought he'd managed a quiet escape after returning Solin to his home, but they had been lying in wait for him when he left the outskirts of the citadel. He'd barely had time to shake his head in the direction of Kelmir, whose eyes gleamed out of the shadows of the trees before he'd had to turn his attention to the fight. The big cat would have been helpful, but Milos had no reason to wish that kind of harm on anyone. Yet. He'd come to find Kira, or at least news of her, and becoming a criminal, or worse, would not likely offer any advantage. Not that they refrained from firmly knocking him about.

The man and woman guarding him were both well muscled, the woman though shorter was wiry and rough looking. Neither of them spoke nor looked at Milos, but both stood poised and ready to move should there be the need to drop him to the ground once more. He wondered again how they seemed to move so quickly, as if he were wading through a morass of wet sand while his attackers were flying. True, they hadn't broken anything that wasn't already broken. He tested his leg again. Odd, Solin's simple touch had appeared to knit the wound, or at least had alleviated the pain surrounding it. Although, it had not increased his advantage against his captors.

He considered his chances of escape, but the odds were against him. His bruised and scratched face provided a clear idea of what his captors were capable of. Besides, where would he go? Perhaps, he could yet use the situation to his advantage. At the very least, he might discover what had become of Kira. He relaxed his arms and stopped struggling against his bonds.

* * *

How many sunspans had Milos spent here answering questions? Why did this man, the one they called Marquon, care so much about his past? His muscles ached and his fingers still tingled, though the bindings that had deadened the blood flow to his hands had been removed once he had been delivered to this place, a low-ceilinged hall filled with rows of tables and benches.

He had been surprised when they'd offered him drink and had refused it until the man sitting across from him had drunk first. Now, he was caught off guard by this latest question. He thought for a moment. What he knew about battle strategy, aside from what he had read in his books and scrolls, was little enough. The battle of Tem Hold had been short and victory won more by guile than by fighting tactics. As any landholder's son, he had been trained to fight and had even proven himself in the final days of the Outlander invasion. Though, he had not fought with the main forces in that conflict.

He thought back to the day of the battle for Tem Hold. The day Kira had saved his life by slaying the warlord, Toril, who would have sliced him open while his guard was down. He shook off the bloody memory of that day. "I am a Holder in my own land, not a warrior," he said. "But I have enough skill to defend what is mine." *When not taken unawares.*

Marquon nodded. "And what of defending what is another's?" he narrowed his eyes in thought.

Milos took a meager sip of the wine Marquon had placed before him. It was dark, fruity and strong. He set the cup down and shook his head. "I'm no mercenary, if that is what you're asking." The bloody field surrounding Tem Hold rose up before him and he saw once more the smoke of the bier that had held Mayet's body. True, she had betrayed him, betrayed them all for her own ambitions, but she had been his brother's widow, and for a time the Lady of Tem Hold. She likely would still be had his brother not died as a result of the ill-fated hunting trip Milos had urged him into.

"You have regrets." The man took a drink of wine. "They haunt your thoughts." His words were emotion-filled and he wore the sour look of a man who has eaten something that made him ill. "I understand." He swirled the liquid inside his cup and stared into the darkness within it. Then, he set the cup down onto the table and stood, rubbing his hand across his eyes. "My people are dying," he said.

Milos said nothing.

"Oh, I know what you're thinking," Marquon said. "This citadel is aged, but it appears to have stood the tests of time. And with the powers that we wield, the strange wonders that are spoken of across oceans, how could we be dying?" His voice was tinged with sarcasm, bending his words toward self-mockery. He crossed the room and stared out an open window at the evening sky streaked with wispy clouds. "Just as the light fades at the end of day, so does our power grow weak." He spoke quietly, as if talking to himself. "A signal that our own setting sun is nigh."

With sudden energy, he rounded on Milos. "And, as if they already smell the blood in the water, the sharks are circling. If we are to survive, if our race would live on, we must find new ways, blaze new paths, forge new weapons." He strode back to the table, placed both hands upon the wooden surface, leaned forward and studied Milos. "We need an army."

* * *

Milos ruminated the proposal. His freedom and return passage to his own land in exchange for his services as a mercenary and combat trainer. He doubted the balance of such an agreement.

His was not a military mind. What he knew of strategy and tactics was only what he had read of in his books and learned from Toril's attack on Tem Hold. His thoughts strayed to his library, his people, his family. If not for the help of the sturdy Gnomes, along with the plan Milvari and Harl had devised to sicken the soldiers with the Demon's Weed. If not for Jolon's sacrifice . . .

Bloodshed and death. Could he bear any more of bloodshed and death?

He recalled the dark blood that had poured from Mayet, the bodies scattered across what had once been Tem Hold's most fertile fields, the smoke rising from

176

pyres, ashes spreading along the river. How long had it been since peace had ruled in his own land? And now, this stranger in this distant land, a land and a people to which Milos owed nothing, was asking him to fight again.

And what of Kira? What had become of the woman he knew and loved, the woman for whom he had left home and hearth? His reason for coming to this distant land.

He considered his response and the possibility of a counter proposal. Surely, agreeing to train these people did not mean he must fight for them, nor need it require him to take part in any more killing. "As I told you, I am no warrior," he said. "But I will consider your request on the condition that you tell me what your people have done to Kira."

"Kira?" Marquon appeared puzzled. "I have no knowledge of any such person."

Milos shook his head. "If you would bargain with me in one moment, then lie to me the next, there is no trusting your word."

Marquon looked startled, then smoothed his features into a blank canvas. "I have no need to lie to you. No reason."

"Then tell me what has been done to her. I know she would seek me if she were able." Milos ran his hand over his face. She must still be caught up in that evil forest of mist. "You must help me find her."

"You don't mean . . . ?" Marquon's eyes grew wide. "Not a coincidence, then. Her return and your appearance."

"Her return?" Milos asked. "What do you mean by that? You do know who she is, then?"

"Yes." Marquon took a gulp of his wine.

"And she is here? In the Citadel?" Milos could hardly contain his excitement at the prospect of finally being so close to finding Kira.

Marquon held up a hand. "First, let us be certain we are speaking of the same woman. Tall, ivory skin, green eyes? Hair cropped short?"

"Yes. Yes, that's her. Tell me where she is," Milos insisted.

"And you were with her in the veil?"

"Before that," Milos said in exasperation. "We entered the forest together, but were separated after . . . the anger and the darkness."

Marquon took another drink. "You. And the Matriarchess. This is an odd turn." He plunked his goblet down onto the table and stared at Milos, a bemused look on his face. "To my knowledge, nothing has been done except to try and help her recall who she truly is."

Milos stared hard at the man. Something in what Marquon said was a key that would fit inside a secret lock, Milos was certain of it. "And who is she?" he finally asked.

Marquon raised an eyebrow and gave Milos an odd look. "Why, she's only the Matriarch's Heir, and next in line for the Guardian's Seat. The populace awaits a formal announcement. It is said she has suffered a loss of recent memories. But I understand there remains no doubt of her lineage." He pulled his chair around and sat astride it backwards, leaning his muscular arms upon the back of it. "If you know her, how is it you do not know this?"

Milos shook his head, his thoughts swimming as if he were once more lost in the fog. Matriarch's Heir? Was this not a good thing? Did it not mean that at least Kira was safe from harm? "She never told me." He thought about the name Kira had first given him when they'd met. Ardea. Recalled her confessing to him that it had been her mother's name. "She only told me that her mother was dead."

Marquon frowned. "She is not. Though some believe she might as well be, that we might be . . ." He glanced around the room, then leaned forward and lowered his voice, ". . . better off had she been allowed to drown herself as she had intended."

Milos shifted in his chair. Kira had said her mother had died in the war with the Outland Raiders. Her orphaning was the reason she had been raised by the healer Heresta. "Her mother attempted to drown herself? But she is alive and well?"

The man rubbed his knuckles against the side of his chin. "Nay, the Matriarch remains alive, but not well. Not well, at all. And there is much more to the story. Much that you should know, if you are to aid us. And I'm bound to be turned one way or another, now that I have started upon this path, so you might as well hear it from me."

* * *

Milos sat in silence. The story the man had told him sinking in, settling itself heavily upon him. He felt the burden of responsibility weighing down upon him, once more. A weight he thought he had escaped when he'd left Tem Hold. Clearly, he had been a fool to believe that he could free himself of the onus of caring for his fellow man, even when that fellow man was of another land, another culture, even another race.

"I will help you," he said finally. "But in return, I would ask your help in seeing . . . the Matriarch's Heir." He could not use the name they assigned her, could not call her Alyana, and stumbled over the title the man had given to Kira. A title she had never mentioned. How could she have lied to him about her mother? He needed her to explain . . . though a part of him was afraid of what he might hear. She had lied to him before, about her name, about who she was. Why wouldn't she lie about something larger, something like this? But the time they had spent together. The days and nights, the long journey . . .

Had he been wrong to leave Tem Hold to follow her? She had never asked him. Never promised him anything. He had never pushed. Not wanting to force her away. But now he needed to know, needed to hear it from her. He swallowed hard, waiting for Marquon's answer.

After an eternity, Marquon nodded his assent. "I know not how to gain an audience with the Matriarchess, but if you will begin to train us, I will seek a way."

Milos slapped his hand down onto the table. The man eyed it for a moment, then slapped the back of his hand against Milos'.

"We have a bargain," he said, a half smile forming on his lips at Milos' surprise. Then he shrugged. "It is our custom."

His bargain struck, Milos wondered how he might rejoin Vaith and Kelmir, or if he should. That these people did not know of Kira's two animal companions might be all to the good. On the other hand, what might the wyvern and hunting cat do if left on their own for too long? They would have no trouble surviving, of that he was certain. Even without Kira, they had proven their ability to work as a team. But Milos worried. What if they hadn't truly understood when he had asked them to wait outside the citadel for his return? What if they decided to attempt on their own to reach Kira?

Marquon waited on him, watching him deliberate. "The thoughts swarm behind your eyes. Is there something else that worries you?" he finally asked.

Rather than answer the question, Milos stood and peered down at his filthy clothes. "I see that not all our customs are that different," he said. "In my country, we prefer to bathe regularly, much as you appear to, as well." He gestured at himself pointedly.

Marquon laughed. "Come," he said, leading Milos from the room. "I will take you to the bathing room. Once you are cleansed, we shall eat and discuss our plans."

CHAPTER THIRTY-SIX

"I should have had her killed as soon as she arrived," Teraxin muttered.

"Why didn't you?" Kavyn asked, striding into the room unbidden.

Teraxin's mood soured even further. The boy had sprung into a young man, but his attitude was still that of a spoiled child. All the mentoring in the world, all the lessons in politics, the teaching and chiding, seemed unable to polish that from him. Lately, he had grown careless in his behaviors, shallow in his courtesies. For several moons now, he had been acting recklessly, as if he already sat upon the Eilaren throne in his mother's place. This comeuppance in the appearance of the Matriarch's Heir would be comical, if it did not also spell disaster for all of Teraxin's well laid plans. Not that the boy's own recent actions weren't a new and greater barrier to the plans he had lain so long ago, when Kavyn had still been a pliant child.

Teraxin began to sort through his own actions. Had he waited too long to remove the Consort? Had Verun's time with Kavyn set the boy's mind in this fashion? No. He chided himself. This was not the Consort's doing. He, himself, was as much to blame as anyone. He'd put too many ambitions into the boy. It had always been a risk, keeping the secret of Kavyn's extraordinary skills, but the gamble had promised such a large payment, he'd convinced himself it would be worth it. Now, however, he was no longer so certain.

He touched the back of his hand to his forehead, long enough for a glancing respect only, and nodded to his young protégé. "I did not hear you knock," he said.

"That's because I didn't." Kavyn smirked and poured himself a measure of wine. He raised the glass to the light and eyed it. The crimson light reflecting through the glass glittered a fierce dark red.

Kavyn took a sip and spit the wine back into the cup. "Not the finest Northland bottling I have tasted." He set the glass onto the table with a thunk and curled his lip. "I don't know how you stomach it."

Teraxin kept his tongue and his thoughts in check. He had not drunk deeply, yet the wine was already going to his head. His mind-shield remained strong, but he did not like to think what might happen should he let his guard down for even a moment with his young scholar. No. He corrected himself. Not a scholar any longer. Kavyn had no desire to be schooled. "When they first discovered her within the veil, I had no idea who she was. Not until the Physica pointed it out," Teraxin said, his skull wobbling on his aching neck. "Meddling old woman that she is." He sank into a chair. He suddenly felt old, as if his bones should be creaking under his weight. "By then, it was too late to simply dispose of her." He shrugged. "Though her mental affliction makes her no better a tool than your mother."

"Thanks to you, the Council now considers her an option." Kavyn snarled. "If not for me, she'd have been placed on the seat of power already." He shoved aside the drift of papers piled upon the table.

"What do you mean?" Teraxin's words slurred. The potent drink had apparently made his tongue thick, though he truly didn't recall having drunk that much. Only a glass or two. Or two of a pair? He could count them. Could he count on them? His thoughts whirred, trying to catch up with the words that floated past him like bright butterflies. He struggled to make sense of what the younger man had just told him.

Kavyn sneered at his teacher. "Her mental affliction is the only saving grace we've had. No thanks to you and your inability to do something as simple as break an untrained mind. Had you done your part before the blood-forsaken Physica got to her . . ." Kavyn paused, wondering what it would take to destroy the woman for good. First things first, he thought, forcing his attention back to the issue at hand.

"If I have to do everything myself, what purpose do you serve?" His fist pounded the table. It vibrated against Teraxin's elbows. "You have been as worthless to me as a castrated breeder," the younger man shouted.

Teraxin was having trouble following the words. His hands tingled. A numbness crawled up his legs and arms. Had the table's vibration affected the floor, as well? He wondered why his head seemed to be filled with down. Too late, his foggy brain scratched at the answer that tickled at the back of his brain. "What have you done to me?" he gasped.

"Me? I have done nothing." Kavyn tilted his head, eyeing Teraxin. "You were distraught at the recent turn of affairs, your loss of influence and position with the

Council." He sighed in mock exaggeration. "Such a waste." Kavyn shook his head.

Teraxin gaped as his protégé's eyes appeared to multiply and the young man's face became a blur. He felt himself slumping and tried to grab the edge of the table, but his arms no longer obeyed him and he fell forward, the side of his face smacking the table with a loud thump. With the last of his will, he sent his thoughts through the air, reaching out for help, but his awareness slammed back into his head with a jarring slap.

"Tsk, tsk," Kavyn said, his voice sugared in sarcasm. "It appears my poor teacher has sampled one of his own poisons." He leaned over Teraxin and pushed his way into the old man's thoughts, searching for the source of his deep knowledge.

But, although Teraxin's mental shield had collapsed and left him open to Kavyn's prying, his thoughts swirled in a fuzzy maze of confusion. Kavyn squeezed his eyes shut, hands balled into fists, and grunted with the strain of trying to sort through the avalanche of memories, thoughts and emotions.

Suddenly, Teraxin grabbed hold of Kavyn's mind, like a drowning man clinging to his would-be rescuer. Kavyn felt himself being pulled downward into a vortex of anger and fear. It required all his strength of will to pull free. Once back inside his own mind, he stepped back, chest heaving, gritting his teeth in frustration. The root of Teraxin's learning would die with him.

"What an unfortunate loss." Kavyn spilled the last of the wine from Teraxin's cup, knocking the vessel onto the floor where it shattered. Then he reached inside a pocket and took out a small phial, setting it onto the table in front of Teraxin's rapidly blinking eyes. He knew it was beneath him to be so petty, but he just couldn't resist. Teraxin had been arrogant to believe he could control someone of Kavyn's talents. Besides, the scrabbling and reaching of his so-called tutor had become more than just annoying. It had finally stretched Kavyn's tolerance to breaking.

It was unfortunate he would not have possession of Teraxin's knowledge source, but it couldn't be helped. Teraxin had to take his own life in an unfortunate accident. A doomed experiment to determine how much poison it would take to incapacitate a grown person, perhaps. Or the actions of a desperate man overcome by life's unlucky turns. It mattered not what anyone believed about this incident. Perhaps the old man might finally prove useful. So many things could be blamed on a man who no longer lived. The death of Kavyn's father had been a teaching experience, indeed. "Luckily, your feeble attempt to find a way to destroy the Matriarch has ended in tragic failure." Kavyn brushed a bit of nothing from the front of his tunic and turned to leave.

Teraxin tried to make sense of what he was seeing. *Antidote.* The word formed as he finally recognized the bottle and realized what it contained. *Antidote.* He told himself to reach for the container, to pick it up, to drink, but his body refused to obey him. *Antidote.* He tried once more to send his thoughts out, to connect with someone, anyone, but all was a mere buzzing like a swarm of angry bees inside his head, the sound of receding footsteps echoing beneath the thrum that closed over him. His final thought, as the room faded to black, was how much the puddle of poisoned wine resembled the spilled blood of the Matriarch's Consort.

CHAPTER THIRTY-SEVEN

Milos wiped the sweat from his brow. The man before him bent forward, catching his breath. The covered space was close and hot, the exterior walls of other buildings making up the walls of the courtyard, across which a heavy canvas was stretched. The canvas kept out the elements, sun and rain, but also the wind that blew from the coast to cool the inlands.

The courtyard stood bare, aside from a few low benches and weapons racks placed against the walls. While technically, this large space was out of doors, it was stifling. Milos longed for the sun on his back, a breeze in his face, but Marquon insisted that drilling within view of those outside their enclave would draw unwanted questions. So, Milos had begun training the men and women to fight, one-by-one, in the close quarters.

Milos still marveled at the light that emanated from the strange glowing stones set at intervals along the walls. According to Marquon, this was a common method of providing light. It required no fuel, only a special type of polished stone and the energies bestowed by a stone adept—a person with some sort of special ability with rocks—to recharge the stones periodically. The more powerful the innate, the less frequently the stones needed to be charged. Only every third stone in this space was lit, which provided barely enough light to train by. However, when he'd asked Marquon about it, the man only scowled and said, "It is as I have told you, we are a dying race." Milos had no idea how the two things were connected, but he had let it go.

Milos sensed the attack before the blow landed, but he'd let his guard down long enough for his opponent to strike a solid blow to his shoulder before he was able to dodge out of the way. *At least it wasn't my skull*, he chided himself for his lack of attention. Even though this was only training, he needed to remain thoroughly alert. "How is it," he panted out between swings, "that your people have not found someone to provide battle training before now?" He swung his staff at the man across from him, who dodged the blow and grinned, proud of the near miss.

"Our people have not had the need to learn physical combat." The man parried another thrust of Milos' stave and returned to his ready stance. "Many, many generations ago, Matriarch Balendri created the veil. Since that time, each Matriarch has acted as Guardian to our realm, shoring up the veil and ensuring the only outsiders allowed through were by delegation and few in number." He considered Milos for a moment, before swinging a hard blow toward his left ear. "Our history tells us . . . we had the art of fighting once, but . . . we turned from . . . physical violence once the veil was in place." He continued to batter at Milos as he spoke, punctuating his words with blows. "The protection . . . of the Guardians . . . allowed the arts to flourish." He jumped up and to the side as Milos swept his staff at his feet, then lowered his weapon in time to block. "This provided us the time . . . and space . . . within which to hone our mindskills."

Milos positioned himself once more at the ready. "Yet, you have your abilities, what you call mindskills, why is it you are no longer able to protect yourselves with those?"

"As Marquon told you, we are a dying race. Our skills are fading. What will we be once we have lost all trace of our abilities as you call them?" The man snorted in derision as he took another swing.

Milos ducked casually and knocked the man's stave to the side. He suddenly recalled the way he'd felt when they had come upon him at the edge of the city, the way he moved like a man trudging through high tide against their swift motion. "This veil," Milos said, thinking hard on his time in the forest and mists. "It creeps inside men's minds." He jabbed at the man, who parried the blow and lunged a quick riposte before nodding assent to Milos. "If that is so, why not take the knowledge of combat from those same men?"

The man's eyes went wide. He scowled, his mouth flattening in anger. "What kind of people do you take us for?" He swung his weapon overhead, bringing it down toward Milos so rapidly, he nearly slipped by Milos' defense. The staves clashed together with a resounding crack.

Three days ago, this same man would have already been sitting on the healer's bench, his bruises being tended, but these people learned rapidly. It was as if they somehow shared what they learned with one another. Milos would try a new trick on a sparring partner and the next would already know to expect it. If it weren't happening in such rapid succession, Milos might be willing to believe they were practicing on their own, outside of this space, but he suspected there was more to it than that.

A sturdy woman with chestnut-colored hair watched them from the sidelines, waiting her turn. Something about her posture drew Milos' gaze. Her shoulders were set and her fists clenched, but her eyes appeared unfocused. He watched her out of the corner of his eye as he swung the staff at his opponent's feet, causing him to jump out of the way again. Her position never wavered, but her breathing changed. The difference was subtle, but Milos perceived it, the same way he would have noted a deer twitch an ear, stiffen its muscles and prepare to leap into the trees.

Now that he'd seen the change, he could sense it. Each time his opponent swung on him, the woman's shoulders tightened. Each time he caused his opponent to dodge or duck out of the way, her breathing became just a bit more rapid. Finally, Milos called time. He approached his sparring partner and began giving him points on ways to fight more efficiently. As he spoke, he watched the woman over the man's shoulder. She had relaxed, appearing to be intent on his every word, taking in his advice as much as the man with whom he had been fighting.

When it became her turn, she raised her weapon in exactly the position he had recommended to the previous fighter. Instead of initiating the combat, Milos leaned on his staff. "How is it done?"

"What?" The woman remained at the ready, her staff raised.

"The learning. You're sharing in the learning, even when you aren't in the practice ring." He scanned her face. "Is it a mind trick?"

The woman sneered. "Not a trick," she said. "We don't perform tricks."

"He doesn't mean that kind of trick." Marquon stepped into the room. "But Tesalin is correct," he told Milos. "We don't perform tricks. Nor is what we do magic, though it may appear so to you. And as I said, we do not pry inside another's thoughts without leave."

"It's like the mist," Milos mused. "Like—" He stopped himself from finishing. He had been about to say it was like Kira's mental connection with Vaith and Kelmir, but he had promised never to reveal her secret to anyone. And though these were her people, though she had lied to him, he could not bring himself to break his oath to her.

"Like what?" Marquon stood just outside the sparring ring, watching him.

"The stones that glow on the walls," Milos replied quickly. "You put your thoughts into them somehow. It's how you knew of me, without anyone sending up an alarm. And when we fight, you share your mind with the others." It certainly sounded like magic.

"Something like that," Marquon replied. "It's a bit more complicated, but yes. We are able to share our minds. It is a very efficient way to convey information. And training." He nodded toward Tesalin who still held her staff at the ready, prepared to fight.

Milos backed up and wiped his face on his sleeve. "I think then," he said, "it is time for you to begin sparring against each other." He stepped out of the ring and handed his staff to Marquon. "I will share what I know with you from the sidelines for a time."

The big man smiled wryly as he took the wooden weapon from him.

Milos watched as Tesalin and Marquon sparred, deftly

dodging and swinging as if they had been fighting this way for seasons, rather than days. They spun and weaved in a graceful dance, the like of which Milos had not seen before. The closest matched combatants he had witnessed before now had been his uncle and father. As a young boy, he had watched them spar in the yard of Tem Hold. They had used any excuse to work out their arguments and frustrations in this way. They gambled over anything, pitting their strength and agility against the first spring foal, a new leathern jerkin, a jug of ale.

Milos lost track of the fight before him, wandering in his remembrances until he heard the thunk of a weapon hitting home too hard and a gasp as Tesalin dropped her weapon and ran to help her opponent, only to be thrown down by the swipe of a staff swung deftly along the ground, which swept her off her feet and onto her back.

"I believe one of the first lessons was never to let down your guard." Marquon rubbed his left shoulder and flexed his arm, moving it in slow circles, checking his range of motion.

"Thank you kindly for the reminder," Tesalin rasped, pushing herself up into a sitting position. "It won't happen again."

Milos found himself beginning to like these people. They took things in stride, without complaint. He crossed the floor and offered a hand to the woman. She took it and rose to her feet with a grunt.

"I see how it is." Marquon stood, using his staff for leverage. "You have a softness for women." He laughed.

Milos felt heat rise up his face. He let go of Tesalin's hand and she gave him a quick nod of thanks and limped across the space to a nearby bench.

"In my realm, we defer to women more readily, perhaps." Milos paused for a moment recalling Mayet, her desperate attempt to reassert her lost position, and what her manipulations had cost her in the end. His jaw tightened. "In some ways, however, some treat them as inferiors, almost as objects."

Marquon had stopped laughing. His eyes held something like understanding. "Anger in your heart will not remedy the past," he murmured.

Milos gave him a half smile. How was it this man seemed to know what he was feeling? "Everyone has bits of wisdom to share with me, these days." He rubbed the back of his neck, easing the tension that had gathered there. "Are you peering inside my mind?" he finally asked.

Marquon's eyes went wide. "I would not do such a thing, even were I able. That is a personal invasion that goes beyond mere rudeness." He dusted off his trousers. "No, I am only empathic, nothing more."

Ah, Milos thought. This explained why his earlier sparring partner had taken such offense to his suggestion. Even to these people, who had such clear abilities to see inside stones and plants, to flit inside one another's thoughts, to share their thinking without speech, an invasion of the mind without permission would be tantamount to rape. "Empathic?"

"I can sense what others are feeling, but I cannot read their thoughts exactly, nor see inside what they think."

"He needs to understand us better." Tesalin called from the side of the room.

Marquon nodded. "Tesalin is right. You are a stranger here and our ways must seem odd to you. Come. We shall eat and I will explain more about our culture."

"And about our mind-skills," Tesalin offered.

Milos followed Marquon across the yard and into a smaller building. A man in a leather apron tended a fire upon which a kettle boiled. The rich aroma of fresh stew filled the room, causing Milos' stomach to growl.

"Well, you don't need to read minds to know that I'm famished," he joked, but his thoughts reeled and spun. What if there were people here who did not share this moral opposition to invading another's mind? Would Milos know if someone slipped inside his mind without consent? A prickling sensation crawled up the back of his neck, an itch like something worming its way through his skull. He glanced out the door. Across the yard, Tesalin looked up and smiled, then returned to cleaning sweat and grime from the practice staves as if she had not a care.

CHAPTER THIRTY-EIGHT

"Come and drink your tea," Devira said, pouring the steaming liquid into a porcelain cup. "It will help you to calm."

"This is a dangerous turn." Zoshia waved her off and continued to pace the floor of their apartments. "A calmative will not help."

"Teraxin was an old man too greedy for power." Devira set the teapot down onto the table. "His passing is for others to regret."

Zoshia stopped her pacing and looked up sharply at her lifemate. "I'm surprised at the ease with which you can say that."

"Because I'm a Physica? And a healer of minds?" Devira scoffed. "His was not a mind that could be healed by any known art, even had he sought for it."

Zoshia shook her head. "No. Because you know what is at stake here, or at least you should. Does it not make you wonder? Why would a man so hungry for position end his own life?"

"Who knows what manner of experiment he was undertaking? The antidote sitting there before him. He could have easily had it in his hand had he thought the need so great." She reached across the dainty table for a honey cake. "I would call it wasteful, if I did not know better. As it is, he will at least no longer be a threat to the Matriarchess."

"Yes," Zoshia murmured. "But I don't believe it was an accident. And when dangerous prey is eaten, it is always by a more dangerous animal."

Devira paused, the honey cake held in mid air, a single bite missing. She swallowed the morsel and set the cake down onto her plate. "If you believe it to have been by foul deed, I know only one person who would be so ruthless."

"Do not speak aloud the name you hold on the tip of your tongue!" Zoshia hissed.

"What will it take for you to see it?" Devira shouted in exasperation. "Who else might he allow to pour his wine? The old manipulator was not inclined toward trust."

"You have no proof of anything untoward. And there is nothing solid on which to balance such accusations. So, it would be better not to speak them out loud," Zoshia said, a warning in her voice.

Devira opened her mouth to protest, but bit back her words. Her lifemate was right, she had no proof. Only the nagging of her heart and the niggling of suspicion that had settled in her brain long ago. "Might you at least increase the Keepers in the Guardian's Tower?"

Zoshia turned and began pacing once again. "How would you have me do that without suggesting I suspect something amiss?" She shook her head. "I will not smear the name of a potential heir to the Seat without due cause."

"I could give notice that the Matriarch's condition is worsening," Devira wiped her fingers on a napkin. "But to reveal how lost her mind has become would give him exactly what he wants."

Zoshia stopped pacing and glared at Devira. "I do not understand why you are so certain it was him, but Teraxin's death is an omen, a warning of things to come. Of that, I am certain. We have the Matriarchess. If you would see our traditions continue as you desire, she is a card that must be played sooner rather than later."

"She isn't ready," Devira said. "She has made great strides, but . . ."

"A blunt knife is not worthless," Zoshia shot back. "Only more difficult to use."

"But I cannot even guarantee you the blunt edge. Not without risk to the girl."

"There is more at stake here than the fate of one girl." Zoshia clasped her hands together. "As you said, our entire way of life stands upon the brink." She pulled her hands apart. "Would you let our people fail, now?"

Devira shook her head. "My oath," she began. But Zoshia would not hear her. She had never seemed to understand. Even with all her knowledge and experience, she could not grasp the charge of the Physicas, the responsibilities they had to their patients. "At the very least," she finally said, "the girl should be given some choice in the matter."

"Yes. By all means," Zoshia said. "Let us ask the child raised by the backward Aestrons, with no memory of her birthright nor her bloodline, what should become of the Eilaren people."

Devira threw up her hands in surrender. There was no arguing with Zoshia when she got this way. And this was certainly not the time to reveal how far the

Matriarchess had progressed in her training, nor the unease Devira felt regarding her inability to fully fathom the girl's skills. Instead, she took a large sip of tea and focused on finishing her meal.

CHAPTER THIRTY-NINE

As the sun lowered in the distant sky, Milos stepped outside the compound.

Tesalin stood beside the gate, speaking with another of the Protectors. "I believe Marquon prefers you stay hidden behind the walls of the compound," she said as he passed.

"He did mention my not being seen by the populace," Milos admitted. "But I need a moment to myself somewhere away from the training grounds and the constant drilling."

"I understand," she said, nodding toward a narrow path that split from the main walkway. "That way will take you down to the water by a less used route. As like as not, you'll be alone at this hour."

The trail wound its way between willowy trees and lush greenery till it finally opened up onto a stream that gurgled and splashed. Tall, cream-colored plants of a type Milos had never before seen grew along the edges of the water. A glister of light and color caught his eye and for a moment he thought Vaith would swoop down from above, but when he searched the trees for the little wyvern, he saw only brown branches covered in green leaves that trembled in the morning breeze.

He leaned down and trailed his fingers in the cool water. Then, he kneeled and dipped his cupped hands into the stream and splashed his face with the cool water, scrubbing his neck and hair.

A noise behind him made him start and he remembered who and where he was, an outsider in the midst of the Eilaren. He slipped down the bank and ducked behind the tall plants.

"No need to hide on my account," a low voice purred.

Milos peered out from the undergrowth, knife in hand. The face that gazed back at him was elderly and wrinkled, surrounded by a halo of white. The man's hair and beard looked like lamb's wool washed to a glowing sheen and combed for spinning. The old man stared at him, and Milos realized his pale eyes did not focus.

Blind.

"Come along," the old man coaxed. "I'll not give out your secret. Though, Marquon should have kept you better hidden, had he not wanted you seen by the likes of me." He smiled as if at some jest. "Besides, I'm quite curious how you managed to bypass the Guardian's Veil."

Milos stepped out of the foliage. "Veil?" He could likely deal with a blind old man, but with what had happened to him recently, he held his knife at the ready.

"You're clearly an outsider . . ." The old man nodded as he spoke, his long, wispy beard bobbing upon his chest. "Yet, you have passed beyond the city's defenses and somehow found your way into our citadel. Either there is a weakness in the Veil, or you are possessed of a most curious skill." His tone grew serious and his voice dropped to a low whisper that Milos could barely hear. "A skill, which we must understand."

"How do you know I am an outsider?" Milos asked.

The old man smiled. "One sees farther with the mind than with a pair of failed eyes," he said.

Milos took a step nearer and peered at the man. Pale scars that had earlier been hidden by the wrinkles in his aged face surrounded his eyes.

"An accident," the old man said, as if he could see Milos staring. His voice had gone serious again.

"Your pardon," Milos said, dropping his gaze from the scarred and wrinkled face. He slid his knife into his belt. "I did not intend to stare."

"Of course, you did. But pardon is granted," replied the man. "I am Kalt."

Milos hesitated, but there seemed no harm in the old man. A name would tell him nothing more than he already seemed to know. And this old man appeared to know plenty, already. "Milos," he told him.

"I would learn more of you, Milos," Kalt said. "I rarely come across anything so interesting on my daily stroll along these waters. Would you care to accompany me on my walk?"

Milos glanced around. He had already risked too much. Clearly, his presence was no longer a secret, but did he dare walk blithely through the citadel with this man?

"Do not worry yourself," the man told him as if reading his thoughts. "My home is nearby and we shall be unmolested."

Milos hesitated, wondering if the old man had invaded his mind, but he sensed no malice in him. Likely, he was harmless and, as far as Milos could tell, no guards had been summoned to take him.

They walked along the river, then followed a narrow path that veered into the woods. The old man strode along without hesitation, never stumbling even as the path wound through the trees and rose and fell with the terrain. Milos watched the trees, half expecting to be ambushed at every turn and narrowing.

The trail widened out and spilled them into a clearing where Kalt paused, placing his fingertips at his temples. A spiral path led inward from the edges of the wood, culminating in the center where a tall tree stood. At first, it appeared that something had been wrapped around the trunk of the tree, but when Milos examined it closer, he found that what had at first appeared to be a single trunk was actually a number of smaller trees that had twisted together into a knotted braid and spiraled upward.

He peered up into the leafy canopy and caught his breath. The leaves were a multitude of shapes and a diverse variation of greens.

"My family monument," Kalt said, as he lowered his hands from his face. "Their spirits rest here."

Milos glanced around, expecting markers or gravestones, but the space between the spiraling path was filled only with low ground cover, thick round-petaled plants that grew in shades of gold and yellow. The path itself was paved with wooden planks, laid in an intricate interlocking pattern that also appeared to twist and braid itself around the clearing.

"Come," his host led on, following the path around the edge of the tree line. "We won't disturb their rest today."

Milos followed the old man, glancing over his shoulder and wondering if the old man could actually rouse the dead in this strange place.

On the far side of the clearing, they passed through another gap in the trees and walked around a tall hedge behind which hid a low-roofed cottage, surrounded by colorful plants. A smooth floor of wooden planking extended from the cottage, protected overhead by a thick bower of twisted vines. Beneath the leafy covering sat a low table surrounded by padded benches.

The old man waved at the table. "Please, take your ease," he told Milos, as he ducked beneath the bower and opened a narrow door. "I will see what refreshment I have to offer a guest." He slipped inside the house, leaving Milos alone.

Milos paced, surveying the garden that grew alongside the back wall of the house. What had at first appeared to be a random assortment of plants, turned out to be a well cared for plot bursting with numerous fruits and vegetables. Some he recognized as similar to the crops grown at Tem Hold, melons and squash, others were odd shapes and colors he'd not seen before.

"Are you a gardener?" Kalt spoke from behind him, and Milos spun to face the old man who had silently reemerged from the house carrying a tray with a large pitcher and several bowls.

"I was a Holder in my land," Milos said. "The people of my Hold produced many crops." He realized for the first time since he'd set off with Kira how much he missed Tem Hold and its people. He wondered once more how his niece and nephew fared. Wondered what had become of the people of the Hold. Were they still working together as he had hoped they would when he'd divided the holding between them? He made the sign of the circle and wished them well.

Kalt set the tray down onto the table and poured water from the pitcher into a large bowl. He picked up a towel and held it in both hands, offering it to Milos. "Please," he said. "Wash and refresh yourself."

Milos hesitated.

"It is an old custom," Kalt said, smiling. "I offer you, my guest, the waters of cleansing and refreshment. Afterward, we will partake of the bounty of my garden."

Once they had washed, Kalt led Milos to the garden where the old man picked an assortment of fruits and vegetables, handing them to Milos to carry to the table. Kalt rinsed each item thoroughly, muttering under his breath. Milos caught only a few of the words, but he knew a prayer of thanks when he heard it, so he waited politely until Kalt stopped speaking and offered him a plate piled high with the fresh picked foods.

"Please, be welcome here," the old man said.

Still wary, Milos took first only those things familiar to him, but once Kalt had partaken of the odd varieties, Milos' hunger overcame him and he ate with gusto.

Finally, Kalt settled into his seat and cocked his chin forward, his lively beard lifting in the cooling breeze that wafted across the yard and stirred the leaves of the bower setting them to whispering. "Now, I would appreciate your sharing with me how you managed to pierce the Veil." The blind man's voice filled with curiosity.

Milos shrugged. "I appreciate your hospitality, and I would answer you, if I could, but I do not know what you mean."

"You came from a far land, did you not?" Kalt scratched at his shaggy chin in contemplation.

Forgetting for a moment that Kalt was blind, Milos caught himself nodding in response. "Yes," he admitted out loud, knowing it was useless to lie about a fact the old man had already discerned the answer to.

"And when you reached our shore, you had no unusual encounters?" Kalt leaned forward and placed his hands upon the table expectantly.

Milos weighed his response, what was the old man

driving at? "There was a sudden storm," he said.

"As, yes. There are always storms offshore." Kalt waved the words away. "After the storm? What then?"

"Always?" Milos asked.

"Often enough." Kalt waved the question aside. "What happened once you set foot inside the boundary?"

Milos thought for a moment about all that had happened and wondered how Dahl and the rest of the ship's crew fared. Were they still on the beach, or had they dared the darkness of the trees after Dahl's return? Would they fall prey to . . . "The boundary," he said suddenly, glancing up at the bower and across the yard beyond the hedge at the towering braided tree. "The forest marks the boundary to this land. The veil you speak of, it's not a physical thing, is it?"

Milos shivered despite the warm afternoon. The chill fog that had held him inside seemed to reach out icy fingers to wrap once more around his mind. He felt it like a physical sensation and barely contained his urge to flee.

"You know of what I speak," Kalt murmured, relief clear in his voice. "Then the Veil remains intact." He appeared thoughtful. "It is a wonder then, that you have reached this city."

CHAPTER FORTY

A light rapping at the door brought Kira's attention back to the room.

"Come in," she called, tucking her amulet into her bodice. If there were more memories to be gleaned from the polished bit of metal, they were locked tightly away and she had yet to find the key to releasing them. Even if the secrets within the locket had been played out, Kira felt better keeping it close to her heart.

Keliss entered the room, carrying a tray. "How are you feeling today?" she asked. This was her customary greeting, but today her voice sounded weary and her face appeared strained.

"I am very well, thank you," Kira said, eyeing the apprentice Mentat. "But what of you?"

Keliss set the tray down and rubbed at her temples. "I'm fine. Merely a headache."

"Another one?" Kira went to Keliss and took her wrist. The young woman's pulse raced as if she'd run all the way to Kira's room, yet she was not out of breath.

Keliss gently extricated her hand from Kira's grip. "Who is the patient here?" she asked, but before Kira could answer, the young woman collapsed to her knees, holding her head and shrieking in pain.

Kira knelt beside her and tried to put her arms around her, but Keliss screamed and slapped her. She tumbled onto her side and began thrashing, legs and arms flailing. She kicked out stiff-legged and knocked into the small table, sending the tray and its contents crashing to the floor.

"Help!" Kira shouted. She grabbed Keliss and tried to hold her down to keep her skull from pounding against the floor, but her thrashing only increased.

The door flew open and three attendants rushed into the room. Two of them reached past Kira and took hold of Keliss. The other, a tall woman with auburn hair, grabbed Kira and yanked her away from the flailing apprentice.

Kira tried to push away. "What is happening to her?" she asked. The woman who still clung to her shushed her.

The two Mentats had taken up position, one on either side of Keliss, hands held against her head. "Peace, peace, peace" they said in unison, repeating the word until it became a rhythmic chant, though the strain on their faces suggested anything but calm.

Slowly, Keliss' thrashing slowed to quaking, then reduced further until it appeared she only shivered on the floor between the two Mentats. Finally, she stilled and, after a few moments, they nodded and the attendant ushered Kira from the room.

Out in the passageway, the tall woman looked her in the eyes. "What happened?" she asked.

"I . . . I don't know," Kira told her. "She brought in the

evening tray, as usual, but . . ."

"But what?"

"She seemed . . . unwell."

One of the Mentats stepped out into the hallway, closing the door behind her. "Tell us what you did," she said, her voice an angry accusation.

Kira backed away in surprise. "I did nothing."

The woman frowned, her eyes narrowing in suspicion. "She was fine when I saw her in the kitchen, preparing your tray," she grumbled. "Now . . . your face is marked and she . . ."

Kira's hand went to her cheek where Keliss had slapped her after falling into her fit.

"She's not merely ill, then?" The attendant beside Kira asked.

The other woman shook her head and glared at Kira.

"What then?"

"Tampering." The way she spat the word gave it an ugly sound.

A knowing look passed between them before they turned their angry gazes on Kira.

Kira's skin went cold. What were they saying? Why were they looking at her that way? Like a . . . criminal. *Tampering.* Her floundering awareness finally reached out and caught the word again. *Tampering.* There was no greater illegal act among the Eilaren than invading another's thoughts without leave. And they thought Kira responsible for such an act?

"I wouldn't—" she began, but their hard looks cut her off.

There had been mistrust of her from the first, but for anyone to think she would do such a thing, would even attempt such a thing . . .

"Send for the Physica," the Mentat said. "But first, confine her to another room." She pointed at Kira.

"Come with me," the auburn-haired woman took her by the arm.

Kira shook her off. "I want to see Keliss."

"Why? So you can finish what you started?"

"No," Kira said. "I want to make certain she is all right."

The woman shook her head. "She is far from all right."

CHAPTER FORTY-ONE

"No!" Devira gripped her lifemate's hand.

Zoshia pulled away. "This is Council business," she rasped. "I cannot allow personal feelings to interfere."

"But a full panel? Can you not convince them of another way?"

"What would you have me do?" Zoshia paced to the far side of the greeting room. The argument had started in their sleeping space, but had moved out here once they had both realized neither of them would sleep this night.

"But they will destroy what progress we have made with her. She has learned much, but there is so much more she needs to know. They'll rip her mental shields to shreds. You know what that means."

"Ardea was clearly lax in her training of the girl," Zoshia said, accusation in her tone. "There is no way to make up for that."

Devira bristled at the insult to her sibling. As much

as Ardea had wronged them all, she was still her sister. "Perhaps, Ardea was right in taking the girl. Mayhap, she knew better than we what we were becoming in our decline."

"Hush!" Zoshia rounded on her. "How often must I remind you not to speak so?"

"What matter can it make? Zosh, don't you see? If we allow this, then we will have become what we feared. The Council has lost sight of who we once were. We have become no more tolerant, and no less brutal, than those who fear us simply for who and what we are." Devira rubbed her forehead. "If she is at fault for Keliss' state, it was not by intent. The fault, as you have pointed out, lies with me."

"If she has tampered, she is dangerous. Whether it was purposeful or not." Zoshia caught Devira's scarred hands in hers and forced her to look into her eyes. "I know what this means, especially to you. But I am bound by my oath to the Council, as much as you are bound to yours. No one can be allowed to behave outside the law. No one. Especially, not now."

Devira nodded and leaned into her partner. "I know," she whispered. "But we had come so close. So close."

They stood for a time, wrapped in each other's arms, Devira's tears dampening her lifemate's collar.

"Come along to bed," Zoshia finally said. "You will be better able to prepare the girl, if you are rested."

Devira reluctantly allowed herself to be led to their sleeping room, but she knew she would not be able to rest this night.

CHAPTER FORTY-TWO

Kira had been left to herself. No guards stood outside her door, but she knew she was watched. She sat in the window seat, searching the sky. Once again, she had no idea what she might be looking for, only that she panicked, worried she might miss something important each time she attempted to focus on anything else. After Keliss' fit, Kira had been confined to her rooms. She might as well gaze out at the sky as to lie abed staring into the shadows that clung to the corners of the high ceiling where the light did not reach.

A rap at her door made her jump. She called out for the visitor to enter, but the door remained closed. The light rapping came again and she hurried to the door and opened it. A young man stood in the otherwise empty hallway. He shifted from one foot to the other, as if his feet wished to run and it was all he could do to keep himself here.

"May I be of some service to you?" she asked.

"I've a message." The boy stared down at his restless feet and spoke so quietly, she could barely make out the words.

"A message?"

He nodded, still staring down at his toes.

Her neck tingled in that way it did when something was amiss. She checked both directions, but no one else approached. "Who sent you?" she asked in a tight whisper.

"Marquon." The boy glanced up at her from under his hazel lashes, then returned his gaze to the floor. "But it's not from him."

The tingling grew and a deep unease thrummed in her chest. "You had better come inside."

The boy cast a wary glance over his shoulder and shook his head. "He asks only will you speak with him."

"Speak with whom?"

"The Aestron," the boy said, then scanned the hallway once more. "The one they call Milos."

Milos! A door inside her swung open and a golden trove of memories spilled out. His face rose up before her, his blue eyes laughing at something she'd said, and a comforting warmth wrapped itself around her.

Voices sounded along the passageway and the boy started. "He will find you by the water." With that, he turned and darted off, head down, dodging past two women who turned the corner at just that moment.

Kira ducked back into her room.

Milos. With sudden clarity, she recalled his smile, his touch. They had set out upon this journey together. How they had separated, she had no idea. Something else from their time together niggled at her, but she could not quite grasp it and she could not imagine anything that could have come between them.

Damn these fleeting recollections. There were still so

many holes in her head. But Milos. His dark hair and blue eyes. His lips. His smile. Those were finally no longer tangled with the memories of fire and blood and the destruction that had surrounded her, no longer churned in a swirl of running and fighting. The distillation of memories had finally separated Milos from Toril in both her heart and her mind.

But now what? It appeared he was safe, or at least free to send her a message, but how could she respond without giving away her only shield, that of pretending to still be unable to remember?

How long could she put him off? There was too much plotting and secrecy here for her to reveal how much she could now recall of her former life. She dared not risk involving him until she had sorted the tangled weave of intrigue. And now, these accusations of tampering.

She returned to the window and gazed out once more, searching the sky for a glittering flash of color, for a part of her soul to wing across the sky and appear. She shook her head. That part of her mind was still a maze of winding stairs and closed doorways. Yet, something hovered there just beyond her reach. Something as important as her memories of Milos. If only she could open the correct door. She clutched at her medallion, grateful for the inheritance that had been bequeathed to her, but wishing the cold metal held more than just her distant past.

She grasped the medallion harder and the room grew hazy, the walls fading into the distance.

A soft growl startled her and she sat up. She turned slowly, peering into evening shadows. A dark patch moved nearer and she wiped at her eyes, trying to see through the wetness that still lingered there. The growl turned to a low rumble that she suddenly recognized as purring and the darkness separated itself from the

S. A. Skinner

shadowy trees and stepped closer. Kira's breath caught in her chest and she froze in place as the hunting cat closed in, its mottled fur catching the evening light like scudding moonlit clouds on a stormy night.

She cringed, waiting for the predator to pounce, but the rumbling sound grew louder and the cat padded lightly forward until it stood directly beside her, then lowered its head to rub up against her leg. The touch of its fur was comforting and Kira reached out tentative fingers to stroke the softness of it. As her trembling fingers connected with the silken fur, she felt her awareness slip and for a moment she saw herself as if through another's eyes, felt her furred cheek brush against bare skin. She jerked her hand away and her brain snapped back into place. She glanced down at the big cat, which had settled onto its haunches and stared at her expectantly.

"How did you do that?" She gazed deep into the cat's eyes, seeking an answer. An odd fluttery sensation nudged at the edges of her awareness. She searched for the cause and found herself once again inside the thoughts of the feline at her feet. There was no fear, nor ire, just a sense of belonging, like coming home on a cold night to loving arms and a warm fire. Kira slipped back into her own mind and slid down from her perch, wrapping her thin arms around the cat, hugging it tight.

"Hello," she whispered into the cat's ear. "My name is Kira, what's yours?"

A knocking sound roused her from her remembrance. The forest receded and she was left breathless, holding the fast fading memory of soft fur and joyful belonging.

Kelmir. I remember you.

Then she pushed her mental shields into place, forcing all she had been back into the dark recesses and allowing her past to become a vast blank canvas once

215

more before opening the door.

CHAPTER FORTY-THREE

Milos took another drink of fruit-infused water. Marquon had offered wine with their repast, but Milos had declined, choosing to stay clear and focused. The itching that had started at the base of his skull still lingered. Marquon had shared much about their culture, but Milos still had questions.

"Your people have talents that are beyond what mine can even fathom. Most of my countrymen fear your borders. The Sunfleet's Captain was barely willing to sail close enough to allow us to come ashore. If not for the storm . . ." He did not finish the thought, suddenly concerned that his host already knew more about him than he should. "Tell me, why is it you now feel the need to learn to fight with your bodies when you can do so much with your minds? Surely, the fading of skills that you suggest would take many years to unfold."

"Our mind-skills have kept the world at bay for a multitude of generations, but now . . ." he swiped his hand through his thick hair, ". . . our skills fade rapidly. Our children continue to be born with affinities, but not with the skills for telepathy, or transference. Only rarely do we see skills that even compare with what was once considered a passing level. Yet, our Council sits and debates, making no decisions. They fight over tradition, and fear to make a change when change is already being forced upon us."

Milos chewed his bread and nodded. He recalled the Holders in his own country. How they despised the changes he had proposed. How he had made those changes anyway. Made them and left the people of Tem Hold to deal with what he had wrought. He swallowed hard and took another sip from his cup. Change did not come easy to many, especially those in power.

"We seem to have more in common than not." Marquon clapped him on the shoulder.

Milos scowled at the man, his jaw tight. He had not spoken the words aloud.

Marquon leaned back in his chair and raised the flagon to his lips to drink. Then, as if just noting Milos' discomfort, he set the wine cup down onto the table. "I didn't pry," he said. "You thought it right at me. It's a common practice to be attuned during conversation. And it's not the words I hear, only the sense of them."

Milos nodded, but he glared at Marquon, letting his mind go blank for a moment before thinking, *It is not a common practice in mine.* Then he pushed out his chair and took his leave. He forced a cloud of images into his mind, thinking hard on seeds, planting, harvest, even crop devouring pests, until he had walked to the far edge of the sanctuary. Hah. Sanctuary. Not for him. For him this was simply another prison, like the one he had wandered inside the veil. The only difference being that there he had been certain he'd had a reason to keep striving. To keep searching.

Before, he had searched for Kira, keeping hope alive that he would find her. Well, find her, he had. Here. Among these . . . odd strangers. People who might bend another's will, perhaps shape another's thoughts, merely by thinking on it. A chill ran up his spine. For all Marquon's complaints that his people's skills grew weak, that they were losing what abilities their predecessors had claimed, they were still capable of more than what, until now, Milos not have considered possible.

Even the least of these people controlled strange skills beyond anything Milos was capable of. More than any such abilities of his own people. Certainly, a few of Aestron's healers had been possessed of abilities beyond the norm. Some, like Heresta, could even foretell the future with some accuracy. But none could wriggle inside and pry into another's thoughts.

A sudden revelation hit him like a heavy stave swung in earnest. They were like her. Like Kira. She was home here. Among her people. She had found what she had sought. Was it any wonder she had not looked for him once she had been welcomed home? How could he ever compare to a man with the mind skills of Marquon, or any of these people? How could he compete?

He scuffed the toe of his boot in the dirt. Then stared at how worn and travel weary it looked. He almost laughed at what he had become. What he had given up. For her. He spun around and strode back to the practice floor, in need of something, someone, to fight.

* * *

Milos sat upon the low bench, still winded from the recent round of practice. Tesalin stood nearby, rubbing her forearm where he had managed to catch her a glancing blow. It would not have landed so hard had she turned and ducked as he had expected her to, but she had missed her footing and the staff had connected with a resounding thump before he could reverse the thrust.

"How does it feel?" he asked.

"Like I've been kicked by a mare." She grimaced and flexed her arm. "Nothing broken, though. It will heal. I'll have one of the Physicas see to it. To ensure proper healing."

"Physica?"

"Flesh healers." She rubbed her arm and grimaced. "Do you not have those with the gift of healing in your land?"

Milos thought about Kira's ability with herbs, the knowledge she had passed on to his niece, Milvari, about Heresta's legacy of knowledge and wisdom. "Healers, we have, though none I know who can heal merely by thinking on it," he said. "But why do you call them flesh healers? Is there any other kind?"

She sat beside him and settled her injured arm into her lap with a wince. "Plant healers, mental healers—"

Milos started. "Mental healers?"

"Yes. Those with an affinity for mental skills."

Milos' brow knitted in thought. "Could they also cloud a mind?" he asked, trying to keep the dark suspicion from his voice.

"It is possible. Those with the affinity for thought healing have been known to help those with traumatic experience learn to let the experience fade, thus diminish the fears, and quell the nightmares that haunt them." She frowned and shifted her arm to a more comfortable position. "It must be a guided practice, teaching the injured to open to the practitioner and follow the paths created for healing."

"And what of those who have forgotten things they

may wish to recall?" Milos rubbed his hands together to keep from making them into fists. "Can they be helped the same way?"

She gave him a funny look. "Have you need of such help?"

Milos leaned against the wall. "No. Not I." He tried to sound nonchalant. "But if someone had forgotten something . . . important . . ." He glanced at her.

"I do not know all the ways of such healing." She cradled her arm and stood to go. "My own skills, such as they are, are only those of reader and I am only able to read what is shared purposefully. If you have need of such knowledge, I suggest you seek the mental healers themselves. They are better prepared to answer your questions, should they deem it proper to do so."

Milos raised a questioning eyebrow.

She started to shrug, but stopped, wincing at the pain the movement inflicted. "While once we spoke of our skills as would anyone speak of the typical senses, hearing, taste, speech, you will find that these days some are less willing to discuss their affinities than others." With that, she marched from the room, clearly determined to show as little pain as possible.

He wondered at her words. These days. She said it as if there were something onerous about this time in their lives. What had changed for these people that they might have gone from speaking openly about their gifts, their "skills" as they called them, to holding their thoughts close, as one might guard a dangerous secret?

These people, this place. Even a person without the ability to read minds could tell there was much more beneath the surface.

CHAPTER FORTY-FOUR

Kira recognized the woman who entered and quietly shut the door behind her. She had met the Second Seat in the Council chambers.

"Good day to you, Matriarchess." Zoshia touched the back of her hand to her forehead and then held it out to Kira. "You appear to have rallied since your recent . . . discomfitures."

Kira raised her hand, brushing the backs of her fingers across the councilor's outstretched palm. "Devira's ministrations have been greatly beneficial."

Zoshia's countenance softened. "Indeed. She is a most talented Physica and a capable Mentat." Her voice seemed to hold a note of pride.

Kira sensed a surprising warmth emanating from the Second and quickly checked her shielding was in place. But no. This was no invasion. Simply an emotional response to the subject of their discussion. One strong enough for Kira to read without trying. She had only a moment to wonder if this were some new development in her capabilities, like the shielding control Devira had finally succeeded in teaching her after so many attempts.

"Please, make yourself comfortable," Kira gestured to a chair, remembering her manners.

"We have much to discuss," Zoshia told her, adjusting her robes as she settled into the cushioned seat. "I hope you are well enough to hear what I have to say."

* * *

Kira walked beside the flowing water, keeping her pace leisurely despite her anxiousness. She did not know how much time she would have before the formal charges would be brought against her, and Milos had not come the night before. A small part of her did not wish to see him. She knew not how she would be able to school her emotions, pretend not to know him, when her memories of him had become so vivid.

Yesterday, she had struggled with her decision to deny him, wanting once more to have him beside her.

And last night, she had dreamed of him. In her dream, they lived in a snug cottage at the edge of rich farmland. They had sat beside the fire, talking in soft voices of the coming harvest. She had been happy. Until a blaze of light had lit the evening sky and they heard the cries of women and children, the shouting of men. Milos had tried to keep her inside, but she had torn herself from him and run outside to find the fields aflame, warring armies silhouetted against the fiery light. The armies clashed together and out of their ranks strode Kavyn, his eyes glittering in the dark, reflecting the burning fields. He waved his arm at the men who clashed and died upon the fiery fields. "This is what you have wrought," he told her. "This is what you bring to us. And in return, I have a gift for you." He held up a bag that dripped with a dark viscous liquid and dumped the contents at her feet. Something round tumbled out and rolled across the ground, stopping at her feet. She stared down into the lifeless eyes of Milos.

She'd come full awake, shaking and sweating and knowing what she must do.

A flash of iridescence caught her eye and she glanced up to see the little wyvern circle once overhead before alighting on a low branch in front of her. The dainty reptile folded its wings and tilted its head, staring at her with its piercing gaze. Kira glanced around to ensure no one was near, then let down her outer shield and held out her arm. Vaith flew to her and landed upon her wrist. Without a leather guard, his sharp claws scratched at her skin through the cloth of her brocaded sleeve, but she cared not. She stroked his neck with her fingers and cooed at him. "Hello, my little princeling."

Vaith pushed against her touch and trilled low in his throat. His sense of belonging radiating in a palpable way.

His head jerked up and Kira heard the crack of a twig breaking beneath a boot. *Go. Hide.* She launched Vaith into the air and snapped her shields into place as a familiar figure stepped into view.

Milos stopped when he saw her, hope clear in his visage. Kira wanted nothing more than to run to him, to hold him, but now, with these charges hanging over her . . . She couldn't risk his safety, too. She forced herself to remain still and assume a blank look. Milos took a single step toward her and stopped, the hope falling from his face.

CHAPTER FORTY-FIVE

"Kira." Milos reached out a hand to her.

"You are Milos?" Kira's voice held no warmth.

He dropped his hand and planted his feet. "You know that I am. Deny that you love me, if that be the case, but do not deny you know me."

"How should I know you?"

Did her voice tremble? Or was he imagining it? She reached up and grasped her medallion, a familiar nervous habit he normally found endearing. Now, it merely pained him.

"If you know Vaith, you know me."

She frowned and sagged, looking sorrowful and confused and he wondered if what he'd said were true or only the hopeful belief of his wounded heart. Then a sound behind him caused him to glance back. A young man dressed in finery stood on the path, watching them. Milos startled at the man's features, how striking the resemblance to Kira. He gave Milos a searching look, then his gaze traveled beyond him to settle upon Kira.

Milos turned back to see that she now stood tall and stiff, her face blank. But this time there was something else in her mien, something that made him want to go to her, to put himself between her and this man who looked so much like her.

The young man stepped up beside him. "Who is your friend, Sister?"

Sister? Milos opened his mouth to voice the question aloud, but a scratching at the inside of his skull gave him pause. He used the only defense he had, letting his anger flash against the prickling sensation until it receded.

As if from a great distance, he heard Kira's voice.

"He is no friend of mine."

"Then shall I call for the Keepers to have him . . . removed?"

Kira smiled, but her face hardened into a dark mask. "I am more than well enough to manage, Kavyn. I am told a Guardian must keep for herself."

The young man's eyes narrowed, but he placed the back of his hand to his forehead and leaned forward in a slight bow. "You learn quickly." He gave Milos an assessing look. "Although, Guardian may be a stretch with the trial at your door."

For a moment, Milos felt as lost as a leaf spinning in a great whirling wind, then he found himself able to gather his senses once more. "I thought I knew the woman I had grown to love," he growled, "but I see now that I was mis . . . led."

Kira flinched, and her eyes grew wide, but her mouth drew down into a hard line. "I know not why you would insist upon knowing me. Clearly, you are from another land, another people, and you have no place here. Do you so seek to elevate yourself that you would attempt to convince a royal heir that you somehow care for her, a stranger to you and your world?"

Her words struck him like a blow and his anger flared. "Excuse me for having mistaken you for someone I thought I knew," he said, his voice dripping with ire. "Of course, you could not be her. The woman I knew was compassionate and caring and not concerned with rank and power." He shook his head. "May Troka grant you all that you deserve." He made a half-hearted sign of the circle before spinning on his heel and leaving the way he had come.

* * *

"Why Sister," Kavyn said, staring after Milos in a measuring way. "You're trembling. I'll call the Keepers and have them detain that invader." He made as if to send for the citadel warders.

"No." Kira laid a hand upon his shoulder to refocus his attention on her. "No, let him go. He's done no harm."

"I disagree," Kavyn said, his lips curling into a sneer. "He has accosted my sister, and the Matriarchess of Eilar. And we should know what such an outsider is doing not only in the citadel, but on the Guardian's Grounds."

Kira had no response for this, but she knew she must somehow distract her brother from calling the guards on Milos. If he were detained, she would be unable to keep their relationship secret. She would not be able to bear it if he were locked in a cell and questioned. Nor did she think his mind would hold against the prodding of the interrogators. She shuddered, wondering if her own mind would stand against the trial they had slated for her.

"Have you seen the Matriarch today?" she asked to change the subject, making the question sound as innocent as she could.

Kavyn scowled, then frowned, his face falling into a sad moue. "Yes. I'm afraid she is less well than ever. Time is growing short. If you are to take your rightful place, you must work harder to regain your lost thoughts and learn the necessary skills." He reached up and grasped her by the wrist, staring intently, as if he might find the secret answers to all his questions in the palm of her hand. "Have you regained nothing?"

Kira tried to pull away, but his grip on her wrist tightened.

He pulled her close and hissed into her ear. "You seem hesitant in your duties. One might think you were not happy to be the heir to the Guardian's Seat. Or is there something else that would keep you from assuming your rightful place? This matter of tampering, perhaps was no accident?"

Kira gasped. All pretense of brotherly love and concern had fled from him. Kavyn's grip tightened and Kira felt a pressure on her awareness so intense she thought she might lose consciousness. Then, suddenly, it lifted like a leaf rising on the wind and her brother looked surprised.

"I don't know what you mean." Kira told him, wrenching her arm free. She rubbed at her wrist and glared at him.

Kavyn's eyes narrowed, then his face grew blank. "I apologize." He touched his chest with the palm of his hand. "I did not mean to push. Nor to harm you." He gestured to her wrist. "It is just that I am overcome by worry for our mother and fear what may become of our land should anything befall her and you are unable to take your place upon the Guardian's Seat." His voice dripped with sweetness and sincerity, but his words were surrounded by dark spaces.

* * *

Kavyn offered Alyana his arm and returned with her to the main keep. Once inside, he excused himself and turned away. He had unfinished business to attend to and was determined to delay no longer.

He headed to the western ell of the upper keep, his step measured and calm, but his thoughts racing. It was clear his sister remembered more than she let on. It was also apparent that she had learned to use a mental shield quite handily. There was much more to her than Kavyn had at first thought. He would do well not to underestimate her again.

Ah, well, they would see if her shield was strong enough to hold against a full panel of interrogators. Kavyn anticipated watching them pry inside her. If he could not himself find a path inside her mind, a panel would be certain to find one. Such a thing had not been undertaken since the Consort's death.

Not that the panel had discovered anything useful then, since all of their energies had been so misdirected. And Kavyn had not been allowed to watch the proceedings, having been deemed too young to be exposed to such a thing. But, now . . . now he would be able to oversee every aspect of the panel's deconstruction of his dear sister's mental shields. If he managed things well, he would even be able to participate. Then all her locked doors would be open to him. He might actually manage to find the root of her power and find a way to place a drain. This would be a special treat, indeed.

CHAPTER FORTY-SIX

Milos struggled to choke down his anger and hurt. What had he expected? That she would fall into his arms? Yes, he had to admit, he had hoped for such a tender reunion. Although, in truth, Kira had never been prone to being so demonstrative. But her actions had always before been those of someone who cared. Had she not shared with him her secret abilities when she had kept that from all others, even Toril, whom she had thought she'd loved before him?

Small kindnesses. Shared secrets. Gentle words. Where had these things fled to?

He strode back to the compound. He would tell Marquon that he would finish the training as promised, but afterward, he would return to his own land, his own people.

"There are ships that come and go," Marquon told him around a mouthful of warm bread at table that evening. "But the schedule of ingress and egress is set

S. A. Skinner

by the Eilaren Council." He sat thoughtful for a moment, chewing his food. Then, he took a swig of dark red wine from the goblet that had been set before him and gazed directly at Milos as if assessing his worthiness before finishing. "And only the Seated One can lift the Veil."

A sudden shiver ran down Milos' spine. Until now, he had avoided drinking the spirits offered, but he reached for a goblet of his own and drank deeply. "This Veil, this thing the Guardian controls, can it change the weather?"

Marquon stared, seeming to take his measure. "It has some physical capabilities. And there is the Net, which keeps the coast safe from unwelcome ships." His words were slow and calculating. "But only an elemental innate, someone with power and skills beyond imagining would be able to use the power of the Veil so directly." He set his knife and fork down and placed his elbows on the board. "A Guardian that formidable has only ever been named in legend."

"But legends are always founded upon fact," Milos said. "Which suggests that at some point in your history, there was one of your race capable of such feats."

"There are many legends." Marquon shook his head. "And, yes, more often than not, there is fact beneath the tale. But our skilled blood grows thin. Our connection to that power has leeched from this land, like good soil runs off in a flooding rain."

"How many of your people can directly mindspeak?" Milos asked suddenly. "Not gain only the sense of the words, as you are able, but to communicate? And can it be done beyond a greater distance than across a room?"

Marquon shrugged. "Fewer now than in my father's time. Ten score, perhaps. Fewer than one in several hundreds of children born today. And not near that

231

many who can, as you say, communicate across a distance."

"How do you know that?"

Marquon reached for the platter of bread and tore off a hunk from a heavy grained loaf. "It is common knowledge among our people, though we are cautious of speaking openly about it."

"But how do you know? How is such a thing measured? Surely a tiny babe cannot speak inside another's mind without language. So, how is it you know how many children are born with such a gift."

"Of course we cannot tell when they are so young." Marquon smirked. "Children only begin to express their affinities as they age. Minor things manifest early, but the larger skills only take shape as they grow."

"When do your children come of age in a skill?"

Marquon's looked up at him. "Why do you ask all these questions?"

"I simply wish to understand," Milos said. "You owe me that much for my pledge. Do I need swear another oath to protect your secrets?"

"At the age of maturity." Marquon slathered his bread with butter. "Those who live long enough come into their full skills some time around a score of years, give or take a year or two."

Milos set down his cup. "Those who live long enough?"

Marquon grunted. "It is as if the island were cursed this past score of turns. Our most skilled men and women conceive, their children are born, but most do not survive more than a handful of turns." He pushed away his plate, his face declaring his loss of appetite.

"A disease that kills only children?" Milos felt his throat tighten, as if someone gripped him round the neck.

"Not always illness. Nor the same illness when it is." Marquon's shoulders slumped. "My nephew, my brother's only son, wandered off in the night. He fell from the heights above the bay." His eyes glistened and his jaw tightened. "He was only seven turns old. And an innate like the boy you saved."

"Solin," Milos said. "He is safe?"

"Yes, thanks to your intervention. For that we owe you a debt already. Although, we might not have become aware of you so soon had the encounter never happened. We would have lost yet another light. Luckily, too, we have friends in many places, or you would be facing the Council, and likely the interrogators now, instead of working with the Protectorate. Ancestors be praised for scant miracles. Yet, there is a darkness eating at us . . ." His face crumpled and he shoved his chair away from the table and rose. "Enough. I have said enough."

Milos watched him go, understanding the other man's need to be alone with his grief and pain. He recalled requiring the same sense of distance when his brother had died. Unlike the women of the Hold, he'd sought solace in silence and comfort in quietude. He sat at the table, sifting all that Marquon had said.

This once great race, with all their amazing abilities, truly was dying. Even without the loss of their skills, the loss of their children must be a terrible curse to live with. His rescue of Solin had been fortunate. Had he not been in the forest, the boy would surely have perished in the boar's attack. But how was it that children of such a tender age were able to wander off from home and hearth, to perish in such strange and terrible accidents? What could cause them to do so?

He thought again about his visit to Kira. Was this what had changed her heart toward him? This great sorrow that burdened her people must be a devastation to her. Not that she had ever claimed to find joy in children herself. Nay, her time with his niece and nephew had proven her awkwardness in that regard. The thought almost made him smile. But then he recalled his home and all he had given up, all he had left behind to join her in her journey to learn of her origins and her people. Devastating it might be, but such a pain as this was one he had once thought they would have shared. Instead, she rejected him.

So be it. He rose to go to his bed. He would finish what he had started here, make good his bargain. Then he would leave this sad, dying land and return to his life among the living in his own.

CHAPTER FORTY-SEVEN

Milos lay on his back in the practice grounds, his chest tight, and worked to suck in precious air. Marquon reached a hand out to help him up, but Milos waved him off as his lungs finally filled. "I have taught you all I know," he gasped. "You, and your followers." He gestured at the others who continued to spar in pairs. He pushed himself up to his knees hands on his thighs. Still panting, he lurched to his feet. "I seek your leave, now, to return to my own land."

Marquon arched a brow. "But what of the Matriarch's Heir?"

Milos bit back the bitter words that rested on the end of his tongue and shrugged. "She has returned to her home," he said. "I will do the same."

Marquon leaned forward and held the back of his hand against his forehead in the Eilaren sign of full respect. The clanging of swords and rapping of staves ceased, as all sparring stopped and the rest of

Marquon's people followed suit.

Milos stood still, not knowing for a moment how to respond, then he returned the salute.

"I would beg a boon of you," he said suddenly, thinking of Dahl and the captain and crew of the Sunfleet.

"Speak your desire. If it is within my command to grant, I will do so." Marquon nodded.

"I would have your aid in releasing the captain and crew of the ship that brought us, that brought me here."

"Release?" Marquon's brow wrinkled in confusion.

"Those who remain within the Veil." Milos grimaced. "If they still live."

Marquon smiled. "The Veil does not kill."

Milos shook his head. "But I was lost within it for days, without the ability to find food nor water."

Marquon regarded Milos kindly. "Nay," he said. "The Veil does not keep prisoners. It merely sends those who cross its path dreams until they are pushed back beyond it again."

"If it pushes them back out, then how came I here into your city?"

"That is a very good question, and one which I had not considered." Marquon looked thoughtful. "I will have to let you know, if I find the answer to that mystery."

"Will you help me to gather the sailors, then?" Milos let his determination color his words.

Marquon crossed his arms. "A passing ship will find them in time," he said, his voice flat.

"In time, some of them may die from hunger, or from the wounds they received in the wreck," Milos said, thinking of the man who had refused Kira's help because of her connection to these people. Prejudice appeared to flower on both sides of the water. But Marquon's people, those of the Protectorate, had accepted him, and seemed in many ways to have grown to trust and, he recalled the salutation of respect they had given him, to even honor him.

"These men came to your shores to bring me here." He did not add that they had also returned to these lands a long lost heir. Kira's new position seemed to be somewhat in question, yet. Which gave Milos a chill when he thought upon it. Politics, it seemed, played a role in every land, and she had made her choice. So, he tried not to let his mind wander there. Instead, he pointed his thoughts homeward. But he could not leave behind the crew of the Sunfleet to fend for themselves until another ship could rescue them. No. It was clear that might not happen for many moons. Besides, they were his countrymen and they deserved better than to be abandoned upon a foreign shore. "I will not leave them behind." He squared his shoulders.

"We have not the numbers to split our fighting force for such a venture. And we still have not solved the mystery of your ability to traverse the Veil unescorted. Who knows what anomaly took place the first time, or whether or not it will hold for you a second time?"

Milos bristled and opened his mouth to respond, but Marquon held up his hand.

"However, even without the ability to read your thoughts, I know you will not be satisfied until this is done." Marquon took a breath and raised his voice so that all could hear. "I will not let it be said that we dishonored our friendship by allowing you to attempt to traverse the Veil unaided. We will help you."

Milos relaxed.

"I will guide you myself," Marquon said.

There were murmurs among Marquon's followers and the tension in the room increased. "Marquon, we cannot allow you to go unaccompanied," Tesalin called out. "We do not know the welcome this Aestron sailing crew will offer."

Marquon shook his head. "We will go in force, to support those who may be stranded in our land while we serve as the new guardians of our shores, as the Protectorate of Eilar."

A chorus of cheers erupted from the women and men surrounding them. Most of whom, Milos recognized as those he had personally trained, but there were others now. Many others who had trickled in to join the militia, who came from all skills—warders, silent guards, stone smiths, element workers—who would work to protect their lands despite the possible repercussions that would likely take place once their government realized what was happening. Milos knew only too well how those in power felt about people taking action without their leave. Right or wrong.

CHAPTER FORTY-EIGHT

Kira stared out of the window, scanning the green-covered grounds and narrow river that led down to the sea.

"You must remain calm throughout the panel's questioning," Devira repeated, as if she thought Kira had not heard the first dozen times she'd said it.

"It is clear you have no great hope that I will undergo the panel successfully. Why do you continue to try to prepare me for a trial you are so certain I cannot pass?"

Devira's face fell, her normally placid mask disintegrating before Kira's eyes. "I do all I can to keep you from being broken." She touched Kira's cheek with the back of a misshapen hand. "There is in you so much of your father. I can see why she loved him." She gazed into Kira's face, blinking hard in the bright sunlight.

Kira reached up and took her fingers, gently wrapping them in her own pale hand. "The Matriarch. She did this to you, didn't she?"

Devira nodded, pulling her knotted fingers free and tucking her hands inside her apron pockets. "I was tending to her and she . . . lashed out."

"How could you continue to care for her after something like that?"

"How could I not?" Devira smiled sadly. "She was driven by grief, in need of healing." She shrugged. "The roles we play are not always the ones we dream of in life, but they are informed by every choice we make and every path we walk. Who we become, who we have been. If we turn our backs on who we are, who knows what danger we ourselves may become?"

Kira shivered, thinking of Toril and what he had become when he had turned away from the people. "That's not really an answer," she finally said.

"I took an oath and I honor it each and every day. I am a healer, with a duality of mind and body skills. One of the last of our people known to have the ability to walk both of those paths. And my family . . . my sister, Ardea . . . her actions are what drove our Matriarch beyond the bounds of sanity. I would not forsake her, nor my oath." She took out her hands and held them up before her. "No matter the cost."

Kira nodded. This, she understood. Oaths. Loyalty. Promises. She would face the interrogators, if only to prove to them she was not who they thought she was. That she would never do this thing they accused her of.

She only wished she could somehow find a way to tell Milos how she truly felt. It grieved her to know her rejection of him would be the last memory of her he would carry. But there was nothing to be done about it, now. Although she trusted Devira, she could not ask her to carry a message to Milos. It would only cause him more pain. Better that he think her disloyal and uncaring, then to have him attempt to rescue her. Or worse, avenge her.

Standing on the balcony, she linked with Vaith and Kelmir. She would not have them caught up in this. She turned her face from Devira so the Physica would not see her tears.

Go. Find Milos. Watch over one another.

CHAPTER FORTY-NINE

Marquon and Milos set off in the direction of the beach. The rest of the Protectorate would follow. Milos had suggested taking a smaller number, but Marquon had disagreed. There was no telling what might greet them on the beach.

So they left in groups of two to four, with the aim of reassembling far outside the citadel. As far as their intelligence went, the Council remained unaware of their doings. But it would not do to draw attention to themselves. Training an army against the wishes of the Council could be judged an act of treason.

They regrouped in the forest near a towering stone obelisk with a great crystalline orb set atop it. Milos had noted these stones when he had canvassed the forest outside the city, and had thought them merely boundary markers or remnants of a time when the city perhaps covered a larger area than the settlement now claimed. Looking closer, he saw now that the orb glowed in the sunlight, casting a prismatic halo of color that threw a shivering shadow on the ground around it.

Marquon laughed when Milos asked bout the odd markers. "Boundary markers. No. These are the Pillars of Eilar. One of them, at any rate." Marquon grimaced. "I share this with you only because you have sworn yourself to support and keep faith with the Protectorate." He grew serious. "And because I know your heart will not allow you to forswear that oath. The pillars channel the energies of Eilar. The Guardian's Seat may be the heart, the Matriarch the controlling force, but this is part of the machine that powers the Veil." He indicated the orb capped stone.

Milos stared at the structure. The stone was smoothed and polished, with fine-lined ornate carvings etched into the sides. The etchings appeared to ebb and flow, as if they were somehow alive, swirls and shapes that caused the eyes to blear when one tried too hard to focus on them. He reached out a hand to touch the stone surface, but Marquon stuck out his arm to prevent it. "No," the big man said. "I do not know what would happen should you actually touch one of the Pillars. Even if you are not harmed, our Matriarch would surely be disturbed. More than she is already." He frowned.

Milos nodded, but kept his hand raised, holding it close enough to feel the energy flowing from the pillar without actually touching it. His hand tingled, as if the shifting patterns flowed off the obelisk and onto his skin. His scalp fairly buzzed and hummed with it.

In the next moment, he was on his back, staring up into a worried face. The mouth of the face moved, but Milos could hear only the susurration of whispered chanting.

"Milos." He heard his name. For a moment, he

thought it was the whispering voice chanting it, but then the worried face—Marquon's face—moved closer and he heard the man calling his name.

He blinked.

"Praise the Ancestors." Marquon reached out a hand to him. "I told you not to touch it."

Milos sat up and grasped the Eilaren's forearm, allowing him to help him stand. "I didn't—"

Marquon shook his head. "Not only did you, but you practically became one with it." He gave Milos an awkward pat on the shoulder. "It was like a sudden gale slammed you up against it, but instead of screaming out and pushing yourself off, you reached around to embrace it." He paused in thought. "I've never seen anything like it. It looked like neither you, nor the Pillar, would let go." He glanced around at the people who had gathered while Milos had been overpowered by the obelisk. "We wondered what should be done," he said. "But before we could act, the hold released."

Milos nodded at the Pillar standing a dozen strides from where he had lain. "And that's how I landed on my back over here?" He swatted and brushed at himself to remove the dirt and leaves that clung to him.

"Release is much too light a word for what actually happened." Tesalin said. "It looked more like you were thrown by an angry stallion." Milos half-smiled at her description. He'd been thrown by a horse more than once in his lifetime. Oddly, though, he did not feel as if he'd been tossed almost a dozen strides to land upon his back. In contrast, he felt invigorated, alive even. Aside from the ringing in his ears, he felt better than he had in days. In fact, all of the bruises and soreness from his recent sparring bouts seemed to be miraculously cured. He hoped that was the case and not that he had fallen once more under the spell of the Veil. Or worse.

He shook his head clear of the ringing and focused on Marquon once more.

The Eilaren gazed at him in speculation. "There is something . . . not . . . quite the same about you." he said.

Milos smiled and gave his arms and chest a pat. "I feel the same as ever," he said. "Well, aside from this odd tingling."

"Just an odd tingling?" Marquon arched a single eyebrow. "The look on your face, especially the ridiculous smile, says otherwise."

Milos reached up and touched his face, he was indeed smiling. His flesh continued to hum as if a fine music played against him. He tried to frown, but the smile snapped back into place. He shrugged. "It is your strange magic," he told Marquon.

Marquon left it be and gathered his people. "We will soon approach a band of stranded men along the south eastern strand," he told them. "They may be fearful, angry, perhaps desperate." He fixed his gaze on Milos before continuing. "This is to be a peaceful meeting, if at all possible."

Milos stopped pushing his fingertips into his face. "I should go ahead of you," he said. "They know me."

"But from what you have said, they may not trust you," Tesalin said.

"Agreed." Milos couldn't argue with her comment, but he owed a debt to the captain if not his entire crew. And there was the ship's boy, Dahl. He would see him returned home to his family, if he could. "They may not trust me, but their captain has proven an ally, if not a friend. I hope to be able to speak to them without hostility, but an armed group of Eilarens stepping out onto the beach . . ." He left off.

Tesalin opened her mouth to respond, but Marquon

raised his hand and held it level with his chest, palm inward. She shrugged.

"Go," he told Milos. "Make your countrymen understand that we are here to help, and that though we come in peace, we are prepared to act, if necessary." He placed his hand on the pummel of the sword that hung at his side.

Such new-forged weapons were a fresh addition to the Protectorate's equipment. They were strong and well-made, and Milos hoped they would not have need of them.

CHAPTER FIFTY

The bright orb of the rising sun blushed the gardens in pinks and yellows. If not for what awaited Kira in the Interrogator's Hall, it might simply be another lovely day. She wondered how many people gazed out at this same pale blue sky but, unlike her, felt the joy of a new dawn, then shook her head. Feeling sorry for herself would do no one any good. Better she should go through the breathing courses again as Devira had instructed her. But her heart was heavy and her thoughts dashed about, seeking solace where there was none to be found.

She dressed in the gray robes that had been left for her by the attendants. They still refused to speak to her and the younger woman kept her distance, performing her duties quickly and nervously.

Kira's thoughts spun out of control even as she went through the breathing patterns. The robes she wore were made of several layers of thin fabric and tangled around her legs when she walked. Even though she had finally found a measure of comfort in wearing the wide legged pants and long blouses of the Eilaren, these robes made her feel vulnerable, a feeling she despised.

She huffed out her breath and, with a growl of frustration, flung open the wardrobe and dug beneath the pile of linens to pull out her trousers and leather vest. Her shirt had been worn threadbare and completely damaged in the shipwreck, so one of the draped blouses she had been given would have to make do.

She was dressed and feeling much calmer when Devira came for her. The Physica's look of surprise quickly melted, replaced by one of understanding. Though her tight lips refused to quirk up in any semblance of a smile, Kira thought she saw a hint of approval in the woman's face.

Not that it mattered.

Let them accuse her. Let them interrogate her. But let them do it on her terms. She would come before them, not as their Matriarch's lost heir, the cause of so much sorrow, but as who she truly was.

She walked beside Devira, barely noticing which turns they took, or how many flights of stairs they climbed. They must be high above the city by now, she thought. Nearly as high as the Guardian's Tower.

They finally stopped before a plain door of solid wood set on heavy iron hinges.

"I must take my leave, now," Devira said. She placed a knotted hand on each of Kira's shoulders and touched her forehead to Kira's. "Ancestors guide you."

Kira shut her eyes a moment, letting Devira's calming energy seep into her. "Thank you for your kindness."

The heavy door swung open and Devira let her go. "I have done my duty in delivering you here, but I will not participate in this. No matter the law." She turned and strode briskly down the hallway.

Kira paused in the open doorway and stared in.

The interrogators sat upon a dais behind a stone table that curved inward like a crescent moon. All wore white robes lined with scarlet, their faces hidden within heavy hoods. Below them, within the arms of the table sat a wooden chair with a high back and square arms.

Behind the chair rose a low gallery filled with spectators, many of whom Kira recognized as the men and women she had seen in the council chambers. The councilors were seated in the highest row, farthest from the interrogation floor. The lower rows contained mostly strangers, though the glaring faces of Kira's attendants also stared out at her.

Beside her, a woman in long robes like the ones they had tried to dress her in, ushered her forward.

As Kira approached the chair, she realized what had at first appeared to be twisted carving in its arms were long scratches. She shivered as she stood before the chair, daring not think what might have caused them.

Upon the dais, the hooded figures faced her. "Sit," someone said. The voice was soft and low, but it grated at the edge of her senses and caused the hair to stand on her neck.

She was tempted to refuse, but the voice though soft was commanding.

Her hands twitched as she sat down. The deep scoring in the wood scraped against her palms. She folded her hands in her lap.

Behind her, she sensed anticipation and a hint of dismay. Perhaps, Devira was not the only one who held misgivings about this form of trial. Not that common opinion was swayed in her favor.

Kira continued to sit up straight in the chair, shoulders squared and head up. Her breathing had fallen into the rhythm Devira had drilled her on. Long steady inhalations followed by a slight pause and a slow, controlled exhalation, repeated over and over as she waited.

It seemed an eon before anything happened. Then, from a door to her left, Kavyn entered. He, too, wore the gray robes like those she had refused. His step was confident, almost happy. He turned his face to her, his mouth quirked up on one side—in a snide wyvern-caught-the-coney smile—and her breath caught in her throat as she realized her brother would be a part of this process.

She forced herself to resume the breathing pattern. *In. Pause. Out. In. Pause. Out.*

Kavyn strode forward and formally saluted the panel, placing the backs of both hands against his forehead as he bowed toward them. They nodded eerily in unison, their movements so precisely matched, it sent another shiver through Kira. She focused on her breathing, finally feeling the calming effects of the meditative pattern take over. Her fingertips and toes began to tingle, her muscles relaxing. A part of her tried to fight it. This was not her way. She had been trained by Toril to be prepared for violence when confronted, to be ready to duck or fight. He had always preferred the fight.

She breathed more deeply and let herself relax further.

"Alyana, Daughter of the Guardians, Matriarchess of Eilar," Kavyn intoned, "you are charged with tampering before this panel and the members of the Eilaren Council. Will you admit your wrongdoing and save yourself from interrogation?"

Kira could not admit to something she had not done. Nor, she knew, would doing so save her. She finished the pattern at a pause to answer as Devira had instructed her. "I have done no wrong."

Kavyn quirked an eyebrow as she resumed her breathing.

"Will you admit your wrongdoing and save yourself from interrogation?" He asked a second time.

"I have done no wrong." Kira repeated her response as required.

"Will you admit your wrongdoing and save yourself from interrogation?" He asked a third and final time, his voice rising in volume.

"I have done no wrong." Kira was surprised at the lack of emotion in her voice as the words of the ritual response rang out through the otherwise quiet room.

Kavyn turned to face the interrogators. "Thrice supplied. You have your answer."

"As we have ever gathered to protect the Eilar," the interrogators intoned as one, "we are gathered now to seek the truth." The shadowed hoods turned as one to face Kira

Malice glinted in her brother's eyes. "All will be revealed." He backed toward the gallery.

A heavy weight pressed in upon her. The air around her grew thick, but she kept up the pattern. Her deep breathing became more difficult, as if the air were solidifying.

I have done no wrong. I have done no wrong. She repeated the thought, again and again, like a mantra as the edges of her vision blurred and the chamber closed in on her. A searing pain struck between her eyes and she gasped. But she recalled her instructions and picked up her breathing once more. Lights flared in her vision. Memories began to churn unbidden.

Kira gritted her teeth against the pain. She struggled to keep to the pattern. Tried not to fight. Tried to let them sift her thoughts without blocking them. It felt as if animals clawed their way inside her head, scratching at her brain, digging through her thoughts, her memories, her most private moments of anger, sorrow, joy.

Milos was suddenly beside her as they rode out from Tem Hold and all the happiness and trepidation she had felt in that moment came rushing back.

Just as suddenly, she found herself inside a darkened tent and Toril was there, his eyes reflecting the firelight, but there was something wrong with his face. It twisted and stretched at odd angles. Then it was her brother's face she saw. Kavyn's fists raised against her. Kavyn's fist's striking. Striking. Striking. Again and again until she screamed.

"NO!" she shouted, rising from the chair, her hands clenched until her nails bit into her palms. "NO!" A fierce wind rushed off her, pushing against the building pressure. "NO!" The interrogators fell back, hands clasping heads. Chairs scraped against the dais with a screech. The arced table shattered and crashed into a heap of kindling.

The spectators and councilors in the gallery gasped in alarm and surprise.

"Stop!" Kavyn shouted. "It isn't possible." He ran toward her, his hand raised to strike her down and slammed into an invisible wall.

A group of warders rushed forward and a gray mist enveloped her. Instinct told her to lash out, but she feared what terrible powers she might unleash, what further harm she might cause. She dropped her guard and let them take her.

CHAPTER FIFTY-ONE

Milos stepped out of the tangled forest and onto the beach where he paused to assess his surroundings. The scene had not changed much since he and Kira had left, who knew how long ago. The sailors had managed to gather up broken pieces of timber and some remnants from the ship's cargo, along with barrels and crates containing rescued foodstuffs. The flotsam and jetsam of the wreckage had been used to build crude shelters and lean-tos. A pile of debris and deadfall had been stacked above the tide line, ready to be lit as a signal fire at the first sign of a passing ship.

The members of the ship's crew Milos could see were in a sorry state. He scanned their faces, searching for the captain. "Ahoy! On deck, boys!" one of the sailors shouted, his voice a warning growl.

In a moment, wary men filled the strand, each holding a weapon or tool, rock or branch. They did not rush him, but stood their ground, clearly waiting to see what he would do. Their fear and anger was so strong, Milos could sense it roiling off them. His skin no longer tingled. Now, it prickled with tension.

He showed them his hands, raising them to shoulder height, palms outward to show they were empty. His sword remained buckled at his waist. He hoped he would not have to unsheathe it.

He stepped forward, walking slowly across the sand, hands still raised. "I seek a word with Captain Salhker," he called.

The men spoke among themselves.

"The Captain is . . . indisposed," a sailor shouted back. "He has taken fever and barely knows his own name nor sun-up from sun-down." The broad shouldered man strode forward, a long pike-like weapon held in both hands. "I have charge of this crew now, so you'll speak to me. If speech is what you are truly after." He sneered as if he had made a nasty joke. Some of the other men shuffled their feet nervously, as if preparing to move.

Milos stared a moment before recognizing the remade gaff and the First Mate wielding it; a surly man who had not taken kindly to Kira and her companions coming aboard the Sunfleet.

Milos wished to stave off a fight. These sea-hardened men might not carry true weapons, but even so, if they clashed with the trained members of the Eilaren Protectorate, there would be bloodshed. Far too much bloodshed. And Milos intended to save both sides from injury, if he could.

"I am leaving this land," Milos told them. "I wish to return home and have been promised safe passage aboard an outgoing ship. I would take you with me."

"Hah!" The First Mate tossed his weapon from hand to hand. "We would gladly return home, but . . ." He turned and waved an arm at the open sea. "Do you see a ship?" He turned to the rest of the crew. "I don't see a ship, do you boys?"

Milos started to speak but the First Mate cut him off.

"Nay," he growled. "There's naught but shattered pieces of our home and livelihood." He gripped the length of his weapon in both hands. "And for some, not e'en that." He plunged the point of the reworked gaff in the direction of two piles of stones.

Cairns.

Milos felt his mouth go dry.

"Nor do we wish to wander lost in dreams of home, only to find we are still stranded in a hostile land." He waved his weapon at the forest.

Milos stepped closer, but the tension in the First Mate's stance told him to stop.

"So, what is it you think you have to offer us?" The First Mate snarled. "And how is it you come from that damnable forest unscathed, and looking well-fed and clean dressed e'en? All else who've managed to wander back out of that infernal place, returned dazed and scratched and worse for wear."

Milos nodded. "I understand your fear—" he began.

"You understand nothing!" shouted one of the men.

"What magics are you under that you return so many days after the rest?"

"And where is the demon?"

For a moment, Milos found himself at a loss.

"Aye," said another. "Where is the red-haired witch? The one who led us here in the first place. What other torments has she in store for us?"

Milos bristled, but kept his tongue in check. "Kira is not with me," he said, "nor is she a demon. These people . . . I admit their ways are strange to us, but . . ." He paused gathering his thoughts, sifting his own feelings of betrayal and newfound friendship. "We need not fear them," he said finally, realizing it was true. "No more than we need fear our own people. There may be good and bad among them, but just as it is with our own kind, some are loyal and worthy of trust."

"They've broken ya. It was only a matter of time before the witch took control of your wits as well as your manhood." There was ugly laughter at this, and one man spat on the ground at his feet, but most of the sailors merely looked angry.

Milos' jaw tightened. Kira truly had stolen his heart, but she had not taken his manhood, nor had she ever attempted to turn his mind. They agreed on many things, and on those they did not, they either tried to discuss the subject openly, or agreed to avoid it. Or had. All this, he reminded himself, was now relegated to his past. His future was before him, and for the time being, these men were a part of that.

"I will not discuss her with you," he told them in a stern voice. "And I will not force you to join with me in taking a ship from the southern port. I only felt it my duty to offer. And that I have done. If any wish to join me, come. If not, I leave you to your signal fire. And your cairns." The last comment was too much and he knew it, but he could no longer keep his anger in check. These men acted as if their loss was the only hurt suffered in this venture. Milos could not resist taking a final jab at them out of his pain.

The First Mate began to run at him, hoisting his arm back to throw his harpoon-like weapon.

Milos grabbed the hilt of his sword and prepared to dodge. He raised his blade into the air, attempting to quell the men, to stop things before they were out of hand, but before he could, Marquon and his Protectorates stepped out of the forest and onto the edge of the sandy beach, weapons drawn.

"So, this is the way of it," snarled the First Mate. "You brought your friends to ambush us."

The sailors shouted out as they ran forward to meet the Eilaren. The men and women of the Protectorate stood their ground, as Milos had taught them, saving their energy for the melee.

The clash of weapons and shouts of men caused Milos to shudder. His memories reeled back to a battle like this, not long enough ago.

And then a shout went up. A high-pitched shout from the ship's boy, Dahl, "A ship! Gray sails! The Outlanders come!"

All fighting stopped as the sailors and Eilaren stared out to sea and the approach of their mutual enemy.

CHAPTER FIFTY-TWO

Kavyn rushed from the Interrogator's Hall, stripping off the ritual robes and dropping them on the floor behind him. He wiped the blood from his cheek where a flying fragment of the table had left a deep gash, nearly missing his eye, and cursed.

He'd been surprised to see his sister in the clothing of the Aestrons. She was more daring and devious than he had given her credit for. And clearly much more capable. She would have made a worthy opponent, had he the time to continue to play. But her display of power had caused too much of a stir.

Had he known what she was capable of, he might not have interfered as he had. But if the panel had pierced her mental guards, they would have discovered her lack of guilt, might even have pieced together Kavyn's secret, and he couldn't allow that to happen. They needed to be convinced that Alyana was a danger to them, to all of Eilar.

He'd intended to get inside her mind before the interrogators could, but she'd been too strong. And better trained than he had anticipated.

Too bad none of the interrogators had been crippled in the energy burst she had caused. That would have ensured her a place in the deepest blockaded cell. Instead, there would be some on the Council still considering her as a potential replacement for the Matriarch. Some who would think the power she held worth the risks. Kavyn could not allow that.

He rushed into his rooms and slammed the door behind him, throwing the lock into place. He would have to set his other plans in motion earlier than he'd intended, but there was nothing to be done about it now. The sensing stones he'd sent would show when he'd managed to make his play. All his plans could come to nothing, if his allies were not in place and ready to strike. But he could afford to wait no longer.

He levered his heavy bed away from the wall and pushed aside the thick tapestry. His fingers slid down the ornate wood panels until he found the nearly indiscernible indents that precisely matched his fingertips and pushed. A quiet snick was all that suggested anything had happened, but Kavyn grinned. He reached down and pulled on the bas-relief of the bottom-most panel, sliding it out from the wall to reveal his most prized possession. The one thing even his mentor had never guessed at. A focusing crystal. A small, yet powerful version of the Guardian's Seat. Anticipation quickened his blood. He longed for the exhilaration of the touchstone's power. Not since that first time he had melded with the stone had this small taste been enough. He needed to sit in that seat, to feel the lifeblood of the realm and all its crystals connected, thrumming for him and him alone.

The touchstone had cost him. And it had taken years of research to discover the secrets of its making thought to have been lost for so many generations. Lost. But not to one who could soar across mental guards as Kavyn could. He had sifted and dug through so many thoughts and memories seeking those bits of knowledge that had been left behind. Tiny breadcrumbs that seemed like nothing until he had pieced them all together.

Killing the artisan who had created it for him had been an unfortunate necessity. He would have liked to have forced the man to create another, larger version. But the fool had decried the work. Had even suggested that something in the stone had been wrong, that Kavyn's design had been horribly flawed. He'd refused to attempt another, and Kavyn sensed the guilt inside the man. The sort of guilt that could drive a person to confess what he had done. Kavyn could not risk having anyone discover what had been wrought. He would never share this rediscovery with anyone.

No. Only he was capable of controlling the touchstone.

He reached out for the stone, his fingers shaking slightly before gripping it tightly. The shock nearly threw him to the floor. Every muscle in his body tensed as he absorbed the surge of energy, but he hung on. Hung on and laughed as his awareness expanded, exploding across space and time.

CHAPTER FIFTY-THREE

Milos gazed out at the tall-masted ship as beyond it there rose another set of sails, and then another. He expected to see the ship turn toward the rocks, the winds and water to shift and roil. But the sea remained calm and the ships showed no sign of slowing. The Outland Raider plowed straight toward them, gray sails billowing in the steady wind.

"Where is the storm?" called a voice from the line of trees. "Where is the Guardian's Net?"

"We must retreat to the Veil!" called Tesalin. "We are too few. We cannot fight against two enemies at once."

"No," Milos shouted. "We cannot abandon these men here. They will be outnumbered and slaughtered."

"We can bring them with us," Marquon said.

"There is no time to make the necessary parting in the Veil," another said. "They will be lost in the dream, rendered unconscious."

"Let them. The raiders too will be lost," someone said.

261

"Nay." One of the sailors spat. "We'll not go willingly into that nightmare, again."

Marquon frowned. "Then we must strike a truce to fight alongside one another."

The sailors glanced at each other, anger and fear casting doubt in their minds.

Milos called out to them. "Each and every one of you knows of the heartless nature of the Outland raiders, how when they came to our shores they struck at village and field, Hold and farm alike. None were safe from their barbaric wrath. Men. Women. Children. The raiders slew all, with no regard to life."

Every crewmember had lost someone in the Outland raids, and the war that had raged for years. Men nodded and gripped their weapons.

The ship's First Mate cursed. "Truce, then," he shouted for all to hear. "Until we clear the Outland threat. Afterward . . ." He shook a fist in Milos' direction.

Milos and Marquon nodded. "Truce then." They strode over to the First Mate and extended the backs of their hands to seal the agreement. After a moment's hesitation, he acquiesced and made the bargain, his lip curled up in a disgusted sneer.

"Now," Milos said. "What do you suggest we do to stop them from landing?"

"If the Guardian's Net does not catch them, there is nothing we can do to keep them from our shore," Marquon grumbled. "I only hope it was not your dance with the Pillar that downed that safeguard. Our people are failing, our Guardian is failing, and now our protections are failing. This is why we formed the Protectorate, for such an eventuality as this." He pointed his weapon at the Outlander ships. "An eventuality we had truly hoped not to see take place. And for certain not so soon."

Milos empathized with this man. A man who would lead his people's defense, all the while wishing he had no need to do so. "You keep saying the Guardian is failing," he said suddenly. "What does that mean?"

Marquon gave him a hard look. "It means, my friend, that had you chosen to remain here rather than return to your own land, you could shortly be our land's next Consort." His face turned hard as he glanced back out to sea, where one of the ships had turned aside. "If we have any land left after today."

For a moment Milos thought the ships might pass the island kingdom by, but the lead vessel swung about and maneuvered close to shore and dropped anchor.

The men on shore watched expectantly. No boats were lowered from the ships. Yet, there appeared to be a great deal of activity taking place. A score of men swarmed around a tall structure that jutted up from the ship's afterdeck.

Then, with a loud thwack, a long arm swung toward shore, releasing a smoking object into the air.

"Catapults and war fire!" Milos shouted. "Drop back to the trees."

The fiery missile arced in a high trajectory, flying toward the shore. The burning mass of pitch and oil fell short, hitting the water with an audible hiss.

Eilaren and Aestrons alike retreated to the edge of the forest and spread themselves along the tree line, staying within sight of the shore.

The ship carrying the catapult continued to fire flaming missiles at the shore. A spreading mass fell onto the makeshift encampment. Dried driftwood and rescued timbers whooshed into flame.

"The Cap'n!" Dahl shouted, pointing at a smoking lean-to at the far end of the beach. "He'll be burned alive!" He scrambled along the shore, running toward the flaming structure.

"Dahl, no!" Milos tore after him. The catapult crew sent missiles crawling further and further up the beach toward the forest and Milos had to duck and dodge flying clumps of burning pitch.

Flames already licked at the lean-to when Milos caught up to Dahl.

"Captain! Captain Salhker!" Dahl shouted, shielding his face from the heat and flames.

"Stand back." Milos caught the boy by the shoulder and yanked him away. He dropped his sword and peered into the rickety structure.

The ship's captain lay inside, his breathing shallow and ragged, and a sour stench rolled out, mixing with the bitter smell of burning oil and wood. Heat bit at Milos and he choked on the dark smoke that billowed all around. He coughed and pulled his shirt up over his face, but it did no good. The smoke and heat clawed at him as he dove inside the rough shelter and grabbed the captain by the shoulders, dragging him outside just as the lean-to collapsed in a blaze. Cinders scorched the bottoms of the unconscious man's trousers and Milos rushed to brush them away.

More fire fell from the sky as Milos tried to hoist the big man onto his shoulders, but the captain's weight was suddenly lifted from him by two ragged men.

"We got 'im now," said the cook's mate, as he and the other man carried their captain up the sand and into the trees.

"Thank you," Dahl said, gazing worriedly after them.

Milos nodded. "Go on."

The boy hesitated only a moment before scurrying after the men.

Milos hurried back to where the Eilaren Protectorate hovered in wait. Meanwhile, the other dark ships had dropped anchor and prepared to offload their deadly cargo.

Marquon waved to one of his men and the slender young Eilaren jogged over. "If the Net has failed," he told him, "we must know the condition of the Veil. If it yet holds, find a Mist Walker to create a pathway through for our allies."

The boy gave a curt nod and turned to go, but Marquon gripped him by the shoulder. "Either way, the Council must be informed of what is happening." The young man blanched.

"Find Kalt and have him make the report. They will still not like to hear it, but they will at least believe it from him. And your mother will not have to know from whence this information came." Marquon patted his shoulder. "Now, go. Quickly."

The youth took off at a run, diving in under the trees at full speed. The slap of leaf and branch faded as he passed further away from them.

"He's a quick lad." Milos gave Marquon a knowing look.

Marquon's mouth drew down into a tight line. "My sister's eldest." He sighed. "I'd not have him with us in a pitched battle."

Milos placed the back of his hand to his forehead and leaned forward. "You're a good man, and a good uncle," he told him.

Marquon frowned. "If I truly were a good uncle, as you say, I would not have allowed him to join the Protectorate to begin with. Though, I know not how I could have kept him from it." He stared down at his hands. "His mother does not know. We swore one another to secrecy on the matter. She will make me burn for it, should she find out. She'll do far worse, if anything happens to the boy."

"Let us do our best then to ensure she has no need to know." A fiery missile crashed onto the beach only a few strides from them, splattering oily flames, ending all talk. Milos and Marquon dove into the trees.

Milos stared out at the sea. The ships had launched their away boats and begun ferrying the raiders to shore. The war fire ship would soon have to let up to avoid burning their own men, and then the close fighting would begin.

Were they so certain of their fierceness and war skills, they prepared to attack the island with a mere three ships? It had not been so when they had come to Aestron. They had come in force, clearly planning to conquer the unsuspecting villages and Holdings by sheer force of their overpowering numbers. Had it not been for the fierce rallying of men . . . He let that thought trail off. Following it only led him back full circle.

"Marquon," Milos said suddenly. "When the Guardian's Net is in place, where do ships normally make landfall?"

Marquon thought about the question before answering. "There are two ports used for trade, where the Guardian's Net is not employed. The largest at the south-eastern shore of the Citadel. The rest of the coast is, or was, protected. Why do you ask?"

"Do you not think it odd that only three ships have come to attack a land this size, and then without hesitation or sending out a scouting ship, choose to land on a shore that would normally be protected by such a safeguard?"

Marquon's brow furrowed in thought. "You are making a point, but one that I am unable to grasp."

Milos hesitated. What if he was wrong? Finally, he spoke. "Either they expected the Net to be inactive," he said, "or there are also ships heading for your open ports. Or both."

Marquon's face hardened. "I need to send another runner," he said between clenched teeth.

CHAPTER FIFTY-FOUR

"Such force," Zoshia said again, flinching as Devira dabbed at her forearm where the bits of debris had struck her when she'd raised her arm to cover her face. "Nothing we have seen these many generations . . . " She seemed unable to wrap her thinking around the display of power that had erupted in the Interrogator's Hall.

Had Devira not seen the devastation for herself, she would not have believed such a thing were possible. Not in this day and age. None had exhibited such power in generations. The light of hope warmed her heart and she felt herself smile.

Zoshia sat up suddenly. "Why did you not warn me?" she snapped.

Devira gaped at her lifemate in exasperation, and reached for her arm. "I didn't know," she said flatly, dabbing again at Zoshia's wounds. They were not deep, but Devira had had to remove a number of stonewood splinters from her arm, and the bleeding had not yet stopped.

"How could you not have seen this in the girl?" Zoshia asked in disbelief. "You worked with her. You delved inside her mind."

"I told you, there were . . . barriers . . . unlike anything I have seen before. And I could find nothing in any of the archives." She folded a clean cloth around Zoshia's arm. "Hold this in place while I wrap it."

Zoshia shook her head, but placed her fingers on the edges of the bandage. "I fear the answer to your prayers has turned out to be the doom of our people. A doom we cannot even fathom."

"Now, who is being dramatic?" Devira said, but she was afraid that Zoshia might be right. The girl would make a formidable Guardian, but would the Council allow such a dangerous mind upon the Seat? And if an entire panel could not control her mental energy, what drastic measures might they take to stop her from being a threat if she chose a darker path?

She tied off the bandage and Zoshia let out a hiss. "Gently."

"It needs to be snug."

"It need not cut off the flow of blood to my hand." Zoshia pulled her arm away.

Devira sat back, startled at the anger in her lifemate's voice. "Zosh—"

Zoshia stood abruptly. "I need to return to the Council Chamber. We have much to discuss."

"Why are you so angry?"

"I'm not angry, I'm . . . defeated and . . . disappointed."

Confusion and hurt twined around Devira and her scarred hands shook. "You're blaming me."

"I'm not blaming you," Zoshia hissed.

"Yes, you are." She held up a hand to ward off her

partner's rising ire. "I'm not prying. Your feelings are so strong, I can sense them without even trying." She stood so she could look Zoshia in the eye. "I did all that I could, without breaking my oath, both for Eilar and for the girl." Oaths, she should have said. Her Physic's oath and the one made so long ago as a loving sister.

"You should have done more." Zoshia's voice rose. "You should have used your skills to spare us all from your family's curse!"

Devira stepped back, the words stinging as if she'd been slapped. "Is that what you think? That we are—that I am a curse to you?" She hugged her hands into her body. "No wonder you made me promise to stay outside your mind."

"Devi." Zoshia took a step toward her. "I didn't mean—"

But Devira didn't stay to listen. She let the slamming of the door behind her be her voice.

CHAPTER FIFTY-FIVE

Kira awoke with a start.

The room was dark and . . . small. She sat up and glanced around. She was in a small mean cell, somewhat like the one she had found herself in when she first arrived in the Guardian's Citadel. But this room felt odd. Cloistered, as if the walls were lined with thick layers of straw. She relaxed her mental shield and heard . . . nothing. No buzz of whispering voices. No distant emotional outbursts. Only silence.

For a moment, it seemed a relief. Then she realized she was completely cut off. She reached for Vaith and Kelmir and the weight of loss hit her like an avalanche. No! She had only just reconnected with them.

She scrabbled for a break in the wall between her and Vaith, frantically searched the blackness for the dark velvet of Kelmir's thoughts. If she could just break through to them. She strained until her head ached and tears ran down her face.

Panic thrust a fist into her stomach and a keening cry rose up inside her. Before she could release it into the world, the door swung wide and a slash of blinding light fell on her. A figure stood silhouetted in the doorway, flanked by two sturdy guards. Kira shielded her eyes, trying to make out the face of the person who stepped quickly inside the room.

"Privacy," the visitor said and the door swung shut, the lock clicking.

"Devira?" Kira's voice cracked.

"Yes," the Physica said.

"What's happened? Where am I?"

"Hush," Devira said. "Give me a moment to shed some light."

There was a sudden flash and Kira flinched, blinking as her eyes adjusted to the brightness.

"My apologies." Devira closed her fingers around the glow stone in her hand and the light faded, glowing red where it seeped through her twisted fingers. The Physica moved closer to Kira and held the light near her face. "You've caused quite a stir." She eased herself down onto the bed beside Kira.

"I'm so sorry," Kira said. "I didn't mean . . . is everyone all right?"

"Minor injuries, for the most part. Although, the stonewood interrogator's table will never be the same." She gave Kira a sad smile. "Just as well. Such old practices do not become us. We might just as soon burn our people at the stake, as others once did."

"Devira," Kira said. "I've lost my . . . sensing."

"Nay, child. It's merely the effects of the damping stones in the walls here. No mental energy can penetrate these cell walls in or out."

"Is that why I can't . . ." Kira swallowed. She wanted to trust this woman fully, but she had been trained for so long to keep quiet about Vaith and Kelmir.

"Ssshhhh," Devira reached out and placed the back of her hand against Kira's temple. *I am here with you.*

Kira heard the words inside her mind and felt comforted.

She leaned into the older woman's touch. *Thank you. I want you to know, I remember. Everything.*

Devira did not flinch nor move away from her. *Good, but you need not tell me, if you do not wish to.*

In a rush, Kira let go of all her secrets, spilling her memories, giving it all to the Physica. All, but her intimate moments with Milos. Those memories, she kept to herself, holding tight to them.

Devira took it all in. A wave of sadness spreading out from her as she saw everything, all of Kira's memories. From the death of Kira's father beside the river, to the death of the woman Kira had known as her mother at the hands of the Outlanders.

Kira left out nothing. Not her affinity to animals, her connection to her companions, not her love of Milos. When she was done, she felt lighter. Unburdened of so much.

"Thank you," Devira said, her voice thick with emotion. "Thank you for your trust. And for returning my sister to me." She let her hand fall to her side.

"What will happen now?" Kira asked.

"I cannot say." Devira shrugged. "The memories you have shared prove to me that you did nothing to Keliss, but I saw nothing that either proves nor disproves that you were responsible for what happened in the Interrogator's Hall. Though, it was not done purposefully, it has created an air of fear. And there is still the problem of what happened to Keliss. And who is responsible." She rubbed at her temples. "Not to mention that I may not be believed and you would have to share your memories at the very least with the First Councilor."

Kira shook her head. "No."

"Why not?"

"Because we have no way of knowing who was involved in my father's murder."

"You aren't suggesting the First could have had anything to do with that?"

"How can you be certain he didn't?"

"There is nothing that would give him cause to do such a thing. Nothing to be gained by it. Not for him."

"Then who?" Kira stopped short. "What happened to Keliss . . . I know I did not cause that, so who did?"

CHAPTER FIFTY-SIX

"Step aside," Devira ordered the guards. "I need to take Matriarchess Alyana to the First."

The guards stiffened. "From what I hear, she's no longer the Matriarchess, and we are under orders to keep her here," the woman said.

Kira stood behind the Physica just inside the doorway of her cell and peered out, her nerves knotted and jumbled.

"You know me," Devira said. "Noan," she called the man by name. "How is your son? Has his collar bone mended well?"

He pursed his lips together and nodded. "Very well, thank you, Physica," he mumbled. "His mam says—"

"We have orders," the woman cut him off, bristling at Kira who had edged into the doorway.

Noan looked at Devira and shrugged an apology.

Devira regarded the woman. "Still angry at me for putting you on light duty last moon, I see."

The woman frowned. "I was fine."

"You were weak from eating that—"

"Don't." The guard said, a warning in her voice.

"As you wish." Devira touched her hand to her forehead. "But I do need to take the Matriarchess to the First."

The woman scowled and Noan, despite looking as though it pained him a great deal to stand against the Physica, barred the way.

A tremor ran through the keep and a sudden dizziness overcame Kira. The world seemed to lurch sideways and she gripped the wall to keep herself from toppling over. "Something has happened."

The guards glanced at one another and then at the Physica.

Devira was silent. Her face was ashen and she shivered, as if an icy wind had suddenly found her. "She fails." Devira's words, barely audible, were formed of breath and pain.

Kira steadied herself. "The Matriarch?"

Devira nodded, her face grim.

Kira stormed out of the room and ran at the two muscular guards. They made a move to bar her way, but Kira refused to stop and they gave way to her, stumbling aside as if pushed. She didn't have time to worry about it as the noise of hundreds of minds crashed in on her almost crushing her before she could put her mental guards in place.

Head pounding, she rushed down the passageway and leaped up the stone stairs, running for the Guardian's Hall without waiting to see if the Physica followed.

If the Matriarch fell, all would be lost.

Once on the main level, she recalled the twists and turns from her first visit to the Guardian's Tower. She ran, feet flying, focused only on taking first one turn and then another before rushing up another flight of stairs.

Devira followed as best she could, but Kira sped up and the Physica soon dropped behind. The foreboding sense of urgency pushed Kira onward and upward toward the Guardian's Tower and the Matriarch.

The halls at this hour were nearly empty, and the few people she passed made way for her. Some appeared fearful and backed against the walls to stay well out of her way. Several glowered at her with outright anger, but no one attempted to stop her rushing through the keep as if a wild animal chased after her. No doubt, they had heard about the fiasco of the interrogation.

Kira still could not make sense of what had happened, but she had no time to worry about it. She needed to discover what had befallen her mother. Kavyn could be up to anything at this point. And she feared what that could mean for the Matriarch.

She sighted the door to the Guardian's Chamber and slowed to a cautious walk. The room, when she reached it, stood silent and dark, as if every illuminated crystal and glowstone had been sucked dry of all its energy. The great door was ajar, deep shadows shifted within. It was as if a blanket of dark wool covered everything.

Kira stepped inside the doorway and peered in.

The Guardian's room held but a soft glow from the huge hearth, the fire having died low. The windows were shuttered, afternoon light barely edging the slats. Within the shadows, a dark shape loomed upon the dais. Kira approached the ornately carved chair, feeling naked without any kind of weapon. "Matriarch," she whispered, reaching out to the hunched figure. "Mother?"

A nearby torch flared to life, casting long shadows across the floor, and the figure in the chair shifted. A low rumble of laughter echoed around the room.

"State your business," a voice called out to her. But before Kira could answer, her brother stepped from the shadows.

Kira froze. A cold prickling wrapped around her. "Kavyn. What are you doing here?"

Kavyn took another step forward. "I think the better questions is, what, dear sister, are you doing here?"

"My business is with the Matriarch." Kira fought the urge to back up.

"Ah, but your business is no longer important," he said. "However, mine is."

He flicked his wrist and the Matriarch's arm jerked. He rolled his head and the Matriarch's head rolled.

Kira gasped. "You're manipulating her."

Kavyn made a pout. "Oh, yes. Someone had to take control of things. After all, our dear mother seems a bit lost in the fog."

"How long . . . ?" Kira started toward him, hands clenched into fists.

"Ah, ah, ah," Kavyn warned. "You wouldn't want our dear mother to throw herself out a window, would you?" The Matriarch's body spasmed and rose from the Guardian's Seat in awkward jerking motions.

"Kavyn, please." Kira reached out to her brother.

"So sorry about Mother not recognizing you," Kavyn continued, "but we couldn't have another heir getting in the way. Especially, not after you began to regain your memories." He turned to look at her and the Matriarch's head swiveled in Kira's direction.

"You were to blame for that, as well?" Kira asked, sensing Kavyn's mind probing at her shields.

"Not at first," he told her, "but when Teraxin lost his hold, someone had to take control and show the old fool how things should be done." He sneered at her, his left hand balled into a tight fist. "No one has the power and skill that I do. Imagine Teraxin's surprise when I sent him into his own dark hole." He frowned. "What I don't understand is how you managed to learn to guard against me so rapidly."

It was Kira's turn to gloat. "You underestimated the abilities of my mentors." The pendant lay heavy against her skin, but she refused the urge to touch it. There was no point in giving away anything to her brother.

Out in the corridor, running footsteps slapped against the stone.

Kavyn's attention was drawn to them as Devira rushed into the room. The Physica's breath came in panting gasps as she rushed toward the Matriarch.

With sudden fierceness, Kira pushed her thoughts against Kavyn's guard, and for a moment felt as if she would break through, but she was snapped back with such force that her skull ached as if it had been slammed into a rock wall.

She hissed in pain as her brother's laughter broke through the pounding of her head.

Like swatting a pesky gnat.

Devira reached the Matriarch, but stopped short, screaming in pain. She held her hands out before her, her fingers curling into tight fists. "No," she snarled, teeth gritted with the effort. "I'll not relive the past." She turned to glare at Kavyn.

"Very well," he said, placing his left fist against his forehead and squeezing his eyes shut.

The Matriarch lurched forward, stretched out her arms, and shoved the Physica from behind. With a startled cry, Devira fell forward down the steps. Her head hit the floor with a resounding crack and she collapsed with a groan.

Kira sucked in air between her teeth. "What have you done?" she demanded, rushing forward to help Devira.

"You have no idea," Kavyn told her between chuckles. "But you will soon understand the extent of my power, and my reach." He raised his left fist and shook it at her.

A black cloud wrapped itself around Kira. She kneeled beside Devira, praying she still lived. The Physica's breath was shallow and rapid, but Kira did not have the strength to move her or to even call for aid. Helplessness gripped her, braiding a tight rope around her heart and mind. Hopelessness engulfed her. All the training she'd received from Devira was nothing beside the years of practice her brother had had. And there was a deadly strength to him. One she could never match.

She thought of all she had lost. Her parents, Heresta, Vaith, Kelmir, Milos.

Especially Milos. She would miss him most of all. She could see him now, one of his rare smiles lighting up his face. She looked into his eyes and saw a reflection of herself, the image of her as he had always seen her, strong, independent, fearless. And in a tiny corner of her mind, a light shone. A light that told her she couldn't give up. Couldn't let Kavyn win. She had to fight.

She reached again for the light that glinted in the darkness, the flame of her own conviction. It seemed a far off tiny glimmer, but a glimmer was all she needed. The darkness tried to hold her back, but she ignored it, stretching toward that light, that tiny spark. Had almost reached it, when Kavyn thrust into her consciousness and twisted. He raked against her thoughts, scalding her mind. The sensation was as real as if he had thrown hot oil on her bare skin. The searing feeling she had experienced when the basilisk had sprayed her with its acidic venom was nothing compared to this. She screamed and heard her own shriek as if from far off.

Fight back! A new voice, one that was familiar. One that had once cooed softly to her and sung lullabies beside her cradle.

She screamed again, and felt the need to retch, but the physical sensation was distant, a pale echo against the shallow pain that ground into her thoughts. She pushed herself, resetting the shields Kavyn had breached. He laughed as he battered against the thin barriers, stretching them to the point of shattering.

If he broke through again, she would be lost.

A brush of warmth blew past her, a gentle but firm touch helped to shore up her weak shield. *Push*, the voice told her. *Here.*

Like a parent taking the hand of a young child, the warm force nudged her awareness toward a cold place. A black spot spider-webbed with cracks of hot light.

Kira probed at the place, pushing against it tentatively. She lurched forward and tumbled down, down into a morass of emotions. Anger. Disappointment. Jealousy. Fear. *The fear*, the Matriarch's voice whispered. *Reach for the fear.*

Kira grabbed onto the emotion and pulled at it like a thread, following it through a tangled weave of knots until she found the frightened boy standing behind a pillar of dark anger. He cowered, shivering in terror.

"I'll never be good enough, never be anything. I'm nothing but a boy," he muttered. "But a very special boy," he told himself. "Teraxin says so. Teraxin is the only one who sees it, sees how special I am. Sees me."

His head jerked up at Kira's approach. He pointed a stubby finger at her. "You!" he yelled. "You are nothing. You will never be anything. Teraxin will see to it."

"I'm sorry you're afraid," Kira said. "I'm sorry you were used the way you were. You should have been allowed to be a child."

"Liar!" he shouted. "You want it all for yourself." He pulled back his arm, making a fist. Then thrust his hand out toward her, palm open. A wall of fire shot from his fingers, the flames wrapping around her and engulfing her.

Kira flung up her arms and braced herself against the flames, but instead of the searing pain she expected, a cool rain fell around her, dousing the flames and cooling the heat.

"Not fair!" the little boy screamed. "You always loved her best." He fell onto his knees, sobbing.

Kira rushed to him and tried to wrap her arms around his skinny frame, but he pushed her from him. Eyes red, face twisted in an angry sneer. "I hate you!" he bellowed. "I hate you all! I wish you were dead."

The cool rain turned to icy hail, pattering on the ground around them and blowing into his face, leaving red marks where the frozen rain struck his skin.

"You never loved me," he said to the sky. His small boy voice grew in volume and deepened to a rich timbre as his thin body morphed into that of the grown man Kavyn had become.

Kira stepped back. She stared at her brother. They faced each other on a gray plain that spread out into the distance. The hail had stopped, but dark clouds rumbled on the horizon, crackling with thunder and lightning. A slim figure walked toward them from out of the darkness.

The Matriarch strode forward. Behind her a rainbow coalesced in liquid strands of color. The sky shimmered and shifted like pigment cast upon a mixture of water and oil that roiled and stirred. Her pale hair and her raiment whipped around her as if blown by a great wind, though the air around them was still as death.

The woman stopped a few strides from Kavyn and Kira. The three of them formed a triangle of bodies in the middle of the endless landscape.

Kira was stung by the woman's beauty and grace. A complete contrast to the shell of a woman who sat upon the dais each day in the Guardian's Seat. "Mother?" she gasped.

"You are every bit the young woman I had hoped you would be." The Matriarch smiled at her.

Kavyn curled his lip. "No greetings for your son, Matriarch?"

"Kavyn," she said. A deep sadness rounded out the timbre of her voice. "You were my last hope. If only I had seen sooner what you were becoming."

"Hope?" He laughed. "Your aspirations for me were never enough."

"You have no idea what I had planned for you," she said sadly. "Had you but bided your time after your sister was lost to us, I could have brought about the change you longed for. But your tutor's reports of your failed progress dashed any hopes I had harbored for you and our people."

Kavyn's face grew red, his eyes flashed ire. "Teraxin was never more than a clever fool."

"He was more than that," she said. "He was the seal upon your fate. Our fate."

Kavyn hissed. He flung out his hands, sending fire belching at both women, but Kira dove toward her mother, shielding her with her own body and a sudden wall of ice fixed itself between them, cooling the heat of the flames and melting into a puddle at Kavyn's feet.

"You're no match for me," he screamed. "Not even with her help."

The Matriarch shook her head. "It appears, she doesn't need my help," she said, in a quiet voice.

Kira drew back, her thoughts spinning and spiraling. The Matriarch reached out her hand and brushed her fingertips across Kira's cheek. "Alyana?" she murmured.

"Are you well?" Her eyes, though they rested on Kira's, focused on something distant, another place. Perhaps, another time. A thousand images exploded in Kira's brain, a kaleidoscope of memories. Kira as an infant. Her father's smile. The nursemaid, Ardea, who Kira had thought to be her mother, bouncing her upon a knee. The face of a little boy, peering at her over the edge of her cradle. Kavyn's face. His puckish lips curled in a sneer of dislike.

Over the boy's shoulder, a woman watched, her face filled with love. The Matriarch, her mother, Kira realized, but without the stress-worn face and weary eyes. Mother and son were a near-matched pair, with their bow-shaped lips and hazel eyes. Kira was startled by the distinct difference between her coloring and theirs. Till her father's face came into her vision, standing apart from mother and son. A delicate pinch between his eyes. Eyes as green as hers, and red-gold hair that hung to his broad shoulders. A young Ardea watched them from the other side of the room, a mixture of love and pain filling her face.

Tears crept from the corners of Kira's eyes, and a hot barb sank into her heart as the vision changed again. The scene by the river. The voices of the men. Ardea sweeping Kira out of her father's arms as he brushed a kiss across her tiny cheek and ushered them off, as if he knew what was coming for him. The sound of knives thrust into flesh. The smell of blood. The taste of salt air and the expanse of ocean.

Kira fell to her knees as the black cloud once more encompassed her, cutting off her thoughts and vision. Again her memories seemed to peel away, leaving raw empty spaces, patches of nothing. She tried to catch her breath, to suck in precious air, but her lungs burned as if the flames that had earlier been sent against her were now roiled inside her chest.

"Fight him," the Matriarch called from the distance.

But she couldn't. There was nothing for her. Nothing but fire and darkness. She was on fire. The world was in flames. Everything was burning. The guardian's room. Kelmir. Vaith. Milos. She could hear their screams, feel their agony. They were dying. All dying. And Kira could not live without them. She choked on her sorrow. "I'm sorry," she whispered. "Forgive me."

It was all Ardea's fault. All of this. She reached up and grabbed hold of her medallion, ripped it from around her neck and prepared to fling it away, then hesitated. There was something she needed to do first. Something that had slipped from her like an eel slides through the water. She needed to remember. Ardea. What was it Ardea had told her? "When you are grown," she'd said, "you will understand the sacrifices women make to safeguard their children and those they love."

The truth dawned upon her and with it a clarity Kira had not known before. The black cloud that had enveloped her awareness, slipped back, like a receding fog. The light that had drawn her in expanded, flowed, refilled the empty spaces, warming and reassuring her. Her vision cleared and the room reemerged.

A clap of thunder rocked the room. The world seemed to quake.

She saw the Matriarch's face twisted in sorrow and anger. Her mouth a taut line, eyes blazing. The Matriarch's voice boomed in Kira's head, echoing inside her skull, "Kavyn! What have you done?" Her words were shredded by sobs and filled with anger and disbelief. "You have destroyed us . . . stripped us of our last protection. And for what? Jealousy? Arrogance? Greed? Ambition? And you call women the emotional sex. Disdain us for our lack of logic. Did you once follow your acts through to their logical conclusion? Did you even consider the possible consequences?" The Matriarch took a deep breath.

There was a pause and the throne room shook. The shutters slammed open. Wind beat at the trees outside and branches bent and swayed, creaking and moaning. The wind reached inside the throne room. Curtains billowed and snapped. Tapestries slapped the walls. The scent of flowers filled the room, as petals swirled in on the wind. Then, the sky darkened and the room shook again.

"What's happening?" Kira cried.

The Matriarch's face softened. Her skin emitted an aura of blue light that pulsed, fading each time, to a softer hue. "Alyana, my little duckling," she said. "I missed you so. And now you deserve the truth."

"It's all right." Kira said. "I know you're not my mother."

"What?" Kavyn's face twisted into a grimace of fury. He lunged at Kira. The Matriarch held up her hand, palm out. Kavyn froze, as if she held him in place. He growled in frustration.

The Matriarch emitted tendrils of light that reached for Kavyn and wrapped around him like twining vines. "Do you not appreciate the taste of the medicine you dispense?" she asked.

He rolled his eyes and grunted, the muscles of his neck stretched with the strain, but he moved but a hair's breadth.

"Yes," the Matriarch said to Kira, deep sadness in her voice. "I should have realized Ardea would give you the gift. You were always Ardea's. Not just to nursemaid, but truly hers. Ardea had been like a sister to me. Her mother was First Advisor to my mother, so we played together, were raised and tutored together. When she fell in love with your father, she moved out of the keep. They both tried to deny their feelings, avoiding chance encounters, but love is a great and terrible thing. A power difficult to deny. And one day . . . When I discovered the infidelity of my Consort . . ." She remained silent for so long, Kira thought she might have drifted off. The dark fog that had embraced Kira's thoughts and clogged her mind began to return, and she felt herself panic, not knowing whether she was still in the physical realm or remained trapped inside herself. But the keep gave another hard shake and the darkness disappeared, flashing out as if it had never been.

Kavyn growled in frustration.

The Matriarch grimaced and continued her tale. "As fate played out, Ardea and I had our lying in at nearly the same hour. Ardea's baby girl was hale and healthy. But my daughter, our hope, struggled to thrive. She died. So soon after her birth." There was a catch in her voice.

Something shifted in Kira's head, as so many things clicked into place. "You and Ardea switched babies."

"It wasn't such a terrible thing. You are after all the daughter of my love and a woman I called my sister by stronger bonds than blood," the Matriarch said in a hushed voice.

Kavyn snorted. "Stronger bonds than blood?" he hissed. "And you call me traitor."

"What I did, I did for the people, not for my own gain," she said. Her voice sounded weak, but there was a fierceness beneath it.

"Truly? Yet you insist that what I attempt would not be for the good of all, for the good of our people?" He twitched, his lips turning up as he struggled to regain control of his own muscle and sinew.

"There is a difference, Kavyn. And had I not sought so

287

desperately to make up to you for what I had done, had I not coddled and spoiled you so horribly, you might actually be able to recognize that difference."

She reached out to Kira, touching her brow with the tip of her finger. "To you, my sister's daughter, I leave this gift." A warm glow surrounded Kira, and a buzzing resonated inside her skull. Something in her shifted, like the click of a lock and another door opened within her. An overwhelming flood of joy swept through her.

The keep shook and the Matriarch sagged and Kira sensed a shift of energy, like the rushing of a stormy wind. When the Matriarch spoke again, her words were slurred and brushed with so much sorrow, Kira's heart felt raw. "Use it wisely."

The Matriarch sagged against the marble arm of the Guardian's Seat, her energy spent. In that moment, the room seemed to wrench and shift. Kavyn was suddenly before the Matriarch, his hands raised against her. The Matriarch gasped, but her sudden look of surprise was immediately replaced by one of stern remonstrance. "Why?"

The joy washed away from Kira, replaced by the need to protect this woman, a woman who had loved so deeply that loss had scarred her for life. She flung out her arms and leaped forward, inserting herself between mother and son.

"I . . ." Kira's muscles clenched. She stood frozen before the Matriarch, her jaw clamped shut and she was unable to finish.

Kavyn laughed. "Two hens with a single arrow."

"There is no more time . . ." The Matriarch's voice cracked, as if she were straining against something, holding a great force at bay.

A blinding light erupted from Kavyn's fist.

Kira's body became engulfed in an aura of bright

pain. She tried to cover her face, but she stood frozen, immobilized. Her body shook, then seized, feeling as if she'd been struck by lightning.

For a moment, her awareness expanded, and she could not only hear, but see everything taking place all at once. The landscape opened up and below her the Councilors and people of Eilar stood looking up in fear at the stormy sky.

Kira found herself swept up over the forest. She soared above a bloody beach, where men and women fought to keep an invading army from landing upon their shores. A glint of dark hair caught her eye. Milos!

He stood shoulder to shoulder with a tall man and a dark-haired woman. Together, they stood before a rush of armed men who waded ashore, grim menace on their faces.

Suddenly Kavyn was somehow beside her. "Ah, there it is," he whispered in her ear. "The chink in your armor. Disgusting, really, that you should find such an inferior being so valuable."

Kavyn's voice floated in and out of hearing, his words a guttural chant. The Matriarch hissed in pain. The horizon flipped, again and again. Kira felt herself spinning with it.

As if yanked at the end of a heavy rope, she was pulled above the world. Below her, the broken ward stones of Eilar stood in ruins, connected by silver threads that gleamed and pulsed.

A blade swung down toward Milos. He parried the strike and brought his sword up for a finishing blow, but stopped mid-swing, as if something barred his way. He stood like a statue and looked upward, as if he could see her hovering there, a question in his dark eyes. His enemy, seeing his opening, grinned and aimed for his heart . . .

Kavyn laughed.

"No!" Kira screamed.

Time stopped, the battle on the beach became a frozen moment. A tableau woven into one of the keep's tapestries.

Kavyn howled in frustration.

Something inside Kira exploded and she felt herself snapped back across the world. She hovered, floating outside her body as she watched the scene in the Guardian's Tower unfold in slow motion.

Kavyn's arms were outstretched, his face twisted in an angry rictus. A fierce white light enveloped him and moved outward.

The Matriarch wilted like a dying frost flower beneath a summer sky. A blue aura, emanated from her, as if her spirit were leaving her body.

Between them, like the moon crossing between the earth and the sun, Kira stood transfixed.

She turned on Kavyn, pushing her mental guards into place and found her strength, not inside her mind, but within her heart. She wrapped herself inside the nurturing of her parents, enfolded herself in Heresta's warmth and wisdom, took refuge within the connection to her companions, and girded herself with the love of Milos.

Kavyn gripped the arm of the Guardian's Seat and raised his left fist into the air, a harsh light glowing from between his fingers. He grunted as if lifting a great weight and opened his hand to reveal a glowing stone. "I won't need an army to destroy you and everyone you love." Energy streamed into the room in ropy strands of silver and blue. The stone pulsed and Kavyn closed his eyes in ecstasy.

Realization hit Kira like a fist. The lines of energy. Kavyn was taking in power, absorbing it into himself through the stone in his hand. She had to stop him, cut him off from the source before he drained all the energy from the land, before the Isle of Eilar and everyone on it, everyone she loved, was destroyed. She had to send the power back into the land.

She dropped her mental shields, opened herself up and reached out with her mind.

As if it were the most natural thing in the world, the force lines began to bend and twist, shifting away from Kavyn. They rushed to Kira, striking her like lightning bolts. Again and again. She cried out each time one of the lines hit her and her body absorbed the energy.

"No!" Kavyn shrieked, trying to pull the power back. But the word caught in his throat, turning into a garbled sound of pain. The pulsing stone in his hand exploded, shards flying outward and he fell to the floor.

Kira screamed, unable to stop the energy that flowed into her remorselessly. The tower shook and shivered. Once more, she found herself connected with everything. Earth. Rocks. Water. Trees. But this time was different. The tendrils that connected her to the Matriarch frayed and fell apart, a single strand at a time. And the line that kept her tied to her brother snapped.

"Our people are in need of a leader. One who can heal this land." The Matriarch's voice grew distant, fading like the call of a bird winging rapidly off into the distance. *You will make an excellent Guardian.* Her words echoed inside Kira's head.

Kira gasped. Her mental shields slammed into place and she was swept back across the wide plain, flying above great expanses of ocean and forest, deep valleys of red-gold rock and snow-topped mountains slid past her. The wind whipped at her face and tears scalded her cold cheeks. It felt as if it took forever and, at the same time, only a moment for all this to pass. Then, she found herself once more in the Guardian's room, almost as if she'd never left.

The room grew suddenly bright, as if a sun had exploded inside the keep. The halo of light that had glimmered around the Matriarch when Kira had first seen her in the mind's realm, now appeared to emanate from Kira's skin.

Kavyn sat slumped against the stone steps. A tendril of drool wended its way from the corner of Kavyn's mouth down his chin and onto his red silk shirt.

"Kavyn?"

He raised his head, but his eyes were vacant, his expression blank.

CHAPTER FIFTY-SEVEN

Milos felt himself released from a stunned state, in time to see the point of a sword flashing in the sun, heading directly for his heart. He swiftly dropped his sword across his body, knowing as he did so, the parry would come too late. Though he could now move, whatever had caused his momentary immobility would still succeed in killing him. A distant part of him saw the blow coming as if in slow motion.

A flash of color appeared overhead and a low snarl rang out. The blade stopped in mid-stroke and was thrust aside as a large dark body hurled against the Outlander holding it. The brawny warrior screamed as sharp claws raked down his side, yet managed to right himself and throw off the hunting cat. Blood gushed from his wound as he swung his weapon at Milos.

Milos pushed the attacker back with a series of powerful strikes, then thrust his sword into the invader's chest.

"I don't know how you found me," Milos said to Vaith and Kelmir, "but thank Troka, you arrived when you did." Vaith screeched and swooped in an arc above Milos. Kelmir padded up beside him and growled a challenge.

From not far off, Marquon called out to Milos. "Are you well?" he asked, panting. The concern in his voice was clear.

"I am now. Someone . . . or something . . ." Milos started. Then he shook his head. "No time, now. Look to your left!"

He dodged an incoming strike from behind, as Marquon spun to fend off the burly man who had run up on them.

Kelmir and Vaith fought beside Milos and the attackers quickly learned to give the animals a wide berth. Milos had just knocked the weapon from the hand of a combatant, when a shout caused him to look out toward the frothing shoreline. Milos laughed aloud and the man he had been fighting turned to look. Then suddenly set off at a hard run.

Marquon dispatched his own foe and glanced at Milos, his gaze quickly scanning the big cat and wyvern flanking him. He raised an eyebrow at Milos. "Are you certain you are well?"

Milos pointed with his sword. "The tides," Milos said, "have turned." He smirked at the groan Marquon emitted in response to his play on words.

The two men stared after the invading ship, which had unfurled its dark sails and was turning from them, heading out to sea. The few surviving invaders sloshed into the surf, some leaping into the boats they had used to come ashore and rowing as fast as they could, others swimming in desperation toward the ship, hoping to be picked up by their comrades.

"You have . . . interesting allies," Marquon finally said, gesturing at Kelmir, who stood beside Milos, panting in the sun.

"You have no idea," Milos glanced around to be sure the invaders were all either escaping or dead, then reached up to allow Vaith to light upon his wrist.

Cheering, the remaining able-bodied members of the Eilaren Protectorate, and their Aestron allies, chased the last of the invaders from the beach.

CHAPTER FIFTY-EIGHT

Kira brushed her fingertips across the Matriarch's cheek. The chill of the dead woman's skin matched the chill of the room, and the hollow place this journey had left in Kira's heart. Aertine and Devira, her aunts, Kira reminded herself, stood in the crowd of mourners, their white robes reflecting the crystal lights that glowed at intervals along the walls and hung suspended from the high arches overhead. There were many dark homes on this day, their owners having given all the light they owned in order to illuminate the Matriarch's funereal gathering.

The body had been tended to by scores of Physica and many others skilled in all manner of arts. Kira had lost track of who and of what purpose each had been, but Devira had explained that, in addition to preserving the body, the people of Eilar came from afar to pay homage to the passed Matriarch. Some out of respect, others out of duty, and some because ritual demanded it.

Matriarch Kyrina had lain in state for the past three days and would be interred at dusk. A low-backed wooden seat had been placed beside the bier, and Kavyn sat propped up in the chair, layers of cotton lace at his throat to hide the dampness of his shirt.

Kira had told the Council what she knew of Kavyn's actions, but as he was now rendered harmless, there seemed no need to take further action against him. Even a fresh panel of interrogators would likely be unable to plumb the fathoms of his lost mind.

Displaying him here seemed like punishment enough to Kira. Not that he'd shown any signs of self-awareness.

Kira shuddered at the memory of their battle in the tower. She sat at the far end of the high-ceilinged room, wearing the stifling Guardian's robes and heavy chains of office. But her own doubts were even more suffocating than the heavy accouterments of status.

During her debriefing with the Council, a conversation that took what seemed like eons though it had only been a few spans. She had spoken cautiously, telling them everything she could. Everything, except the secret of her birth. That information weighed heavier upon her than the chains of office, but the Matriarch had kept the secret, even after her proclaimed heir's disappearance. Kira had no idea what harm revealing the truth might do, so she'd decided to bide her time.

Meanwhile, following protocol, she had spent the past three days sitting in this room. Since then, aside from the councilors, and a few brief exchanges with Devira, who was still mending from her fall, Kira had not spoken with anyone, except the messenger who had been charged with finding Milos, delivering her message and returning with his answer.

Milos lived, as did Vaith and Kelmir. For this, above all else, she was grateful. Through all that had followed in these past few days, the latter two had stayed close, prowling her rooms and the keep gardens, seeming content to be reunited with her once more, yet fearful of being parted again. They had free run. The Eilaren's ready acceptance of Kira's gift and connection with her companions had been a surprise and relief. Now, her heart was nearly whole, but for the empty place where Milos belonged. She tried to temper the hope that surged inside her, hope that the hole in her heart would soon be filled once more.

Until the interment, there wasn't much for her to do but think. So she spent the time reviewing every action that had brought her here. Every thought. Every choice.

If but a single thing had been different, would she now be sitting here? An imposter upon a foreign throne? If she had never come here, would Kavyn have acted as he had? Would he have destroyed the Warding Stones, the last bastion of protection this land and its people had had?

She shifted the weighty chains of office on her shoulders. She would have preferred not wearing them, but the First had insisted. The Matriarch had passed without the formal naming of an heir. Kira's complicated status was an issue the councilors had sharply debated, and not all were happy with the final outcome, but one thing was certain, she could not leave this land and these people now. No matter what it cost her. Her connection to the force lines was too great. And she was needed here. She worried what the people would think were they to become aware of her non-Guardian blood. Yet, she would do whatever was needed to help keep them safe and make the land whole once more.

She thought again of Milos, wondering if he had received her message. Would he come simply because she had asked?

The sound of the reflection bells roused her from thought. Finally, the large doors at the opposite end of the room opened inward and a procession of women and men marched slowly forward to take up the Matriarch's bier.

Kira stood, waiting for the signal to follow them out to where they would lay the body to rest beneath the Guardian's memory marker. Kyrina would be lain to rest beside her ancestors, a long line of women, marching back in time. A line which, unknown to anyone but Kira, had now been severed.

CHAPTER FIFTY-NINE

Kira stood in the garden, waiting, nervous and tense. Her last meeting with Milos had not been a good one. Would he come now? Would he forgive her for denying him? The rushing water of the wide stream gurgled and splashed, but did nothing to calm her agitation and sense of foreboding.

She had sent word to him as soon as the invaders had left their shores. He had responded that he would come to her as soon as he could. That had been more than three days ago. The young man who had carried the message had been nervous and uncertain. In the few moments she had been allowed with him, Kira had tried to pry some information from the boy, but he had merely mumbled and shuffled his feet. It could simply have been that the boy was afraid to speak to her, but Kira had worried on it. What if it had been something more? What if in addition to everything else, things between her and Milos had been irreparably changed?

He'd been angry enough when she had forced him off the ship before seeing to her own safety. Denying him in the garden, no matter her reasons, could be felt as a betrayal of his trust in her. Kira knew only too well that feeling and how difficult a wound it was to heal.

The last rays of the low sun did little to warm her chill heart and she wrapped her light cloak about her. Summer had flown from the land, almost as if it too were afraid of the changes that had come to Eilar.

The crunch of gravel underfoot alerted her to his approach. She turned slowly, afraid it would not be him.

Milos stepped into the open and stopped, staring at her, as if he thought she would once more turn him away.

"I was afraid you wouldn't come," she said.

"As was I," he admitted in a low voice.

There was something different about him now. Something she could not place, but clearly sensed. She saw the bandages on wrist and neck, but that wasn't it. This was something . . . deeper.

"I'm so sorry," she said it in a rush, afraid he might leave before she could finish. "I was afraid—"

He stood his ground, but his face grew clouded. Anger and confusion warred on his countenance. "I never gave you cause . . ."

His whispered words tore at her heart. She wanted to run to him, to throw herself into his arms. But her feet betrayed her, keeping her rooted in place. "No," she said, the meaning of his words finally sinking in. "Not afraid of you. Afraid for you."

His eyes narrowed. Was that hurt?

"You should have been . . . neither," he said gruffly. His gaze pierced her. He appeared tired, beaten.

Suddenly, she could not stand to be so far from him. She rushed forward, and in the same instant he strode across the open space, closing the distance between them. They held one another close. His warm lips sought hers and for a long moment they were lost to the world around them.

Finally, he pulled his face from hers. He wrapped his arms even tighter about her and kissed her forehead. Kira heard his breath catch in his throat and hot tears rolled down her cheeks. "Kira," he said. "Kira," he repeated, his voice gruff with emotion. "I thought I had lost you."

"And I thought you . . ." she could not bring herself to finish. She pressed her face into his neck, muffling her sobs.

He leaned away and reached to wipe the tears from her face, wincing with the movement.

"You're hurt," she said, stepping back to better survey his wounds.

"That would explain the bandages." His mouth quirked up in a wry smile.

Kira nodded at him. "There is something different about you, but it is not your humor," she chided.

"There is something different about me," he agreed, letting his hands fall away from her.

Worry scratched at her like a mouse gnawing a seed. "What is it?"

His brow wrinkled, as if his thoughts had fled just as he would have gathered them in. "I cannot rightly say." He glanced around the garden. "It is nothing," he said with a shrug followed by another wince of pain.

"You need to stop annoying your wounds," Kira scolded.

"I hear," he said, with a frown, "that the Eilaren have a new Matriarch."

Kira pursed her lips, but said nothing.

"It is true, then?" His hands fell to his sides. "You've

taken the Guardian's Seat?"

"I didn't take it!" she protested. But she knew the words were only half true. No matter the outcome, her actions, her choices, had been the cause of it. And Kavyn. It was not as if he had been suited to the role. Beyond that, now he drooled and lolled like a newborn, his mind broken. As he had intended hers to be.

"If you did not take it, then you need not accept it." Milos sounded hopeful.

Kira glanced at the keep, the tall corner tower with its high windows that housed the Eilaren seat of power, then returned her gaze to Milos. "Someone must sit in the Guardian's Seat."

"Let someone else do so, then. Anyone else." He reached out, wrapping his warm hand about her chilled fingers.

Kira considered his words. What was there that she could do here? The Veil was broken. The stone workers had not the knowledge nor the skill to repair the warded columns. Yet, the Guardian's Seat could not remain empty. Her people needed a Matriarch, and even without the proper bloodline, she had been chosen, connected to the land by a bond that felt unbreakable.

Fate and the wheel had already turned.

Her heart ached. She wanted nothing more than to be with this man, to return to the way things had been before they had come here, before she had been passed the Matriarch's mantle. "I cannot abandon my land, and my people." Kira nearly choked on the words, the bitter truth of them a sour dreg she dearly wished not to swallow.

"Kira, I am taking the sailors home. Those who survived."

"But . . ."

He shook his head. "I hadn't . . . believed . . . I needed

to see you . . . to hear it from you. But . . ." he spread his hands.

"Milos," she whispered. "Please stay. The Consort's chair—"

"No," he cut her off, his voice hard, his face a stiff mask. "No," he repeated, this time more quietly. "I did not follow you from my home to sit at your feet. I thought . . . I wanted . . . We have always been . . ." his words trailed off.

"It need not be forever," she said, but her words felt empty of promise. How could she know how long it would be? What could she offer him? She could not leave these people, this land, helpless. She must do what she could to protect them, though she had little idea how she would accomplish it. She had committed herself to this.

The Matriarch's secret chafed at her. She had not asked for this. She hadn't even been born to it. If not for the pact between her mother and the Matriarch, she would never have been pulled into this. She railed at the injustice of it. This was not her task. She was not even of Guardian blood! Yet, her fingers, her very skin, tingled with the force the Matriarch had entrusted to her, and the power of the land that thrummed in tune with her pulse. What else could she do? She must do everything in her control to fulfill the promise of the Guardians.

She shivered and pulled her cloak against her skin, but the thin cloth held no warmth for her and neither did the sorrow in Milos' visage. "When?" she whispered. "When will you go?"

Milos licked his lips, his hand reaching unconsciously to touch his bandaged shoulder. "As soon as the ports are reopened and the wounded men well enough to travel." He swallowed nervously. "Kira, won't you please come with us?" He pleaded with his eyes as well as his words. "With me?"

She shivered, uncertain if it was caused by the evening chill, or just the sensation that she were dying, bit by bit. The cold crept up her limbs and into her heart. She couldn't speak. Couldn't bear to tell him no. Instead she swept an arm out to indicate the city. "It's dying," she murmured. "They are dying."

"And you would prefer to stay here and die with them than to return with me to our land?" He spoke quietly, but hurt and anger tinged his voice.

"This, this is my land," she said. "I owe—"

"You owe them nothing," he growled, his fingers wrapping themselves into fists.

Kira flinched and he paused, composing his features, relaxing, forcing his hands open.

"It appears," he said, "that all of your memories remain intact, after all."

His words fell on her like a blow and she felt the blood rush into her cheeks. "Indeed," she said. "I have recovered more than I knew I owned. And not all of them pretty." She stared at the running water, the path that led beside it, the tall rushes growing along the edge . . . "There are some I wish I could give back."

"Kira," Milos said, his voice softening. "I'm sorry. I know you. I know your heart. If you feel you must stay here, for whatever reason, then you must do what is in your heart."

"And you, Milos. What is in your heart?"

"I would have things as they were for us before we came here. But that cannot be. We have crossed an ocean and I have once more spilled blood." He wiped his hands on his trousers as he spoke, as if he could remove the death from them. "You . . ."

He took her hand in his once more. "My heart desires

to be with you, Kira. You are the only woman I have ever truly loved. But my heart also says that I was rash to leave Tem Hold as I did and . . . I need to return."

"Are you saying that leaving Tem Hold with me was a mistake?" Kira tried not to show the hurt his words caused her, but her voice cracked, giving her away.

"I am saying I need to return to my home. You of all people must understand this." He brought her hand up to his cheek, closed his eyes and rubbed his face against her knuckles. Finally, he opened his eyes and stared into hers. "If you are set on staying here, then I will not dissuade you. But I cannot remain. I am not material for a Matriarch's Consort."

Kira felt as if her heart had turned to ice and had been cast down onto the rock-hard ground to shatter at her feet. Tiny splinters of frost wormed their way through her blood, freezing her to the core. "So be it," she said, gently pulling her hand from his grasp, ignoring the pain that bloomed in his eyes. "It appears we are no longer traveling in the same direction."

She turned and walked slowly away, destined for the Guardian's Tower. When she reached the archway that led from the garden, she looked back to find Milos gone. The garden stood empty except for the dying autumn leaves that fluttered silently to the ground.

* * *

Acknowledgements

This book would not exist, if not for all of the readers and fans who waited in anticipation—and with varying levels of patience (smiley face)—and continued to ask for more of Kira's journey. I think you wanted to know, even more than I did, what she would do next. I'm sorry it took so long to find out. Thank you for being so steadfast.

Thanks to Dawn V. and Linda J. for your encouragement and your generous (and too kind) feedback on the manuscript. You gave me the courage and motivation to keep going exactly when I needed it.

And thank you to the fabulous team at Brick Cave Books, I would be lost without you.